WHITE OAKS

Jordan King

Edited by Benjamin White

Published in North America and Europe by Running Wild Press. Visit Running Wild Press at www.runningwildpress.com Educators, librarians, book clubs (as well as the eternally curious), go to www.runningwildpress.com.

ISBN (pbk) 978-1-955062-16-9
ISBN (ebook) 978-1-955062-17-6

For Jody

ACKNOWLEDGEMENTS

First, I have to thank Craig Clevenger. I had an interest in writing from an early age, but I never had the determination to do anything about it until I read *Dermaphoria.* The elegant way he built the oppressive, grimy, and beautiful landscape in that book just flipped a switch inside me. I'm not sure how you ever really thank someone for that properly.

Thank you to the LitReactor writing workshop. Such a fun, helpful, and talented group. Big thanks to Jessica, Hannes, Repo, Brenna, Red and many others for putting so much time and effort into helping me become a better writer. I posted a short story (which would eventually become this book) on LitReactor and received a lot of praise (and a lot of helpful criticism). It was a story I could never walk away from, in part because I was so encouraged to continue by a group of people I'll probably never meet in real life.

I can't say enough about the folks I met at Miami of Ohio while working on my MFA in Creative Writing. Thanks to Eric Goodman for seeing something in my writing and taking me into the program. Thanks to Keith Tuma for a lot of things but mostly for making me read publicly when you knew I'd rather crawl into a hole and die. It was painful, especially for the audience, but by the end, I never felt more comfortable in front of others. Thanks to Amy Toland and all the other staff at Miami who were always there, always helpful and always making us feel at home. Thanks to all the faculty at Miami, but especially

Jacquelyn Mitchard, Hugh Sheehy and Alissa Nutting, whose guidance and encouragement meant more to me than I could ever put into words. Thanks to all the other students at Miami, who brought so much joy, wonder, and weirdness into my life. Letta, Andrea, Brian, Alex, Katey, Lincoln, Matt L., Kim, Roy, Bing, Heba, Gavin, Ray, Jason, Whitney, Michael, Katharine, Nancy, Bob, Bill, Jaurice, Jessica, John, Meredith, Sally, Tonja, Andrew, Kinsey, Leah, Matt H., Paul, Casey, Margaret, Matt B., Andy, Tyler, Megan, Recarlo and…gosh I hope that's everyone, but it probably isn't. Also, thank you to Karl for sharing your disturbing family history and letting me use some of it in this book.

Of course, I have to thank Jody for always being there to listen to me talk out plot problems, read drafts, help with research, etc. To Julia and Abby; watching you become the women you are has been one of the true joys in my life. To Logan; keep doing what you're doing and you won't need to wait nearly as long for your dreams to come true. Whatever it is people are looking for, you have it, and not just in your music.

CHAPTER 1

"Do you know where you are?"

The answer to that was a simple no, but it wouldn't be helpful to say that out loud. I scrambled through fragmented memories, trying to recall the last thing I'd done. There was little to go on, so I shook my head, and he jotted a note.

"I'm in a hospital," I said, far too late. It was more a question than a statement.

"What hospital?" he asked, pen hovering over the paper.

I shrugged, and he added more notes to the record. Somewhere outside his office, a door slammed, and the noise was followed by a muffled argument. He looked over my shoulder, frowned and let out a long sigh.

"Excuse me for a moment."

When he opened the door a woman shouted, "I knew it." I turned around to see who it was, but the door closed, and I was alone again.

With the unexpected free time to gather my thoughts, I tried to uncover something, anything, that might explain my being there. There was a crushing headache that lasted for several days. A back spasm in the middle of that week. A mound of pills in my hand, more than once. Bright lights and a nurse with a fluffy blonde ponytail bouncing from shoulder to shoulder as she walked away. That was all I could salvage. I'd overdosed again, but that was the only thing I was really sure about.

There was more shouting outside the door. It was the mystery woman. "You said there'd be no more. You said we were stopping this."

Stopping what, I didn't know. The doctor said something in response that was unclear. I was only half paying attention anyway.

His office walls seemed closer than they were at first and all I could think about was getting out of there, wherever there was. The lone window in the office was too small for anything larger than a malnourished cat to squeeze through.

He came back in and apologized for the interruption. "Now, where were we?" he asked and picked up his pen.

"What was that about?" I asked.

"Nothing that concerns you."

Under his lab coat was a light brown sweater with a badge pinned to it. I couldn't read the name on the badge. Every time I tried to focus on it, the letters doubled and vibrated. If he'd told me his name before, it'd slipped my mind. His beard, the same dingy white as his lab coat, swallowed up the bottom half of his face.

There was nothing soothing or reassuring in the room, and no personal effects. Every wall was covered with multicolored vine wallpaper. It seemed like the vines might grow heads that would sprout fangs. My fingers dug into the arm of the chair.

"Something wrong?" he asked.

"Did you tell me your name? I can't remember." It was a stupid question to ask, but it came out before I could consider how it'd sound.

He offered a little smile, and his crow's feet spread. "Doctor Edwin Sawyer."

I nodded. "Right."

"So, you know you're in a hospital, but not which one. Do you know *why* you're here?"

Another simple answer.

Drug overdose.

The whole answer was more complicated. I wasn't sure where to focus my attention. Another wrong answer and I knew I'd condemn myself to whatever the place was, if only for a few days, but possibly even longer. Though I had no interest in staying in the hospital, there wasn't much for me to go home to. In a brief moment of clear thinking, I considered that it might be best to stay and take the opportunity to get clean. I'd tried and failed so many times before. Maybe it was my last chance to save myself and prove that my father had been wrong about me. The thought came and went as soon as a shiver ran up my spine and the all-too-familiar hunger for opioids shouted protests at clear-thinking-me.

"I took too many pills."

His pen continued to hover, and he looked at me through his wild eyebrows that hung down like bangs. I hadn't noticed until then that I was wearing pajamas that didn't belong to me.

"I was in a lot of pain," I said. "Couldn't sleep. I wasn't trying to hurt myself, if that's what you're getting at. Just needed to sleep."

Things were starting to come back to me, and that was the truth. It wasn't a conscious suicide attempt, but the amount used could have brought about that result, so it was hard to know how to feel about what I'd done, and what my true intentions might have been. Lucky wasn't the right word. Maybe fortunate? I'd been fortunate enough to survive multiple overdoses, but knew my behavior was going to catch up with me eventually.

He continued to stare at me. I didn't know what he wanted to hear, and the uncertainty made me even more uncomfortable. My will faltered and I broke eye contact to study my new slippers.

"It was an accident," I said.

Finally, he put pen to paper and scribbled for what felt like several minutes. It was either my release, or condemnation. He capped the pen, set it down, and leaned back in his chair, fingers tented in front of him.

"It's very difficult for me to accept that it was an accident when you've already overdosed two other times." His finger tent pointed at me. "At least two times that we know of. I suppose there could have been more."

I didn't respond and hoped that any kind of expression that would have confirmed that there had been more remained hidden.

"You were in pain?"

I nodded.

"What kind of pain?"

I sighed and absently rubbed my right shoulder. "Here," I said. "Base of my skull, shoulder, neck, arm, upper back. Sharp. Radiating. Stabbing. Constant."

What kind of pain? It was a question I'd heard a hundred times. On a scale of one to ten. Smiley face to frowny face. Words, numbers, and labels that never seemed to make any real difference when placed on my chart.

He stuck the finger tent under his chin and took a deep breath. "What's the diagnosis?"

I shrugged. "There are a lot of things they can't explain."

"What are some of the things they can explain?" He asked.

"Degenerative disc disease, arthritis, herniated discs, pinched nerves, early onset severe osteoporosis, which they found when I had x-rays after a bad flare up. Two of my vertebrae had collapsed in on themselves and left little shards of bone poking into neighboring nerve groupings. Apparently, the x-ray showed evidence of previous breaks. They couldn't quite grasp how I was walking around with a broken back for a couple years. That's just the easy stuff."

"You keep referring to *them*. Who are they?"

"My doctors at the veteran's hospital. At least tell me this isn't a VA hospital."

"We have no affiliation with the VA." He scooted his chair back a little, opened one of the desk drawers and brought out a bottle of water. I was ready to accept it greedily, my mouth was full of paste, but he cracked it open, took a long drink and didn't offer me anything. "So, that's it? You're in pain all the time and they just feed you pills?"

I didn't respond.

"What medications are you taking now?"

"I have prescriptions for Percocet, Vicodin, Cyclobenzaprine, Ambien, and uh." I looked over his shoulder and tried to convince myself that the wallpaper vines weren't moving. "I think that's it."

"How did you get prescriptions for Percocet and Vicodin at the same time?"

"Because the VA is a cancerous mass of incompetence."

He chuckled, but it seemed more at me than my dig at the VA. "So, you intentionally sought out multiple prescriptions?"

I didn't respond, but my silence was answer enough. He scribbled in his notebook again.

"Are you using any recreational drugs?"

"Currently or ever?"

"Currently."

"No," I lied.

"What about other prescription medications? What else have you been given?"

I let out a long slow breath and wiped my hands on my new pajama pants. "I already mentioned a few, but in the past, I've taken OxyContin, Tramadol, Neurontin, Robaxin, Gabapentin, Lortab, Amitriptyline, Codeine, Lyrica, Zoloft, Ambien."

"You already said Ambien." His chin rested on his hand, and his eyes were bleary, like he was bored.

"I think you get the idea," I said and looked at the floor. There was a long gap in conversation while he wrote down everything I'd said, every mannerism, and every changing facial expression I wasn't paying attention to. I used to be a very controlled person, but now had probably given away every secret I'd spent years protecting. The only noise in the room was his scribbling.

"Are those from the war?" he asked, and I looked back up at him.

"Those?"

A look of impatience crossed over his features, and I decided not to test him further.

"Yes."

"Where?" he asked.

"Afghanistan."

"Want to talk about it?"

"Not particularly, no."

"Have you ever felt like you were in that moment again?"

"What do you mean?" I wiped sweat from my forehead and stilled my leg, which was bouncing up and down nervously.

"After coming home," he said. "Did you ever feel like you were back in Afghanistan on the day you were injured? Just sitting in the living room watching television, or looking for cereal at the grocery store?"

I shrugged. The first year had been the hardest, but moments like the ones he was asking about still happened on occasion, even though I'd been out of the Army for more than a decade.

He took a handkerchief from his breast pocket, blew his nose, and neatly folded in his boogers before putting it back into his pocket.

"Do you ever have nightmares about the incident?"

"The incident. That's an interesting word choice."

He ignored my sarcasm. "Have you had any inexplicable emotional outbursts when you were in a situation that reminded you of the incident?"

I didn't respond.

"Is that a yes?"

"You have a booger in your mustache, Doc." He pulled the

handkerchief back out to finish cleaning up the booger that wasn't there.

"So," he prodded. "What about those nightmares?"

"Who cares if I have nightmares sometimes? Who doesn't? And, yes, I can be a little skittish at times, but no worse than most people out in the world. There was nothing I could do that day. There was nothing any of us could have done any different. It just happened. I don't dwell on it."

That was a mix of truth and blatant lies. There really wasn't anything we could have done different, but I thought about it all the time and dreamed about it often.

"I can see some of the exterior damage just by looking at you," he said. "But have any of these doctors found a source of the pain and given recommendations for treatment?"

"There are several things that they've found but no specific recommendations other than things that treat the symptoms. Early on they said I was too young for surgery and that my body would heal itself. A few years later, they said it was too late for surgery and that I'd be dealing with the symptoms for the rest of my life, barring some new medical discovery."

"So," he said and leaned back again. The finger tent returned, and he targeted me with it. "You've been experiencing constant pain that no doctor has been able to really figure out in the last ten plus years, and now you're sitting in my office, in a mental hospital, because you've just overdosed for the third time. Do I have that right?"

I sighed and shook my head in disbelief at what I just walked into. "More or less."

"Well, maybe all those doctors have just been looking in the wrong place. Welcome to White Oaks," he said, and stood up.

"What about my meds?"

"What do you mean?"

"I have multiple prescriptions, how do I retrieve my meds or get new scripts here, I don't know how it works."

He looked at me with a mix of resignation and disbelief. "Mr. Miller, you're in this facility in the first place because you've abused your prescriptions to the point that emergency room intervention was required on three separate occasions."

"Just because I've abused them doesn't mean the prescriptions aren't legitimate. I'm in constant pain. I have regular muscle spasms. I have issues sleeping." Though I'd briefly considered using my time there as an opportunity to get clean, the addict inside me was actively rebelling against the idea. I was already starting to detox at that point and would have done just about anything to avoid diving further into the process.

"I don't think continuing your VA prescriptions is a good idea. Personally, I don't think you should be on anything right now. Maybe we can work through your issues when you have a clear mind."

"So, you look at my intake paperwork and have a ten-minute conversation with me and you think over a decade of well-documented medical issues are just in need of a good cry and group therapy session?"

"Getting agitated is not going to help you. In fact, there is a guard right outside this door, who can hear me right now, and he will come in and subdue you if you continue to get agitated." A little twinkle in his eye told me he wanted me to lose control, that he wanted the guard to force me out of that room and into a locked cell.

"So, I just get to detox off of everything I've been taking, cold turkey?"

"We'll keep a close eye on you, Mr. Miller, I can promise you that."

CHAPTER 2

If there were any private rooms at White Oaks, they weren't for the patients. We all slept in the same open, rectangular room broken up by dull grey pillars and lined with old windows. There were only about a half dozen patients. The beds were a bit scattered, with plenty of space between each one. Everyone was already asleep when the guard escorted me onto the ward. I got into my new bed and pulled the covers over my head.

My skin crawled. Sweat poured off me, soaking the pilled itchy sheets. I froze then burned in waves. My eyes swelled and head pounded. The muscles in my neck and back slowly grew tighter with every hitched breath, sending explosions of hot needles across the side of my face that alternated between each eye. The swarming warmth of it touched every bit of connective tissue and ran throughout every diseased cell.

Every time I shuddered with the need of a half dozen drugs that suddenly weren't coursing through my bloodstream, those explosions intensified and coursed down my arm into fingers that hadn't returned home with me from Afghanistan.

Eventually, the lights clicked on and blinked to life, and a man I'd learn to hate in minutes spoke up for the first time.

"Wake up," he said. The voice was distinct, like there were bees in his throat. "Wake up," he said again, sending another wave of burning sweat into the sheets.

"You don't look so hot." He was standing over me. "You're Jason, right?"

I nodded.

"Another badass soldier reduced to…well," he said and shrugged, disgust in his bloodshot eyes. "Whatever this is."

The insult rolled off my shoulders. I didn't care what he thought of me, but even if I had, my mind was occupied entirely by the detox.

"I'm Charlie," he said and extended a hand. I took it and he pulled me up to a sitting position hard enough to elicit another wave of pain.

"Pleasure," I said through clenched teeth.

He chuckled. "Yeah, we'll see. Looks like you could use a good meal."

"I'm not really hungry."

"All the same, it's time to eat and medicate."

"Medicate with what?" I asked, a little too desperately.

"Doc Sawyer said nothing for you, at least not yet. For the others? It's a long list," he said and walked away.

I hadn't met any of the other patients yet, though they'd given me plenty of sideways glances, like they could smell sanity on me, an outsider.

We got into a line up against the wall and waited for our marching orders into the cafeteria. After one of the guards passed by, there was a tap on my shoulder, and I turned around to face the patient behind me.

"Haven't seen a new face in a while," he said.

"Just got in last night. Jason Miller," I said and held out my hand. He looked at it like it was a disease bomb that would explode STDs all over the room. He dug his hands into his armpits.

"Kevin," he said.

"Nice to meet you, Kevin. What are you in for?"

His eyes darted around the room. He was tall, probably six foot six, give or take. Despite his obvious issues, he was well-groomed and in good shape. There was a dog tag tattoo on his right forearm.

"Were you in the military?" I asked.

His eyes stopped darting around the room. "Army," he said and stood up a little straighter, hands no longer dug into the safety of his armpits. "Explosive Ordnance Disposal. You?"

"Infantry. 10th Mountain."

He smiled and held out his hand, which I took in my own. It was warm and clammy.

"Where'd you serve?" I asked.

"All over. Two deployments to Afghanistan. Four to Iraq. Last one was in Fallujah. IEDs really shook my brain up there," he said. "What about you?"

"Twice to Iraq, Baghdad and Mosul. My last deployment was to Afghanistan, the Korengal Valley," I said.

"Korengal? Shit, that's tough," he said, and I nodded in agreement. "I almost bit it outside Najaf, but some kid took the worst of it when a mortar hit nearby." He paused, clearly trying to remember a specific detail. "Brandon. From the Hundred and First, I think. Man, what was his last name? Real good kid. Got hit early on too." He scratched his cheek and something in his eyes changed, like they were suddenly seeing a place other than White Oaks. When he spoke up again, his gaze was still off somewhere else and his voice was slow and monotone, like he was stuck in a dream. "Man, I can't remember his last name. Said he had a brother named Kevin too though, I do remember that."

The single file line waiting for the cafeteria had finally started to move and I turned away from Kevin and started shuffling along with everyone else.

"How's the food?" I asked Kevin over my shoulder, though I'm not sure why. All I wanted to do was get back into bed and shiver, sweat, and ride the detox misery out as quickly as possible.

"I've had worse," he said.

I was about to ask how long he'd been at White Oaks when a loud crash shattered the peace of our quiet shuffling. The noise startled me, but it threw Kevin into a blind panic. The culprit was the metal trash can I'd soon learn was Charlie's preferred form of wakeup call on the ward.

Kevin was on the floor covering his ears and making pinched grunting noises. He was clenching his jaw so hard I thought he'd crack some teeth. I tried to comfort him, but my touch only made things worse. Charlie and two other employees, who were all neck muscles and biceps, sauntered toward us. The other patients stopped shuffling and some were being driven into their own forms of madness as Kevin wailed, rocking himself back and forth on the floor. The combined screaming echoed throughout the room, it bounced off the walls, and my head started to throb.

"Did you do that, Charlie?" I asked when he stepped in front of Kevin.

"Just a little joke," he said. "Didn't know he was going to be such a little bitch about it."

I didn't know what else to say. Unless I was just being naïve about mental healthcare, no real mental hospital employee would ever intentionally set off a patient, so either Charlie was an aberration, or the whole hospital was.

The room was in almost total chaos at that point, and the yammering insanity that filled my ears wasn't helped by my sweaty junkie shuffling withdrawals.

Charlie and the two walking protein shakes leaned down and jerked Kevin off the floor. They rounded the corner and his screams slowly started to disappear into the bowels of the hospital. It was only then, when we could barely hear him anymore, that the group calmed down and started the slow shuffle again.

The cafeteria was the blandest room I'd ever seen. The walls were a dirty white. There were no windows, just flickering artificial light tubes and lines of plastic picnic tables bolted to the floor. When we arrived, I got out of line and went to the end in order to be the last person to sit down. I wanted to make sure to find an empty corner to sit in where no one would bother me, so I could push food around the plate while I shook and sweat, silently praying for time to go by faster. If I was lucky, my stay at White Oaks would only last a couple days, until I finished going through withdrawal and could convince Dr. Sawyer that I was a productive and sane member of society. There was no way to know, at that point, just how little power and control I had or how unlikely it was that I'd be leaving there any time soon.

After getting a tray of food, I sat at the table farthest away from everyone else. I had a rubbery pancake, a couple pieces of floppy bacon that looked like they'd been cooked in the microwave a week earlier and a peach cup with a tear off plastic film. The flimsy plastic spork was in no way dangerous to anyone or even the pancake. After applying the single serving of syrup, I tried to cut off a bite and the spork just bent. I wasn't hungry anyway, so I dropped it on the plate and pushed the tray to the other side of the table.

I burned with fever and started dripping sweat, then got cold with a shiver that started in my toes and rushed throughout my body. The muscles in my neck seized and a supernova blasted from that spot, blurring the room into a kaleidoscope.

Black specks swirled across my vision and flew in and out of the walls. The crackling static swarmed around me causing my skin to spark and pop.

The static stretched down the room and swarmed one of the other patients I hadn't even noticed yet, but he didn't react to it in any way, like it wasn't even there.

I'd never hallucinated like that before, but also hadn't been sober for that long in over a decade. The delicate processes required for a human mind and body to function properly must have been as scattered as my thoughts, as panicked and damaged as my heart.

I blinked and the static moved to the next man down the line, a guy who sagged everywhere and was down to his last few strands of grey hair. The swarm went up the man's nose and his eyes lit up. I blinked again and they were gone. All at once, I seemed to turn into the swarm. The room spun and shrank down to the size of a drop of fluid on a microscope slide.

***

There was an IV in my arm when I woke up and I reached for it until Dr. Sawyer spoke up. "You will have to thank Michael when you're well enough to go back to the ward," he said.

"Michael?" I asked through a fog, my words thick and slow. My lips stuck to my teeth as the words came out.

"One of the other patients. He saw you collapse and called for help. How are you feeling?"

I groaned an empty response.

"I told you we'd keep an eye on you, didn't I?"

"Water," I said.

He walked around to the other side of the bed and held a child's sippy cup of water to my lips. "When you're well enough to go back onto the ward you can thank him," he said.

"Thank who?"

"Michael, remember?"

"Who's Michael?"

"Just get some rest, Mr. Miller. We'll talk more later."

CHAPTER 3

There were no clocks or calendars anywhere in the hospital. Not in the recovery room, or in Dr. Sawyer's office, and not in the main room where we all stayed. What felt like two days in recovery before returning to the ward could have just as easily been twenty. Right from the beginning, I had no real concept of time.

I was brought back onto the ward by another orderly, James, who sported a patchy beard, a Southern drawl, and tattoos that were either done in prison or in his second cousin's living room.

As soon as we walked through the door, James pointed at the withdrawn figure in the corner of the room. "That's Michael over there," James said. "He's the one that called for help."

James locked the door while I went to thank Michael. My eyes were burning before I got over to him. The whole room reeked of bleach.

Kevin was resting his forehead against the concrete wall.

"Hey, man," I said. "How're you doing?"

He didn't respond, didn't even register that anyone had said a word. There were dark circles around his eyes and his lips were cracked dry. It would be another three days, as far as I could judge the time, before Kevin said a word to anyone.

Michael sat on the end of his bed gently rocking back and forth. His hair was full of collected grease and dandruff. Every bone was visible, he was so skinny.

"You Michael?"

"You're not like the rest of us," he said.

"How's that?"

He didn't respond.

"I just wanted to say thanks for helping me out the other day in the cafeteria. Doc Sawyer told me you called for help," I said and stuck out my hand. "I'm Jason."

Michael ignored my hand. "You're not like the rest of us," he repeated, and then looked around the room.

"I understand if you don't want to shake, it's no big deal, just wanted to say thank you."

He grabbed my wrist when I started to walk away. "First chance you get, you run. Just run away from here." He let go of my wrist. On the other side of the room, Charlie was watching us. He said something to James, who then turned and started to head in our direction.

"Not what you think," Michael whispered. He had straightened himself and looked a little calmer, but a big tear ran down each cheek. He finally made eye contact. "This place is not what you think."

"Y'all look thick as thieves over here," James said.

"Just thanking him for helping me out the other day," I said. "Were you going to show me around, James?"

"Sure thing," he said. "You smoke?"

"Yeah, please tell me we can smoke here."

"Just not inside, come on."

"Thank god. That's the first good thing I've heard in days." I brushed off what Michael had said pretty much immediately. It was a mental hospital, after all. There were bound to be some unusual things said. He seemed genuine, but I didn't know him at all, and I might reconsider what he'd told me if he gained my trust. Then again, I had no intention of being there long enough to get to know any of them.

James gave me the breakdown of the place as smoke billowed and mixed with the cold air into plumes above our heads. It drifted across the unkempt lawn through tree limbs and on to places I couldn't yet go.

No one could turn the lights on or off, the access for the switch was behind another locked door. Lights on at seven, lights off at ten, every day on the nose. Meals were the same. Always a crooked mumbling gaggle of patients waiting in a sort of line to be allowed to eat whatever horrid plastic concoction they'd decided to serve at seven-thirty, twelve, and six every day. Always the same. Meds came on a squeaky rolling cart right after lights on and right before lights out. Always the same. Smoking privileges, outside only three times per day as long as you behaved.

"You about done?" he asked. "Time to go back in."

"All right," I said, taking a string of quick puffs before stubbing my cigarette out in the ash can and digging my hands into my armpits. I often trapped my hands there in the early days at White Oaks to avoid looking too fidgety while the detox ran its final course.

"I forgot about games," he said as we walked back toward the building. "There are a few puzzles, chess board, checkers and cards that you can have access to any time. Again, as long as you're behaving. Give me or Charlie any problems, or any of the other staff, that'll be the first thing you lose."

"Understood," I said, but left out the *you stupid hick* that went through my head.

While he fumbled with the keys to unlock the door, I looked around and for the first time noticed the tall security fence topped with razor wire. I stepped inside and James locked the door behind us.

"I've never been to a mental hospital before," I said, "but the level of security seems a bit much."

He shrugged but didn't address the comment. "It's almost time for group," James said as he unlocked and opened the ward's thick steel door. The smell of bleach punched me in the face as soon as we walked inside.

"You guys ought to consider toning down the cleansers a bit," I said, but James' attention was elsewhere. He was fixated on the patient across the room who was writing on the wall in the most exquisite calligraphy I'd ever seen with what appeared to be his own feces.

"Damnit, Stephen," James yelled and ran across the room.

Stephen had an exploded shit stain on the seat of his pants that streaked down his leg into a loose pool at his feet. When he exhausted the ink, he bent down and dipped an index finger into the pool and stood back up. He turned around and looked at James with an empty expression. His tangled hair shot in every direction. It looked like he'd used some of the excess ink as hair mousse. Stephen looked at his caked finger, then back at James.

"Do not," James started, but before he finished Stephen wiped his finger on James' shirt and smiled.

I liked that smile. The little *fuck you, James*, even though at that point there was no particular reason other than intuition to dislike James. I'd like the smile less later when Dr. Sawyer told me why Stephen was there and I realized that the razor wire and lock on every door might have been a necessity, at least in Stephen's case.

Stephen's smile widened while taking in the expression on James' face that I could only wish to see, then Stephen bolted, and James chased him. They ran in circles around the room, as the other patients hooted and cheered until James employed an old playground move and kicked Stephen's shit pasted shoe causing his right foot to click off the heel of his left. Stephen crashed to the floor and slid into the crumbling plaster wall. Despite the hard fall, Stephen cackled with delight until James came down on top of him.

"Mother fucker," James shouted and dug his knee into the small of Stephen's back while pulling his arm awkwardly until there was a pop.

Stephen screamed and James took a handful of hair and mashed his face into the floor. "You're going to pay for that." James yanked him up.

The walking protein shakes whose names I hadn't learned yet surrounded them and the three of them, under Charlie's supervision, rushed Stephen into the bathroom and threw him to the tile floor, then turned on the shower. The door swung shut behind Charlie and for twenty minutes we all stood silently listening to the four orderlies yell at and beat Stephen, and probably wash him and themselves in between.

My amusement turned to anger as we listened to Stephen's screaming. The anger intensified when I noticed the other patients sitting around passively, like nothing was happening. The only one who didn't seem okay with it was Michael. He sat on the bed with his head in between his knees, rocking back and forth, pressing his knees against his ears to drown out the noise. He looked at me, and I could sense some kind of inexplicable apology.

Then the bathroom door flew open, Charlie stormed out, and Michael put his head back down.

Charlie looked like a pissed off bull seeing nothing but red when he came back into the room. It was unwise to get involved in any way, especially with violence, and doing so would only extend my stay at White Oaks. I didn't even know Stephen, or any of the others, and the truth was that my anger was selfish. Granted, it was wrong for them to beat Stephen so viciously, regardless of the infraction, but what really pissed me off was that I was there in the first place. I didn't belong in a mental hospital. There were some issues I wasn't dealing with in a healthy way, no doubt of that, but they had no right to keep me there and the asshole storming out of the bathroom with a helpless man's blood on his knuckles was the personification of that. If I didn't respond to that feeling right then, I'd end up with my head between my knees like Michael, and that wasn't going to happen.

With the possible ramifications completely ignored, I walked toward

Charlie, fists clenched and eager. By the time he saw me coming it was too late for him to react. I took a quick step forward and delivered an arching punch to the soft spot where the jaw and earlobe meet. Charlie immediately collapsed to the floor, his head audibly cracked off the hard surface.

No one moved or said a word. James and the other guards were still in the bathroom with Stephen. By the time my heart slowed down and I noticed the quiet, a needle was sliding out of my arm. Dr. Sawyer had come out of nowhere.

CHAPTER 4

Maybe I'd been hypnotized and divulged this all to Dr. Sawyer, or maybe I was dying from whatever he injected me with and images of the past flew through my mind, a last chance for inevitable shame and regret. It could have just been a nightmare. After Dr. Sawyer injected me and the world went black, I was on my last walk through the mountains of Afghanistan, over ten years before my admission to White Oaks.

***

The IED went off after five hundred and twenty-four minutes of continuous walking through jagged mountain ranges that would exhaust mules before it exhausted us.

The golf ball sized devices we all had pinned to our gear were to measure the force of an explosion, and provide an instantaneous battlefield diagnosis of traumatic brain injury (TBI), although many of the devices proved faulty over the years. They were worn in triplicate, creating a Bermuda Triangle across the chest. It's where the person I used to be disappeared and was lost forever.

There was the crunch of earth beneath boots, and then a pop and the ground shook. The horizon turned on its side and the next thought not prickling with static was about the clouds swirling into different shapes above me.

After tending to injuries much worse than mine, the medic wrapped the gouge in my leg and what remained of the fingers on my left hand. One of the thousands of pieces of shrapnel whizzing in every direction went through the meat under my chin and came out just below my left eye. It was one of those objects with an inexplicable trajectory that we'd all learned to stop questioning and just accept. He inspected the wound long enough to confirm that it looked worse than it was, and then checked the golf ball device to make sure I wasn't exposed to enough of the concussive force for traumatic brain injury. He tapped me on the shoulder, shoved a Fentanyl lollipop in my mouth, and then moved on to the next delirious soldier.

What the devices couldn't detect were the internal injuries to soft tissue, muscle, and the discs in my spine. Those injuries didn't fully reveal themselves until after Landstuhl and Walter Reed, where they couldn't even get incompetence right.

On one of my last days at Walter Reed, there was a Purple Heart ceremony. It was pinned to my hospital gown by Congressman Whoever. It must have been an election year. He waltzed into my room all smiles and feigned reverence and brought a journalist with him. She took our picture and asked me what it felt like to be an American hero.

"I wouldn't know," I told her, but said nothing about the smell of burnt flesh or how the most critical part of myself broke when I killed my best friend.

Ten years went by in a blur of appointments at the veteran's hospital, when I was lucky enough to get one. The morbidly obese nurse practitioner I was initially assigned to rolled into the exam room on her Government Issue mobility cart. She suggested I lose a few pounds and quit smoking, as if she were an authority on healthy lifestyle choices. She was the first in a long line of incompetent, overworked medical staff.

Ten years of tests, x-rays, and blood work. MRI's – lying in a tube of sporadic drumbeats – the buzzing that always caused my stomach to turn and vision blur. Physical therapy, trigger point injections, battlefield acupuncture, radio frequency ablations, and epidural injections. It all amounted to nothing more than the perpetuation of frustration and misery.

Outside of the doctors, tests, and procedures, I did everything I could think of. Only the highest quality supplements and organic food went into my body even though the grocery bills took up the vast majority of my meager income. I gave up alcohol, caffeine, sugar, and processed foods. I took one thousand milligrams of all-natural vegetarian formula high potency calcium and magnesium to support bone, muscle, and nerve health. For potassium, which among other things assists in normal muscle contraction and relaxation, I ate two bananas every day. One in the morning, one at night. An apple in between for good measure. The herb rhodiola to support a healthy response to the stress all the pain and failed treatments caused.

Thirty minutes of stretches and breathing exercises twice a day. Yoga. Meditation. Bike rides and walks in the park. I went to counseling every week and volunteered at homeless shelters. I read to children at the local library, but had to keep my incomplete hand in my pocket because it was too distracting for some and too distressing for others. It was hard enough for them to look at the scars on my face, but the mangled hand put it over the top for most of them.

None of it changed the progression of symptoms. It got to the point – after all the appointments, treatments, and attempts to remove the unexplainable devastation from my life – that the only way I could function, the only way I felt like a less-shattered version of myself, was to be high on whatever I could get my hands on. All my efforts and positive thinking had failed, and I just gave up. I had become a wraithlike shell of the man I once was.

Memories of those days, those nights, when I ingested as much as I could to mask the symptoms, were like the faded edges of an old photograph that would crumble to nothing as soon as I grabbed hold and tried to make sense of it.

It never stopped. Every day was the same exact battle, not only to outlast the pain and have some normalcy in my life, but to outlast the overwhelming desire to numb it with anything within reach. Regardless of my weakness or strength, my personal failings or successes, the pain was always there; taunting me, tempting me, driving me mad.

Headaches that lasted days at a time exploded every nerve; turned every vein and fiber in the back of my eyeballs into frayed sparking electrical wires that told me the apocalypse had come.

The endless, suffocating pain in my head and shoulder jolted down my arm into hot needle fingertips that weren't even there anymore and drowned out everything else.

When the pills didn't do enough, I would drink myself into a black hole to mask the pain but would still wake up with crackling embers behind each eye, and razor blades wrapped around my spine. Only then I'd have to add a hangover to the list of symptoms that made me want to eat a bullet.

The first overdose was on Cyclobenzaprine, a muscle relaxer I relied too heavily on to reduce the unexplained tension in the muscles from the base of my skull to the curve of my right shoulder.

The muscles would, without warning or reason, grow rock hard to create the earth ending headaches that lasted for days. When it was really bad, the muscles would clinch around the nerve grouping that sent explosions of hot pin pricks coursing through every cell of my right arm and into a tingling hand that wouldn't wake up for days at a time, except to burn.

When the screaming in my head from Monday went to crushing and desperate on Thursday, I swallowed an uncounted handful of muscle relaxers.

An hour later, maybe two, maybe twenty, I tried to stop myself from falling in the street. How I got on the street in the first place is still a mystery to me. My feet were thousand-pound blocks of stone, dragging beneath me too slowly to reach the door before oblivion.

My vision mutinied; the surrounding area of brick buildings, trees, and abandoned shops bounced and swirled around me in slow motion. Then my eyeballs slipped from their sockets and slid down my throat. In my blindness I could feel myself wobbling, being held in place only by the blocks of stone that were my feet. Then my vision came back, and I was peering up at my own pallid sweaty face.

The stone that encased my feet turned to lava and scorched the retinas that materialized in my toenails. My knees finally buckled, and I dropped onto the grainy cement below.

How I got back into my apartment without a trip to the emergency room is as much a mystery as how I got on the street in the first place.

The years floated by on a belching ocean of sedatives. My thoughts, especially in the morning, drifted to my nightstand where a pistol waited patiently for me to work up the nerve to exercise the only viable option left. There would have been no question about intent if I had taken the gun out of the nightstand drawer and turned myself into a statistic. Intent had to remain gray, or so I told myself, if I ever wanted to get past the guard at the gates of heaven. Assuming there even was such a place.

Sleep was the only thing to ever bring complete relief from the pain, but even then, I was haunted by nightmares. I saw limbs scattered about the mountainside. I saw everyone lost that day and all the days before it when even more were lost. I saw the things I did to survive that made sense, and the things I did to survive that I could never tell anyone who wasn't there to understand them. The world was just blood and teeth and screams, but every night I was desperate to see them again because, despite the restlessness of the sleep, it was the only time I could escape the pain.

There was enough OxyContin sitting on the nightstand to sedate a herd of elephants. For my second overdose, I opened the bottle and shook enough onto my palm to bring that relief.

I stared with glassy swirling eyes at the magnificence of its beautiful pale blue long enough to convince myself that I would survive another dose.

CHAPTER 5

Whatever Dr. Sawyer injected me with started to wear off. When I tried to move, I found myself restrained, lying on a table in a room that skipped and swayed every time I turned my head or thought too hard. Blurring around the room by the table were Dr. Sawyer and Charlie. At first, I couldn't make out what they were saying, but it was clear that Dr. Sawyer was trying to talk Charlie out of doing something.

Seconds floated by on tendrils of dust drifting from a ceiling hovering a mile above me. Then the table I was tied to moved and I was facing them both. Fingers snapped in front of my face; the sound echoed inside my head.

"Can you hear me, Jason?" I finally heard Dr. Sawyer say.

I nodded; the room vibrated inside my head as I struggled to focus. With surfacing clarity, I asked Charlie, "How's the jaw?"

"It's the only shot you're ever going to get," Charlie said. His face was expressionless, eyes empty, like he thought I was nothing and intended to treat me as such. "And it's fine. Lucky shot is all, punk ass, I wasn't even looking."

"How's Stephen?"

"We'll get to Stephen," Dr. Sawyer said and stepped between me and Charlie. There was a long quiet before Charlie stepped back and leaned against the wall, his face in the shadows.

"Charlie is right," Dr. Sawyer said. "You won't be hitting another guard. Not if you have any self-interest."

"That's a little sinister sounding, Doc. What are you going to do? Drug me and tie me to a table?"

"We'll do whatever is necessary."

There was something behind the words that I sensed but couldn't flesh out. There was a long pause in the conversation that only served to draw out my sense of disquiet.

"So, what about Stephen?" I asked. "Can you tell me how he is now?"

"You shouldn't care about that asshole," Charlie said. Dr. Sawyer looked at him hard and Charlie leaned back against the wall.

"Again," Dr. Sawyer said. "Charlie is right. Stephen doesn't deserve your concern. You know, I'm not supposed to do this, confidentiality and all, but since you're new I'll make an exception." Dr. Sawyer leaned against the wall next to Charlie.

"The least offensive crime Stephen ever committed was actually his first," he said. "One day his mom came home from work early and heard a child's muffled screams. Stephen was twelve at the time. She searched the house but found no one. Finally, she traced the noise to the attic. She pulled the steps down from the ceiling and went up, where she found Stephen with the neighbor's six-month-old boy. The baby had a rag over his face to muffle the screams." Dr. Sawyer stepped closer to me again. "Stephen had been poking the baby with a safety pin, just to see what it felt like to hurt something. His mother beat him half to death. Had him committed that day."

"Can you take me off the table now?" I asked. The doc breaking confidentiality was enough of a red flag by itself, but him using Stephen's past to justify the assault made even less sense. Assuming what he told me was true, what Stephen did was horrendous, but he did it when he was twelve years old, and it justified nothing. There was no way anyone would ever be okay with the hospital staff beating patients, no matter the reason, and regardless of how bad their past behavior might have been.

"You're right," Dr. Sawyer said. "We are going to be late for group session. Of course, whose fault is that? I'm going to give you something else just to loosen you up a bit more." He produced a syringe out of nowhere. "After group session, you tell me of any side effects, okay?"

"You doing a study?" I asked, ever the smartass.

"Something like that," he said and then the room went back to being blurry and timeless.

I woke up in the main room sitting in a circle with all the other patients. Someone was behind me, holding my shoulders so I wouldn't fall out of the chair. Dr. Sawyer was on the other side of the room in a chair just like mine with a slight smile on his face.

"Looks like we can begin," Dr. Sawyer said. "Our newbie is awake."

I heard what he said, or heard some version of it from another dimension as my mind drifted somewhere out in the dark quiet of space. He kept talking, though some of the syllables went the wrong way as they echoed around eternity, so I only caught pieces. He told the rest of the patients that I'd been punished and warned and that any such behavior would *blah blah blah*.

"Now that we have that out of the way," he said and shuffled some papers. "Right, last time, Kevin, you were wondering why none of the patients ever have visitors. Would you like to continue there or should we move on?"

Kevin didn't respond. Maybe his mind was floating through the same space mine was.

"Kevin?" Dr. Sawyer said and sighed after staring up at Charlie, who was standing somewhere behind me, for a long time. It looked like Dr. Sawyer was irritated with Charlie, like he'd done something to Kevin to cause the lack of response. Maybe the trash can incident on my first day? If that was true, did it mean Dr. Sawyer wasn't as much of a dick as I thought, or was there another explanation for the long, cold stare? I could've been overcomplicating the situation internally because my seemingly disembodied brain was floating through another dimension while I sat in a mental hospital unable to support my own weight. The only things I could really feel were the cold metal folding chair through the paper-thin pajama pants, and the incredible, restrictive weight of the two hands pressing down on my shoulders.

"Moving on then. How about you, Leonard? You're next up to talk if you want."

I hadn't met Leonard yet and wasn't sure which of the out of focus faces belonged to him, but apparently, he was sitting right next to me because that's where the wavering distorted response came from.

"The medicine you're giving me," Leonard said. "What is it?"

"We don't talk about medicine during group sessions," Dr. Sawyer said. My head started to clear enough for me to wonder why we couldn't discuss things like medication in group. Medication was a big part of life in a mental hospital; it had to come up at some point.

"My dream," Leonard said without addressing the warning. "It was too real to not be real." He paused and seemed to be considering something of great importance. "Maybe it wasn't a dream at all, but something I can only see now with the new eyes you gave me."

"New eyes?" Dr. Sawyer asked then scribbled furiously on his notepad.

"I felt them inside for so long. I always knew, but then I saw them. Something was moving under my shirt, so I lifted it up and there was a beehive of little boils and blisters, thousands of them, all over my chest and stomach. I picked at one until it broke open. Inside the skin and puss was this little multicolored insect with a needle-pointed nose just digging into me. I picked it off and when I crushed it, there weren't any guts or blood, the bug was a machine and it broke into little pieces of metal and sparks."

The only thing I could focus on was Leonard's eyes. Everything else had started wavering again. His eyes seemed to sink into his skull as his pupils dilated and contracted rapidly, one and then the other, but when I blinked he looked normal again, or as normal as a man telling that kind of story could appear.

"The more I dug for them," Leonard continued. "The more I found. Thousands of them. Everyone that I killed seemed to duplicate as soon as I crushed it." Leonard wiped sweat from his face and frowned hard, like he was trying to remember some detail that was just out of reach. "There were so many. I couldn't stop them all and they just went inside me." He lifted his shirt to show his destroyed chest and stomach. "I know what you're doing, Doc," Leonard said. "I know."

Dr. Sawyer looked at the self-inflicted damage.

"Good lord," was all he said.

CHAPTER 6

The next few days were a blur. The symptoms from detoxing seemed to worsen every night. I spent most of the time in bed sweating, slamming down water, then rushing into the bathroom to throw it all back up.

Although I wasn't given any kind of meds, I could have sworn they were injecting me with something at night. I'd wake up with sore spots on my arms and butt cheeks where bruises would form, and then the rest of the day was forgotten in irretrievable darkness.

Eventually, I found myself in Dr. Sawyer's office again.

"How do you feel, Mr. Miller?" Dr. Sawyer asked.

"Could you stop calling me Mr. Miller?"

"Why?" he asked, uncrossing his legs and pushing back from his desk.

"Because I asked you to." I turned my gaze from the crack in the floor to his face for the first time since coming into his office.

There was a sudden rush of warm air from a large air vent above me. My hands and feet were always freezing. "*Cold hands, warm heart,*" my mom used to say. Damn I missed her. So, the air could hit my feet, I scooted the chair back and then slipped my hands under my legs to help warm them up.

"You don't like it?" he asked.

"No, I don't." That was a lie. It didn't bother me one bit that he called me Mr. Miller. After years in the Army, I was more than used to formality, but I was beginning to grasp the depth of his stick-in-the-ass mentality and poor bedside manner. I guess he figured when he was dealing with crazy people, he didn't need to worry much about that. I made the request to irritate him, and to avoid answering his questions. In truth, I hadn't heard a single word he said.

"Why?"

"I don't know," I said and shrugged my shoulders. "Too formal, I guess. If you're going to go digging around in the darkest corners of my consciousness, we should be on a first name basis."

He smiled thinly and nodded. "I want to know how you're feeling right now."

"About what?"

"About anything. Your life. How you ended up sitting in this room right now. Your choices. Anything at all," he paused. "Jason, you need to take this more seriously or your stay at White Oaks will go on much longer than you'd like."

"It's already past that point," I said and crossed my arms. After a long silence, I asked how long he'd been counseling for.

"Why?"

"Because you're not very good at it."

"Why do you think that, Mr. Miller?" He put a strong emphasis on the *mister*. I couldn't help but laugh.

"Other counselors I've seen had patience. They listened. They never prodded and forced things the way you do."

He set his pen down, clasped his hands in front of himself and said nothing.

"Are there any women here?" I asked, my arms unfolding so my hands could rest on my legs.

"Patients?"

"Any women in any part of the hospital."

"No," he said, but something in his expression changed.

"Hmm. I heard you arguing with a woman the day I was admitted."

"No such thing happened. You weren't exactly in the best state of mind when you came in," he said. "Don't change the subject. We're talking about you, or trying to anyway."

I sat back in the chair and refolded my arms, having no interest in making things easier on either one of us.

Eventually, the silence got too boring, and I started to feel like a brat sitting uncooperatively in the principal's office. What I wanted more than anything was to leave, so I decided to play along. I'd give him some access and pretend to receive actual therapy in order to get out of there as soon as possible.

"Fine," I said. "You want the truth?"

"I know you're uncomfortable and angry with me, but I really do want to help you."

Somewhere in the back of my mind, alarm bells went off. Outside of him being a bad counselor, there was little to justify the feeling, but I didn't believe for one second that his motives were altruistic. I didn't know what he wanted or why, but his words sounded empty and rehearsed.

However, despite my reservations, there were no substances rushing through my blood stream for the first time in years and it allowed me to think clearly for a change. That unfamiliar clarity caused me to acknowledge the possibility that I might have been the one who was untrustworthy and had questionable motivations.

"The truth is that sometimes I can still feel the vibrations inside my head."

"Vibrations?" he said, cocking one eyebrow.

"From the bomb. From all the bombs. The bullets. All of it."

"No, Mr. Miller, go back further."

"What do you mean?"

"I can't even imagine the things you've been through and seen, and we'll get to the war, but I don't think that's why you're here or why you've been using so heavily for so many years."

There were things I wasn't ready to talk about, and things that no one would ever know, especially not him. There had to be something else, something real, but for the longest time, as I studied the swirling patterns on the tile floor, I couldn't think of anything. Then it hit me. I opened my mouth to speak, closed it again and furrowed my brow.

"Take your time," he said and waited for me to gather my thoughts.

"You asked how I feel, but I don't really know how I feel about anything."

He didn't respond, just continued to watch me think things over.

"I've been in this fog for so long that I don't really know anything about myself. Like I've been on autopilot for decades. An autopilot designed by the biggest moron imaginable, just circling around and around."

"What kind of fog?"

"My childhood lingers on the other side of the fog. It started to form when I was about fifteen, I guess. Before that is so much clearer. I was clearer. Better.

"I played baseball from an early age. I was a decent hitter and outfielder, and had a good arm. Pitching was my favorite." I felt an old version of myself smile at the memories suddenly pouring in. The smell of an oiled baseball glove and freshly cut grass. How my hands would sting when I didn't hit the ball with the sweet spot of the bat. The sound of my dad cheering when I struck someone out or made a diving catch in left field, his voice distinctly drowning out everyone else's.

"My dad wasn't quick with compliments. If he said I was good at something, he really meant it. He said he could tell from an early age that I had something the other kids didn't.

"I was a good student. Had a lot of friends. Even moving around to different bases there was always a lot of camaraderie. All the Army kids were in the same situation and we always stuck together, even though we usually only knew each other for two or three years before one or the other had to move along."

"Was it just you and your dad?" Dr. Sawyer asked.

"No, both my parents were in the Army."

"No brothers or sisters?"

I shook my head. "Anyway, my mom got out when I was ten. My dad retired when I was fifteen and everything changed after that."

"How?" he asked, shifting in his chair.

"They were civilians then. The rotating circle of friends, all the camaraderie, it was gone. It was really different. We moved back here, or not far from here anyway. Everything I knew, the life I was accustomed to, all changed. It was a bad time for change too."

"Why's that?" Dr. Sawyer asked.

"Because I was a teenager, which means I was a dumbass and just itching to rebel against anything. After that, it's a pretty typical dipshit teenage-boy story. I didn't want to play baseball anymore. Met some new friends who were even bigger dipshits. Me and a couple other guys started forging documents. Pretty straightforward stuff at first, permissions slips, altered report cards. Eventually we got busted making fake IDs. Started drinking, doing drugs. Lots of drugs."

"Like what?"

"Pretty much everything but heroin."

"Pretty much?" he prodded, his pen hovering over the paper.

"Acid, mushrooms, pot, and booze primarily. But I tried almost everything else at least once. Crack, meth, cocaine, all kinds of different prescriptions from my friends' parents' medicine cabinets. It wasn't a side hobby either. When I went to school, which wasn't very often, I rarely went sober. Didn't do my homework. Didn't do much of anything really. The relationship I had with my parents got bad pretty quickly. To tell you the truth, from about age fifteen to nineteen is a total blank. I did nothing but get high, and whatever I needed to do to get high more, whether it was work random jobs or steal. When I should have been growing up, learning about myself, the world and forming some kind of general plan for my life, I was smoking weed and dropping acid and staying in that perpetual fog."

I felt safe sharing that with him because it was all very general. There were far worse truths to share outside of the teenage adventures, but I'd only tell them to the right person at the right time and only if my hand was forced.

He rolled his eyes and let out a long breath. "Yes, you were quite the dipshit," he said and smiled. Fucking smiled at me; it was unbelievable, like he was playing with a toy or something. That's how it felt, like I was his entertainment, his lab rat. I shouldn't have been mad; after all, he was right to agree with me. I was a jackass, but something about that smile just made the alarm bells go off again.

"Your pattern of behavior may have started there, but you know what?"

"What?"

"It's good to have the history, but I think your reason for such abuse is somewhere else in your past." He cocked his head to one side and narrowed his eyes. "It's not the war either, is it? Or not entirely." He paused, and I shifted uncomfortably in my seat. "You can tell me anything and it'll never leave this room."

"You know what," I said. "I'm done talking."

"You sure?" His smile immediately no longer playful.

I didn't respond.

"Charlie," he shouted to the goon waiting outside the door. His eyes never left mine. Charlie opened the door without a word.

"Please take *Mister* Miller down to the Thinking Room."

"What's that?" I asked and hoped my tone didn't reveal that whatever it was scared me.

"Just a place where you can think about what you want out of your time here and what you expect to gain by being uncooperative."

Charlie dug his fingers into the soft tissue below the armpit. "Let's go, *Mister* Miller," he buzzed in my ear.

The Thinking Room was nothing more than a concrete floor and cinder block walls that went up at least twenty feet. There was a drain in the center of the room. No bed, no toilet, just walls and floor. Charlie shoved me into the room.

"Sleep tight," he said and slammed the door.

CHAPTER 7

When I got out of the Thinking Room the next morning my back hurt so bad from sitting on the hard floor overnight that I could barely think straight. The pain needed to be worth something, and it seemed obvious that I'd be taken back to Dr. Sawyer's office so he could explain the lesson behind the punishment. But if there had been a lesson, he never told me what it was. Perhaps the lesson was that he had all the power, and if I wanted to stay out of that room, I'd do what he asked, when he asked. I would become much more familiar with that room over time.

On my way toward the television area, a kid wearing a lab coat, who looked to be in his twenties, stepped in front of me.

"What color is a banana?" he asked and held his clipboard up, ready to take notes.

"What?"

"What color is a banana?" he repeated slowly as if he thought I had a learning disability.

"Who are you?" I asked.

"Craig," he said, as if I should have known.

"Jason." I held my hand out and he looked at it, wrinkled his nose and took a step back. I dropped my hand and walked around him.

"You didn't answer the question," he said to my back.

I sat on the couch next to Kevin. "What the hell is that about?" I asked him.

"What, Craig?" he asked, gesturing at the orderly with a slight nod.

"Yeah, as soon as I walked in the door, he asked me what color a banana is."

"He's always asking weird questions like that, not sure why." He wiped his nose on his sleeve. "He's here every couple weeks. Just wanders around asking us all weird questions, and then we don't see him for a while."

"Who was the first President of the United States?" Craig asked another patient from across the room.

"How long have you been here?" I asked Kevin.

He stared at the television, which was playing *SpongeBob Squarepants*, the episode with Pantera as the special musical guest.

"Um," he said and glanced in my direction for a half second before his attention went back to the television. "I don't know."

"You don't know how long you've been here?"

He shrugged. "Six months? I don't know, a year maybe?"

I didn't know what to say to that, so moved on. "Dr. Sawyer said something the other day about people not getting visitors. Is that true? When was the last time your wife visited you?"

Kevin's head swiveled to face me, his eyes big and wet. "How do you know about her?"

"You're wearing a ring. Just assumed."

His expression darkened and he looked back to SpongeBob.

"She's dead. My wife and two girls."

"Oh my god, man, I'm so sorry." I was curious about how, but we barely knew each other and regardless of our surroundings or his mental state, it was too soon to ask such a question. It could have been something he had no involvement in, or could have been another story like Stephen's. Maybe I was the only, or one of the only, patients at White Oaks without a criminally violent past and that's why security seemed to be so heavy at the facility, because it needed to be.

We watched cartoons in silence for another two hours until James called the next group to go out for a smoke.

Outside, I stared across the grounds at the collection of black walnut trees on the other side of the fence. They stood between the white oaks surrounding the perimeter. Some of the limbs were hanging over the razor wire fence and I could see some walnuts decaying in the grass on the hospital side. I assumed James would say no if I asked to walk over, so I just watched the tangled jagged branches sway in the breeze and tried to remember the exact smell from the fleshy, blackening husks. Maybe a little bit like a spicy orange? That seemed wrong, but it was close.

Black walnuts were my mom's favorite. After Dad retired and we moved back to Ohio, they bought an old house in the country. It was surrounded by corn and soybean fields with neighbors set apart by miles. In our back yard was a massive black walnut tree. My mom always gathered whatever nuts the squirrels and chipmunks didn't beat her to and added them to her homemade ice cream.

I stubbed out my second cigarette and continued contemplating the gently swaying trees when a back spasm worse than any I'd experienced in years came. It started slow. The back of my neck got hot, and my face started to tingle. The muscles in between my shoulder blades cramped and I heard a pop. A jolt of electricity went from my spine to phantom fingertips and my vision doubled. My spine felt like it was coated with broken glass, and every breath, every movement was a mistake I could never take back. A low groan escaped my throat and I bent over.

"You okay?" James asked.

I didn't respond right away so he walked over and pulled me up by the shoulder. I screamed and another jolt of electricity went up my spine and pierced my eye like a thousand scattered needles.

My drug abuse had obviously been unhealthy and dangerous, but it didn't come out of nowhere. Episodes like that were indescribable misery and not having any medication at all was a blessing and a curse. Sure, I wasn't a junkie anymore, but I also had nothing to treat any symptoms, which were returning and worsening faster than I could deal with.

"My back," I said through clenched teeth.

"All right," he said, turning to the others. "Thanks to Jason, our smoke break is over early."

James was the only person bothered by that. The other patients, two I hadn't met, and Michael, who didn't smoke but went outside with us for a change of scenery, stared at James with contempt. Michael stepped forward to help me walk in, but I held up a hand in protest.

"Thanks, man, better not to touch me right now. Just need to take it slow." I started to shuffle along the path back toward the building.

We reached the door, but had to wait for James, who stayed behind to finish his smoke. He was deliberately stalling and the only thing it accomplished was causing me additional discomfort. Like Charlie with the trashcan on my first day, James was intentionally tormenting me and there was no reason for it. No explanation or excuse.

"Hey, we don't mind," one of the patients I hadn't met said before James got there. "He's a jerk."

"Thanks," I said. "What's your name?"

"Corey. Friends call me CJ."

"Good to meet you CJ," I said, and he smiled.

Most of the scattered teeth left in his mouth were crooked and grey. His clothes, if you could call the uncomfortable cheap pajamas we wore clothes, hung off him like he'd recently dropped a hundred pounds. His skin was almost transparent, like God covered a skeleton with dirty Saran Wrap and sent it out into the world. He looked like a Halloween decoration more than a man, but I liked him right away.

"Let's get you inside," James said and slapped me on the back.

I wanted to scream again, but not as much as I wanted to bludgeon him. Michael winced and shook his head, then joined me in staring daggers at the back of James' head.

When we got back to the ward CJ asked if I wanted to play a game of chess some time. "Definitely," I said. "For now, I need to lie down though."

"Raincheck," he said and pointed a finger gun at me, a big smile painted on his Saran Wrap face.

"Raincheck," I said. He pulled the trigger and walked off.

"James." I slowly lowered myself onto the bed. "Can you get the doc for me please?"

"You bet," he said and mumbled something else I couldn't hear when he turned to walk away.

Two hours later, Dr. Sawyer came onto the ward. The two hours had passed slowly, felt more like twenty, but I was able to measure the time by counting the number of Seinfeld episodes that played on TV. The last episode to play before Doc showed up was the one where George's fiancé died from poisoning after licking all the stamps for their wedding invitations. By then, I was wishing for stamps of my own.

"James said you're having back problems," Dr. Sawyer said, his age-stained hands dug into the pockets of his sweater, which was the color of dead grass.

"Can I get something for the pain, Doc?"

He sighed.

"Come on, man. I've been off all forms of medication for a week. Give me a break."

"You're not just putting on a show to get drugs? You're really hurt?"

"This is the worst spasm I've had in a long time, but this shit happens regularly. Pretty sure I mentioned that before."

He surveyed me for a moment, and then took a knee. "Where's it hurting?" he asked and pressed on my shoulder. I pulled in a quick breath.

"Please," I said. By then beads of sweat were standing on my forehead and the sheets were damp.

"One dose of muscle relaxers and Percocet today. One more tomorrow *if* you need it. That's it. I have a plan for a more long-term solution for you. We'll discuss that tomorrow."

CHAPTER 8

Hours before anyone else woke up the next day, I lay there hoping Dr. Sawyer would hold to his promise of another dose. My back had improved a little overnight, but everything still ached and the fingers that weren't there buzzed with activity.

I stared for a long time at the ceiling air vent on the far wall by the TV, which looked big enough to get through. I thought I could climb up through the vent when everyone was asleep and find out where it led. Maybe it would take me into the pharmacy and I could determine my own dosage for a while. Maybe it'd take me to an exit and I could discharge myself, but every door I'd been through so far required a key to open, even from the inside. I'd noticed the last time we were outside smoking that the razor wire fence didn't extend over the employee parking lot, so if I found a door that led to that, and the door didn't require a key, maybe I could get out. I'd have to wait until my back improved to find out.

When the lights finally came on and the medication cart rolled out of the locked pharmacy, I sat up with slow, measured movements.

Craig, the temp with the weird questions, pushed the cart over to CJ's bed first. Craig held out the paper cup with pills and CJ shook his head.

"What's the problem, CJ?"

"I lost another tooth last night. Found it on my pillow when I woke up," he said and held out his hand, I assumed with a tooth in it.

Craig sighed. "And?"

"I keep having those dreams and I just," CJ said, swiping a hand down his gaunt face and crossed his arms. "I don't know. I just don't feel right."

Craig set the cup of pills back on the cart and pulled out a clipboard. He asked a battery of questions about side effects and wrote down everything CJ told him.

"Okay," Craig said. "I'll discuss this with Dr. Sawyer this afternoon, we have a meeting, but for now you need to keep taking it."

CJ shook his head and continued to hug himself.

"I know you're frustrated with the side effects," Craig started, but CJ interrupted him.

"Frustrated? I'm losing all my teeth!"

"But your OCD is practically gone," Craig said as if it were some kind of consolation.

"Craig, I've been taking OCD medication half my life and none of them have done anything like this."

"Take it now and I'll talk to Dr. Sawyer about it later, like I said. Maybe we can figure something else out."

CJ sighed, rocked back and forth on the bed and fidgeted with his shirt. Finally, he tossed the pills into his mouth, chased them with a cup of water from the cart, and watched as Craig moved on. When he got to my bed, he gave me the other dose of muscle relaxers and Percocet I was promised.

Craig's lack of concern for CJ's symptoms, the almost irritated dismissal of it was something I couldn't think of a reasonable explanation for. He seemed to be having a severe reaction to his medication. It was possible the medication was responsible for his overall extremely unhealthy appearance. That reminded me that Dr. Sawyer planned to discuss a new medication for me at some point that day. If I had more information to go on, that might have been more unsettling than it was at the time, and with fresh drugs in my body, whatever concern that did pop up dissipated pretty quickly.

I walked over to CJ's bed, where he sat, head in hands.

"Want to break out the chess board after breakfast?" I asked.

He looked up at me and smiled, careful not to expose the few teeth he had left. His skin was somehow drawn even tighter across his sharp features and his eyes weren't just bloodshot, they were almost completely red.

"Sure thing," he said.

"Are you okay?" It was a stupid question, he obviously wasn't. As if the missing teeth and almost transparent skin weren't enough, the red in his eyes, like every blood vessel had burst overnight, were haunting.

He shrugged but that was his only response.

The ward door opened, and Dr. Sawyer came into view. "Mr. Miller," he said and motioned me over. "How are you feeling today?"

"A little better."

"Good," he said. "Come. Let's talk about that plan I mentioned yesterday."

We got to his office, and he asked me to have a seat. Unlike my first time in his office, the wallpaper was just wallpaper and nothing was nearly as ominous as I'd remembered.

"You know firsthand that this country is dealing with a serious crisis with opioids," he said, and I nodded. "A lot of doctors overprescribe, and regardless of the patient's intentions at the beginning of treatment, opioids are addictive and many patients, like you, end up abusing the medications."

I nodded again. "Okay."

"We have access to a new kind of pain medication, and I think it could really help you. It's non-narcotic and is not addictive."

"Sounds kind of boring, Doc."

He didn't find my comment amusing. "Would you rather I put you back on opioids until you kill yourself?" It came out almost as a shout, like he was genuinely angry.

His newfound concern for my health and well-being confused me. For the first several days he'd been hostile, threatening, and abusive and though I had nothing really substantive to go off of, I thought he meant me more harm than anything, but the shift really confused me. Was I imagining his hostility because I was angry about being there and having to actually deal with my problems without the buffer all the meds had been providing me for years? Was he genuinely concerned and really trying to help me? Or was it all a front, just a different kind? Maybe I'd been unfair, and too quick to judge. I really didn't know what to think at that point.

"Wouldn't you rather have a medication that treats your pain without turning you into a junkie?"

"Of course, but," I said and paused.

"But what?"

"CJ has been having issues with his medication. I heard him talking about it with Craig this morning."

"CJ isn't on the medication you're going to be on."

"Is anyone?" I asked.

"No."

"What kind of side effects should I expect?"

"As with any medication, it varies, but the side effects should be minimal. Maybe a little nausea."

"Okay," I said. "That sounds good. When do I start?"

"Soon, but it will take a few days to get into your system and start working, so if you have any other issues like you had yesterday, I'm okay with very small doses of opioids to get you through it, but only if it's absolutely necessary."

Dr. Sawyer led me back to the ward and I asked CJ if he was ready to play.

"So," I said after we set up the board and he moved the first pawn. "What was that about earlier with Craig?"

"They started giving me a new medication for my OCD. Within a few months I've lost more than half my teeth and I have all kinds of other weird side effects. It's been getting worse in the last few weeks."

"Other side effects like what?"

"You don't want to know, and I don't really want to say."

"Fair enough." I moved a pawn. "Your turn."

The first couple hours of the day, after medicating and eating what passed as food at White Oaks, were the quietest. Everyone's meds had kicked in by then and most of the patients were either watching TV or staring out one of the various windows around the room.

I still didn't quite know what to make of the meeting with Dr. Sawyer. The idea of having a medication that helped manage my pain but didn't cause me to repeat the same behavior I'd been repeating for years was intoxicating. It felt good to be figuratively intoxicated instead of my normal state of literal intoxication, however, I had had enough experience with doctors and drug companies to know not to trust them. Also, even though my initial impression of Dr. Sawyer had been challenged, I still felt something lurking in the shadows of White Oaks.

CJ sneezed hard. A tooth plunked off the chess board and landed in my lap. I picked it off my pajamas and when I looked at the board it was speckled with blood.

"I'm sorry," CJ said.

"You don't have to apologize," I started to say, but before I got out the last word CJ's eyes rolled back, and he fell out of his chair. His body went stiff, except for his right hand, which shook uncontrollably. A pool of urine formed under him and spread. I called for help and knelt down beside him. I tried to soothe him, telling him everything would be okay, even though it clearly wouldn't be.

Charlie and Craig rushed onto the ward with a gurney, hoisted CJ onto it and rushed back out of the room.

***

Not long after CJ's removal from the ward I stood at the far end of the designated smoking area as far away from everyone else as possible. I focused attention on the black walnut trees on the other side of the fence.

At first, I didn't see the man standing under the trees. Maybe he'd materialized out of nothing. Maybe he'd been there the whole time. Under the trees, with his fingers leaking through the chain link fence, was my friend Tony from the Army. We'd served together in Afghanistan. Tony stood there watching me; his years-old, sand-brown t-shirt was still tucked into fatigues, the pants still bloused over highly polished boots. He shouldn't have been there.

Tony was dead.

He rattled the fence, shaking it back and forth. He was yelling something, but I couldn't hear anything but the rattling of the fence. The inside of my head started to vibrate, and my ears rang the same way they used to when someone fired a fifty-cal before I had the chance to put in my ear protection.

I glanced away from Tony when James called out that the break was over, and it was time to go back inside. When I looked back to where Tony had been, he was gone.

"Come on, man, let's go," James said. "It's time for group."

I nodded and started to shuffle in with the other patients, though I stayed at the back of the line in order to sneak glances back to where Tony had been standing. He never reappeared.

The folding metal chairs kept in the supply closet were out and in a circle in the middle of the ward. We each took seats and waited to get started. I stared at the floor and thought of Tony. I tried to convince myself that it was just my imagination. There had been other times, I thought I saw him, but never quite as clearly as that day by the fence under the black walnut tree.

Dr. Sawyer got the meeting going. "Jason, you seem troubled. Why don't we start with you?"

"I'm not troubled," I lied. "Just thinking."

"You'll have to excuse me if I don't believe you. Please, go ahead and get us started. What's troubling you?"

"I said I'm not troubled."

He sighed loudly and shifted in his chair. He dug his fingers into his beard and looked like he was about to lose what remained of his patience. I wondered if my lack of cooperation during group would just land me in the Thinking Room again. I didn't want that.

"Fine, Doc. You're the boss," I said.

I looked around the room at the other patients and staff. The walking protein shakes were standing a few feet outside the circle of chairs, both of them with arms crossed.

I knew what I wanted to talk about but had never told anyone about Tony and wasn't sure I was ready. "What's troubling me is that I haven't met everyone here yet."

"Really," Dr. Sawyer said. "That's what's bothering you?"

"Yeah, I mean I've met Michael, Kevin, Leonard, CJ, and Stephen. I met you, of course, and Charlie, James and Craig, the man with the weird questions." The other patients snickered. "But what about those two?" I asked and pointed to the other guards standing outside the circle.

"That's Lee to your right," Dr. Sawyer said as Lee nodded. "To your left is Randall."

"Pleasure, gentlemen," I said, not even trying to hide the sarcasm. "And, what about this fella?" I was pointing at the one patient I hadn't met yet. He was a small man with wiry hair and eyes so big they looked magnified, the same way it looks with someone wearing thick glasses, but his eyes were just naturally oversized, no prescription required.

"That's Clint," Dr. Sawyer said. "Now that we have that out of the way, how about you answer my question for real."

"I don't know what you're talking about."

"James said your mood changed after the smoke break. He said you were fine when you went outside and almost pale, like you'd seen a ghost, on the way inside."

"I'll have to thank him for that later," I said, rested my elbows on my legs, and put my head in my hands for a long moment before sitting back up.

"I was thinking about my friend, Tony."

"And?"

I didn't respond. From the other side of the circle of chairs Michael said, "It's okay, Jason. You can tell us anything."

Dr. Sawyer glared at him, but Michael maintained eye contact with me until I nodded and silently thanked him.

Randall, apparently tired of standing, pulled out one of the extra folding chairs and sat in between Clint and Dr. Sawyer. When he sat down the chair basically vanished, all covered in an instant by his almost cartoonish muscles. There was a vein on his left forearm that doubled in size every time he opened and closed his fist, which he was doing over and over again. It took me a second to realize he was watching me watch him. I cleared my throat and went back to my story.

"Tony was my best friend in the Army. We served together in the Korengal Valley."

"What happened to him?"

Shifting in my chair I flexed, then relaxed, my right hand, which was starting to go numb. I could almost smell the dirt in the air from our outpost in Afghanistan.

"He died," I said.

"How did he die?"

I shifted again and scratched my head. A couple chairs away, Kevin was staring at the floor, eyes wide and jumping up from the focal point to quickly gaze at me before darting back to the floor. I cleared my throat, opened my mouth to continue, and then closed it again.

Deep in the past, I could hear boots shuffling in dirt, overlapping manic voices and cheering.

Surprising me the way I was trained at the Fort Benning rifle range to be surprised when an M16 rifle pops off a round as an unconscious result of a gentle squeeze of a trigger, I heard my own voice explain, "One of the things people don't understand about war is the boredom. It's either intense and scary and exhilarating, or it's so boring that hours feel like days. There were days when the fighting just went on and on. Other days were so boring we'd openly wish for battle, just so we had something to do."

After a long pause, Dr. Sawyer encouraged me to go on. Other faces, blurred by the tears suddenly standing in my eyes, nodded their own encouragement. A tear slipped from one eye and slithered down my cheek. I absently wiped it away and continued.

"We had to kill the time some way, and there was so much testosterone and anxiety that we often killed the time fighting each other." I looked around the room. "In a sporty way, I mean. Not really *fighting* fighting."

"Where did you say you were?" Clint interrupted.

Dr. Sawyer stopped him. "Jason has the floor, Clint. No crosstalk."

I paid no attention to Clint. "We had tournaments. Like gladiators. There had been dozens of those fights without incident, and when the fights ended, there was never animosity. We were brothers. We were all trained in hand-to-hand combat. It was just something to relieve the boredom."

With the exception of Kevin, I had their rapt attention. Kevin was chewing his fingernails, anxiously bouncing one leg, his eyes focused continuously on the floor having stopped glancing up at me.

"One of the go-to moves for just about any of us was to put pressure on the carotid artery with a forearm. If you do it right the person loses consciousness in a few seconds. If you hold too long though, it can be deadly." My voice cracked on the last word, and I had to take a few seconds to compose myself.

"He was my best friend. I couldn't count the number of times he saved my life. Couldn't count the laughs we shared. I didn't mean to hurt him," I said, tears streamed down my face, so many of the words caught in my throat. It was all coming out, unexpected, and full of hurt.

"I held too long. I didn't mean to." My face tried to contort, but I stopped it, and sat up straight. I let out a long breath, shook my head, and cleared my throat. "I let go as soon as he went limp, just like a dozen other times with a dozen other guys. I let go and jumped up. Everyone was cheering and slapping me on the back, but Tony never got up."

What I didn't tell them was that the others lied on my behalf. They all knew it was an accident. They said Tony collapsed while filling a Hesco barrier. Must have been heat stroke, they said, and I went along with it. Tony's family would never know how he died.

Even though the others knew it was an accident and knew how much I was struggling with what happened they never looked at me the same way. I had become worse than a replacement.

"What did the Army do about it?" Dr. Sawyer asked.

I shrugged and let out a low sob. "Nothing really. It was an accident, and they needed every able-bodied soldier in the field. A week later we got hit by the IED and my time in the Army was over."

"Why are you lying?" Clint asked me from across the circle.

"What?"

"Clint," Dr. Sawyer shouted.

"Don't protect them. We need to get the truth out."

"Protect who, jackass?"

He leaned forward in his chair and lowered his voice, as if doing so would make it so the others in the room wouldn't hear him.

"You were never in Afghanistan. You were on the alien mothership with me. That's why you're missing fingers. You cut them off yourself to get rid of the tracking devices in your fingernails. I did the same," he said and pulled open his cheeks so I could see the holes in his gums. "I did the same, but they planted mine in my molars."

Clint turned to Dr. Sawyer. "You can't allow this, Dr. Sawyer. You know what I saw. You know what I've been through."

Suddenly, Randall, the granite pillar of an orderly, who was sitting between Clint and Dr. Sawyer, joined the conversation. "Motherfucker, quit talking across me, your breath smells like zoo dirt."

I wanted to laugh, it was the most unexpectedly hilarious insult I'd heard in years, and Clint was so red he looked like an angry tomato, but I couldn't stop thinking about Tony and what he might have been doing with his life had I not ended it.

Thinking about that made it hard to laugh.

CHAPTER 9

The routine at White Oaks started to sink in. I had been through extensive counseling before, and although I'd never told the story about Tony to anyone else, I felt no lighter having unburdened myself. If anything, the weight of it increased.

I'd been playing a game of solitaire on my bed but was distracted by staring at the air vent and considering the possibilities. My desire for pain pills, however, outweighed everything else at that moment, even escape. The best case scenario I was practically salivating over was raiding the pharmacy and then escaping. It wasn't just the relief from pain I sought, but the high that I was missing – like I was missing my absent friend, Tony. The conscious realization of that brought out both shame and the immediate dismissal of that shame with excuses for why it was reasonable to start taking drugs again, why it was acceptable.

Stephen plopped down at the foot of my bed, breaking the trance. "I'm not crazy, you know." His hair was going every which way. His eyes darted around the room, on the lookout for what, I didn't know.

"Says the person who painted the walls with his shit the other day."

"That was just a game," he said, then winced when he smelled his finger. Maybe he'd been painting again.

"Then why are you here?" I asked and absent-mindedly shuffled the cards in my hand. "If you aren't crazy, I mean."

All around us was the perpetual soundtrack of the ward, which was the shuffling footsteps and delirious mumbling of other *not crazy* patients.

Stephen looked around the room to make sure no one was eavesdropping and leaned toward me.

"I drank his screams," he said, as if those were the magic words that would explain the inner workings of his mind to me.

"You what now?"

"The Thompson baby, from next door, silly."

At first, I didn't know what he was talking about, and then I remembered the day he painted the walls and got attacked by the guards. The day I knocked out Charlie, got strapped to a table and was threatened for my troubles – the day Doc Sawyer confided in me about Stephen. I wondered how Stephen knew I knew. He probably didn't but was just in a mood to explain his not-crazy presence in a metal hospital.

"I just wanted to know what it felt like," he said. "That's all it was, but my mom was so angry. I didn't hurt him, not really, but, oh, how…he…howled. It's really his fault. If he didn't scream so much I would have just quit." His eyes danced with excitement around the room and he pulled on his hair. "I pushed that safety pin into him over and over again. He kept screaming. So I kept drinking."

There was a crash of something falling somewhere. I didn't know what it was, but it startled me.

"That's a fascinating story, Stephen, but I'm a little busy right now," I said and gestured to the cards spread out in front of me.

"Fine," he said, got up and walked away.

***

Charlie and James were the only guards on duty at night. After a couple weeks of observing the pattern, I knew there after lights out there would be a bed-check, and after that there was about a two-hour window of opportunity to explore where the ventilation shaft went. No one manned the pharmacy at night, and I hoped the vent would lead me there. The pain in my back, neck, and arm had become unbearable, and not having access to any pain meds was only making me angrier that I was still locked up.

About an hour after lights out, James came back onto the ward to check on us. When he left the ward again and bolted the steel door behind him, I knew I had two hours.

None of the other patients stirred when I opened the large vent panel and pushed it into the shaft. I pulled myself up, my back temporarily ignored, then peeked back into the ward to make sure no one had woken up and to verify the direction I needed to move in order to reach the pharmacy.

A couple days earlier I had been left alone in Dr. Sawyer's office. He went into the hall to discuss something with Randall, interrupting our session. I was only alone for about ninety seconds, but it was long enough to see and pocket the pen light he had on his desk.

After clicking on the light, I stuck it in my mouth and started crawling. I was grateful the vent was big enough for me to fit in a crouching-crawling position. If I had to lie on my stomach and squirm my way through, I would have gotten too dirty for them to not notice it.

I had no idea where exactly the ventilation shaft led, so I crawled slowly to lessen any noise. For all I knew, I was crawling along right above Charlie and James, so I had to take it slow. By the time I reached the vent leading into the pharmacy, I was drenched with sweat. I didn't have a watch, so I tried to keep track of time by counting, but lost count somewhere around the first hour mark. That barely left me with enough time to find meds, pocket them, and slowly crawl back onto the ward before the next checkup time.

There were two pharmacy doors. One on the ward side, and one directly across that I hoped would take me to an exit that would lead outside the ward. At first, I was excited, but, disappointingly, like the door leading out to the smoking area, it required a key to open, even from the inside. It didn't matter right then because even if I could open that door, I wouldn't have had enough time to keep traversing the vents looking for another way out. That would have required too much time and risk. The next bed check was too soon.

So, twenty minutes later, with my pen light between my teeth, I was back inside the ventilation system returning to the ward. I had a sandwich bag full of muscle relaxers and four different kinds of painkillers. By the time I got back to the ward, and closed the vent, my back was crying for mercy. I pulled two Percocet tablets from the bag, popped them in my mouth, washed them down with a handful of water from the bathroom faucet, and slid under the covers.

Just then, Charlie put his key in the lock and opened the door.

My heart was pounding, I was breathing heavily and sweat poured out of me. When Charlie made his way toward me, I had to force myself to breathe slower, quieter. His flashlight lingered on me, but then he passed, circled the rest of the ward, and went back out the main door. I slept like the dead the rest of that night, having finally gotten some relief from the pain.

In the morning, Dr. Sawyer started me on a regimen with the new non-narcotic pain killer. If he mentioned a name, I couldn't remember and wasn't listening for one anyway. I was too busy enjoying a blissful high from an old friend.

He said it'd be a few days before the medicine would start working. During that time, I kept to myself as much as possible and snuck pills out of the plastic bag hidden in my pillowcase at an alarming, though not surprising, rate. Despite being back in the fog of opioids, the thoughts of escape didn't go away. They still weren't letting me out and had given no indication that a release would be happening any time soon.

Obviously, I'd failed to maintain my sobriety for long, but after dealing with the constant pain for just a few days without any substances, I realized how impossible the idea of permanent sobriety was unless the medicine Dr. Sawyer started me on really worked. If it did work, I could get it on the outside too. If they had access to it at White Oaks, I thought, it must have already passed human trials and been cleared for the market. Maybe it was just so new that my doctor at the VA hadn't heard of it yet. I wasn't sure if I should stay long enough to see if it worked, or if I should just try to escape as soon as the opportunity presented itself.

***

There was so little to do on the ward. After watching Kevin and reflecting on my own issues, I started to think about the wars and their meaning for the first time in years. When you're in the middle of a war, the reasons and explanations rarely matter. What mattered were the men and women by your side and protecting each other. The big picture stuff we'd just leave to the leaders and politicians.

After 9/11 what we were doing in Afghanistan felt right. We eliminated terror cells, hunted Bin Laden and those like him, liberated villages from Taliban control, and helped them dig wells and build schools. As soon as we invaded Iraq, things got murky for me. Iraq's involvement in any kind of terrorist plot or hidden weapons of mass destruction was never clear enough for the invasion to make any kind of sense.

I felt so little pride in what we had called accomplishment. We weren't the lost generation, we weren't the greatest generation, we weren't even the forgotten generation – we were the wasted generation.

It was hard to think clearly about anything related to the war. Whenever I thought about it, things would come back in scattered fragments. Tony was often the first thing to come to mind, and I'd do anything to divert my thoughts from him. I'd think about how my face tingled after battles, and how my hearing would be turned down a few notches. The dog I shot in an alley when I found it gnawing at a little girl missing the lower half of her face. The seemingly endless card games we played when boredom made us all restless. Inevitably, my thoughts would drift back to Tony, and that's when I'd grab another pill, or beer, or both.

***

The stash of pills I had hidden in my pillowcase got smaller as the days passed. I started to wish I'd taken more from the pharmacy, but considering they hadn't noticed them missing by then, I figured I'd have another opportunity to get more.

Boredom was almost as much of an enemy as Dr. Sawyer and Charlie, and passing the days sitting in that familiar old drug-infused fog made the slow passage of time more bearable.

After taking a couple more pills out of the bag in my pillowcase, I cupped them in one hand and went to the bathroom for a mouthful of water to wash them down with. When I walked out of the bathroom Charlie was standing by my bed, hands on hips.

"What the hell is that?" he asked, pointing at the bag of pills sitting on the middle of the bed. I never took the baggie out of my pillowcase. He must have seen me get that last dose. I'd been getting away with it for long enough that I had become complacent.

I didn't respond, just stared at him. He grabbed the bag of pills and stormed over to the pharmacy.

Sitting on the bed, I put my head in my hands. Getting the pills seemed like a good idea at the time. When I'm dealing with the level of pain I was prior to raiding the pharmacy, logic and reason go out the window. I never thought about consequences, before or after. All I thought about was stopping the pain. When Charlie found the pills I so carelessly flaunted, the possible consequences were severe. Best case scenario would be that my reckless decision had just added a few weeks, maybe even months, to my stay at White Oaks. That is, unless I could find a way out.

One episode of *Law and Order* later, Charlie came out of the pharmacy. "Come with me," he said. I followed him without argument. When we got outside the ward, Randall and Lee were waiting and they followed close behind us.

We got to Dr. Sawyer's office. "Wait here," Charlie said. He knocked twice and opened the door without waiting for a response, and then closed it behind him.

My heart was thudding so hard I could feel it in my eyes. I cursed myself for my weakness and carelessness. There was a simple story and one I was going to stick to. The pharmacy door was left unlocked one day, that's all there was to it. I was in a lot of pain and I couldn't sleep. I paced the ward in the middle of the night and out of desperation tried the door and it happened to be unlocked. Maybe it just didn't latch all the way shut. I took a lot of pills and I'm sorry, *grovel grovel, beg beg.* With any luck I'd be out of trouble fast and my stay at White Oaks wouldn't be extended as much as I expected it to be.

Charlie opened Dr. Sawyer's door again and said, "Bring him in."

Randall grabbed me by the meat of my left arm and pushed me into the office even though I didn't try to resist.

"Where'd you get these?" Dr. Sawyer asked. The bag of pills, now only a dozen or so in total, sat on his desk.

"The pharmacy."

"How did you get into the pharmacy?"

"The door was unlocked."

"Really," Dr. Sawyer said in a mocking sing-song voice. He dropped his glasses on the desk and pinched the bridge of his nose.

"I was in a lot of pain the other night, and I couldn't sleep. I was pacing the ward and out of sheer desperation checked the door and it was open. I grabbed some pills and left."

"Charlie," Dr. Sawyer said. "It sounds like Jason thinks you failed in your duties and left the pharmacy open for all."

"I don't know how he got in there, Doc, but I guarantee you I never left the door unlocked. Never."

"What day did you get them?" Dr. Sawyer asked.

I shrugged and wiped my face. "Not sure." He stared at me for a long time, saying nothing. His eyebrows twitched their disapproval at me.

"It was probably Craig. That's when I got in," I said and cleared my throat. "On one of the days Craig was in charge of the pharmacy."

"I see, and just so you know you didn't just take *some* pills." He held a piece of paper in front of his face. "Charlie ran an inventory, and we are missing twenty muscle relaxers, fifty Percocet, thirty Vicodin and twenty-five Tramadol." He dropped the paper on his desk. "And in this baggie here," he said and waved it around. "There are only fifteen pills total." He looked over my left shoulder where Randall stood and nodded.

I turned in time to see the cattle prod in Randall's hand.

When I woke up, I was naked and sprawled on the floor of the Thinking Room.

For the next few days, which felt like a very slow month, I sat on the cold concrete with nothing to do but think and pray for death as the pain in my back got worse with every maddeningly uncomfortable second.

Each morning they'd give me my one non-narcotic pain pill along with a slice of white bread, a hard-boiled egg, and a small glass of water. At night, I got another pill, a small bowl of plain rice and a juice box. The same two meals every day. The only light that entered the Thinking Room was when James or Charlie brought my meals.

I would never tell them the truth about how I got into the pharmacy, no matter how many days I spent alone and freezing in the Thinking Room. The pharmacy door was left unlocked, end of story. I had to keep the ventilation shaft in my back pocket, because it might be the only way I'd ever get out of White Oaks.

CHAPTER 10

Breaking into the pharmacy was one of the worst ideas I ever had, but it was so similar to other things I'd done over the years that the idiocy and carelessness wasn't the least bit surprising.

The pain was severe and almost constant. That was true. The consistency of it broke me, and turned me into a man I could barely make eye contact with in the mirror. That was also true. The harder truth was that I only made things worse. Constantly abusing my prescriptions not only solved nothing, but landed me in White Oaks. If I'd been stronger, more responsible, I might have never even known White Oaks existed. All I wanted to do was get the hell out of there, and stealing from the pharmacy was the one thing that would absolutely guarantee me more time locked inside.

Once I was back on the ward, Michael told me that all the other patients had been questioned to find out if anyone saw how I got into the pharmacy, but if any of them had, which was doubtful, they kept it to themselves.

I stayed in bed, cocooned under the thin sheets and scratchy old blanket, all day. I didn't go outside to smoke, watch TV, or play any games. The only time I left my cotton cave was when I had to pee and when I was forced to come out for the evening group session, where I said nothing and wasn't engaged by anyone. My chair was just outside the circle and I sat there, staring at the floor, hating everything about myself.

Hours after the others had gone to sleep, I laid in bed alternating between cursing myself and staring greedily at the vent shaft cover. The non-narcotic pain medication began to work. I was so distracted by my own self-loathing that I didn't notice it at first, but the muscles in my neck had relaxed a bit and the nerves previously sparking and sending jolts of pain down my arm dimmed, like an old TV screen slowly darkening after being turned off. There was still a haunting ghost of activity, but it was in the background. The relief only caused the shame to deepen. It was an underserved reprieve. Not long before dawn, I slipped into a restless, chaotic sleep.

When I woke up, everyone else was still asleep, but there was a hint of light coming in through the windows so it wouldn't be long before the lights flickered on. I got up and stretched; my back creaking like an old unlubricated hinge. Outside the window above my head, I breathed in the ghost of fresh air sneaking in through the old window as I watched the mist burn away from the unkempt grass beyond the fence line.

The lights blinked on, and I heard the rattling of keys. Charlie opened the door. Behind him, being escorted by James, CJ walked back onto the ward. We made eye contact right away, and even though he looked like a walking apparition we both smiled. I raised my hand and he nodded in response.

Charlie buzzed for everyone to get up. When he passed anyone who hadn't immediately sat up, he grabbed the sheets and ripped them off. "Come on," he hollered. "Everybody up."

"Well, good morning, Charlie," I said, drawing out the *good* an extra beat or two.

He glared at me and waved a dismissive hand.

"He's in a mood," James said. "I wouldn't test it with him today."

"He's always in a mood, James. And since when do you care?"

"I'm headed to the pharmacy," he said, with a slick grin. "Need anything? Couple dozen Percs maybe?"

I ignored that and turned my attention to CJ. "Where've you been? Are you okay?"

"I'm okay," he said and smiled without showing his teeth, assuming he had any left. "Just glad to be back on the ward. A little weird to say that, but I am."

"I know how you feel."

He furrowed his brows.

"Thinking Room," I said and left it at that.

"Oh," he said. "Joy."

Michael appeared on our flank, shuffling quickly over. "CJ!" he said and hugged him.

"Hey, Michael." Even though I'd only been there a few weeks, I knew CJ didn't like to be touched but he returned the hug. Michael was often the exception to his, and most everyone's, pet peeves and obsessions.

After the medication cart came and went, everyone trickled over and welcomed CJ back to the ward. It was good to see him again, but the sight of him was disturbing. Whatever form of recovery he'd gone through didn't seem to do him much good. His appearance had been frightening since the day we first met, and it had steadily worsened.

CJ was a tough, serious-minded chess opponent, but even though I only beat him sometimes, he never lost his temper or spewed crazed conspiracy theories. We often played without much conversation. It's not that we didn't talk because we had nothing to say or didn't like each other. There was always some kind of noise on the ward, and we were comfortable enough with each other that we could enjoy some quiet without it getting weird. In that regard, he reminded me of Tony, who I would often sit with in total silence, especially at night after a long day of battle or boredom, watching the stars and chain smoking.

In the cafeteria, we all sat together, even Clint and Stephen, and had a temporarily pleasant breakfast of oatmeal goop, spongy eggs, and floppy bacon. I missed real food and hadn't enjoyed a solid bowel movement since arriving at White Oaks.

"So, Kevin," CJ said. "I like the new hairdo." Everyone laughed but me. I hadn't noticed before, but he'd apparently started growing new hair.

"Oh, thanks," Kevin said and rubbed his new patches and strands. "Doc said it was an unexpected side effect, but that doesn't make any sense. I think they're giving me something else."

What was left of the color in CJ's face drained and his eyes dropped to the plate of half-eaten food. "A lot of that going around," he said.

"Maybe you shouldn't swallow whatever cock-shaped pill they put in front of you, Corey," Stephen said without looking up. He was making a little sculpture of, well, who knows what with his food.

"Very nice, Stephen," Leonard said.

"Nobody's talking to you, fat boy."

Leonard flushed and started to fidget. He intertwined his fingers and twisted his hands back and forth, mumbling to himself. The pleasant breakfast was apparently over.

"When are you going to start telling the truth about your fingers?" Clint asked me.

"Don't start," I said, without looking at him.

"I'm just saying."

"Don't start," I yelled, emphasizing each word with a smack on the table.

"That's it," Charlie buzzed from across the room. "Breakfast is over, let's go. I don't got all day."

Back on the ward, I ignored the TV and watched Clint from across the room. I failed from the beginning to not be bothered by his crazy accusations. His bulging eyes took up a disproportionate amount of real estate on his otherwise small, pinched face. The neck on his shirt was stretched out and it hung down in a wrinkled V exposing a thick rug of chest hair. He caught me staring. I continued to watch him with a blank, empty expression. His bug eyes darted around the room. He hugged himself, started rocking back and forth, and shook his head in big swinging repetitive motions.

"No," he said and continued gyrating.

I said nothing and stared at him.

"No," he said, much louder and shaking his head so violently back and forth I was worried he'd snap his own neck. Worried wasn't the right word. Hopeful wasn't either, but it was closer.

"Charlie," he screamed. "Charlie, make him stop!"

Charlie walked over, along with Randall, who grabbed Clint's head to still it.

"What's going on, Clint?" Charlie asked irritably. "What's wrong with you?"

"Dead eyes," Clint said. "He's watching me with those dead eyes." He tried to pull away from Randall's inescapable grip. "Don't you let him read my thoughts," he screamed as James slid a syringe into Clint's arm. "Too important." He continued to struggle. "Too important. Too important. Too important." With each utterance, the words slowed and blurred together as the Haldol, or whatever, slithered through his blood stream. I finally looked away from him and leaned back on the couch next to Michael.

"What's all that about?" Michael asked.

"Don't know."

"Why'd you break into the pharmacy?" Michael asked. The words came out tentatively, like he was worried the question would anger me.

"Because I'm in constant severe pain and they won't give me anything for it," I said, but didn't look at him. After a long silence, I added, "And because I'm a drug addict."

"They're really mad at you."

"I'm not too thrilled with myself either," I said and finally looked at him. "Not that I care what the staff thinks."

"You should." He sat back on the couch and pulled his knees up to his chest. "They don't care what happens to you. Just play along. Maybe you'll get a chance to get out of here."

"What do you mean, play along?"

"It doesn't matter. Nobody believes me. No one ever believes me."

"I'm going to go see if CJ wants to kick my ass in chess," Leonard said. I'd forgotten he was sitting on the other side of me on the couch, and his interjection startled me. He got up, picked at his shirt, and shuffled over to CJ's bed. "Up for a game?" he asked. CJ got up slowly, his right arm pressing against his stomach.

"He really is good," Michael said.

"I know. I rarely beat him."

"You've beaten him?"

"Only a couple times, but yeah."

"Dang." He was looking at me with bright admiration.

"You've never?"

"Not even once," he said.

"Why are you here?" I asked. "I mean, you seem perfectly normal to me."

He looked at me and offered a little half smile that exposed a deep dimple on one cheek. In a wavering sarcastic voice while rolling his eyeballs around like a dazed cartoon character he said, "Thanks, but I'm delusional."

I laughed, and his smile widened into full double dimple territory.

"I'm sorry," I said and held my hands up. "I didn't mean to."

"No," he said. "Don't be. Laughter is the best medicine, as they say." He hugged his knees tighter and rested his chin on them. The smile faded. "Not that Dr. Sawyer would ever prescribe it." After a long silence he said, "It all started when I was a little boy and saw two men in dark suits and sunglasses sitting in a car outside our house. They were parked on the street outside my window, just staring at our house."

"What happened? Who were they?"

He shook his head, dropped his knees, and sank, deflated, into the couch.

"I told my parents, but they just thought I was being paranoid." He watched Detectives Stabler and Benson question a child predator on the television for a long, quiet time, and I gave him his space.

"They followed me for months," he said as soon as I quit waiting for him to talk and had gotten back into the show. "One day, I was home alone. I was sick and both my parents were at work."

I shifted my position on the couch to face him.

"I looked out the window, and there was no one in the car. When I turned around, they were in my room. I tried to run. Tried to scream, but I was just frozen." His eyes were wide, afraid, and in the past. "Their faces were expressionless. I thought if they took off their sunglasses, they wouldn't have eyes, just holes. After that, I just went blank. When I woke up, my head hurt and I was so thirsty, but they were gone."

"What happened after that?"

He simultaneously shook his head and shrugged his shoulders. "My parents said it was just a dream. When I told them I wasn't sleeping, they said I was making it up. My baby sister had just been born, and they thought I was just trying to get attention."

"Did the men in suits ever come back?"

"All the time." He looked around the room and ran his hands through his curly hair. "My parents got tired of dealing with me. My sister was normal. She didn't complain about strange men without eyes sneaking into the house."

"How old were you? When the men first came, I mean."

"About eight. After my sister turned nine, my parents said they had enough. They had me committed so someone else could deal with my little delusions," he said, finger quotes in the air around delusions. "They committed me and went on vacation."

"That's messed up, man. I'm so sorry."

"Thanks," he said and hugged his knees again.

"Have they ever come to visit you?"

"The men in suits or my family?"

"Family."

"No one gets visitors here," he said. "Besides, they never came home from that vacation."

"What do you mean?"

"You remember that flight about fifteen years ago that left from Ireland and disappeared somewhere over the Atlantic?"

I blew out a long breath. "Aw, Michael." I didn't really know what else to say.

"They never found it, you know. How do you lose an entire airplane?" he asked. I just shook my head.

"After they were buried," he said and sighed. "Well, after the state buried three empty caskets anyway, I got transferred here. Been here ever since."

"That's a strange connection we all share," I said.

"What's that?"

"It seems like all the patients at White Oaks are all alone in the world."

"We're the perfect patients," he said, using those air quotes with his fingers again. "If there's no one out there in the world to come looking for us, to visit us, they can do whatever they want. Who's out there to care?"

Leonard came back over and sat down next to us. "CJ beat me again," he said. "He doesn't look very good though, and said he had to lay down again."

I wasn't sure if what Michael said about us being the perfect patients for them to do anything they wanted to was one of his so-called delusions or not, but it felt like something said by a perfectly sane person. It felt right, but even if it was right, I still didn't know what it meant or what to do about it. Pairing that with what he'd said to me the first time we met, about getting away from White Oaks, didn't help clarify anything.

***

Sleep eluded me that night, in part because I couldn't stop thinking about what Michael said, and also because CJ was wheezing. His breathing was watery and strained. I sat up on my elbows and looked over toward his bed. Someone was standing over him. I pushed myself all the way up and rubbed my eyes. When I opened them again, the figure was standing next to me. I jerked back and fell out of the bed, pulling the covers off with me. The metal posts squealed on the floor, but no one stirred.

Outside, clouds melted away from the moon and the light illuminated the figure. It was my mom. She was covered in patches of dirt and mold. Her veins were black and bulged everywhere. A needle dangled from her arm.

A clump of dirt fell from her thick auburn hair onto my bed and a bug skittered in and out of her locks. She opened her mouth wide, too wide, and leaned forward. A cold, lifeless and odorless rush of air escaped her mouth. There were no distinguishable words, just overlapping static and echoing whispers. I covered my ears and mashed my face into the mattress.

A hand fell on my shoulder. A sound I'd never heard before, one of pure terror and desperation, escaped my mouth and I pushed the hand away. I looked up, and my mom was gone. Charlie shined his flashlight in my face.

"You all right?" he buzzed.

I put my head between my knees, squeezed them together and let out a sob.

"What's going on?"

I lifted my head up, tears and snot all over my face and shook my head. "My mom," I said in a wavering voice and looked over to the other side of the bed where she'd been standing. "I don't know." I wiped my face. "She."

"You saw her?"

I didn't respond.

"Probably from the medicine Doc put you on," he said. "Hallucinations are a possible side effect." He scribbled a note on his clipboard, flicked off the flashlight and left the ward, locking the door behind him.

Dr. Sawyer hadn't mentioned hallucinations as a possible side effect. All he told me was that a little nausea was possible. He'd lied, and I didn't know why, but there was no reasonable explanation for it. Adding that lie to everything else caused me to feel the same kind of thing I used to feel when our unit went on one of the long treks through the mountains of Afghanistan, when you could tell that something was off and could expect an ambush to begin.

The razor wire fence and high security doors. The treatment of the patients. The horrendous and inexplicable side effects some of the men, especially CJ, were experiencing. The Thinking Room and unambiguous hostility. They had me on a medication I'd never heard of, and after more than a decade of constant doctor appointments, there had never been any mention of any kind of highly effective non-narcotic pain medication. Whatever it was, it brought my mom back from the grave, if only in my head. I had to get out of there. I didn't know what they were doing to us, but it seemed clear at that moment that something was very wrong about White Oaks and those in charge of it.

I crept over to the vent, moved the cover and pulled myself up. In the dark, I felt around for the pen light and when I found it, clicked it on, replaced the vent cover and started crawling. Since I couldn't get out through the pharmacy without a key, I had to at least try finding another way out. When I got to the turn that led to the pharmacy, I paused. Despite the feeling of alarm and the desperate need to get away from White Oaks, the addict in me was still tempted to hit the pharmacy first and get a supply to take with me on the run.

While the debate about what to do raged inside me, I heard voices coming from farther down the vent shaft. That settled the debate. I turned away from the path leading to the pharmacy and moved slowly toward the voices.

I came to a bend in the vent and the volume of the voices increased. I turned off the pen light, held my breath and listened. The vent was still illuminated by a glow coming from the opening where those voices were. I took the turn and slowly crept toward the light, my heart pounding and my face slick with running sweat.

The voices belonged to Charlie and Dr. Sawyer. His office was right outside the ward, next to the pharmacy. Charlie must have gone to report my hallucination right away. I moved slowly, trying to not make a sound, until I was looking down into Dr. Sawyer's office.

"Thanks for letting me know," Dr. Sawyer said. "You need to keep an eye on him. He's an uncooperative little fucker. I'm starting to wonder if it was worth it to bring him here."

"Yeah," Charlie said. "Especially since bringing him here caused Ava to rebel. That's trouble we don't need."

"Ava," Dr. Sawyer said and chuckled without humor. "Speaking of uncooperative little fuckers. We've got a company man coming by tomorrow to help us out with her."

"In what way?"

"You'll see. Once he's done, we'll be able to give her a little bit of her freedom back."

"We should have just gotten rid of her," Charlie said.

"It's hard enough to get people cleared to come here, and I need her help in the lab."

"You think she'll play ball?"

"She won't have much choice if she wants to get back into the company's good graces."

"All right," Charlie said and turned to leave. "I'll keep an eye on Jason and let you know if anything else happens. I'm gonna grab a smoke."

"See you tomorrow, Charlie. I'm about to call it a night."

"All right, boss, have a good one."

My head was spinning. Now that Charlie was gone, I was afraid that any movement would be heard. I tried not to breathe, or inadvertently dislodge any balls of dust that might fall through the vent and drift down to his desk.

I didn't really know what they were talking about, but none of it was good. Ava must have been the woman Dr. Sawyer tried to convince me I'd imagined. The one he'd argued with the night of my admission to White Oaks. It sounded like they had her locked up somewhere in the facility, if that's what Dr. Sawyer meant by saying they could give her some freedom back, so she could help in the lab, whatever that meant.

At that point, I didn't care what it meant. I didn't care what they were doing; I just knew it was bad and that I had to get the hell out of there immediately.

Dr. Sawyer hung his lab coat on the rack behind his desk, grabbed his briefcase, turned out the lights and left the office. The keys rattled as he locked the door. I waited for a few minutes to make sure he was gone, and then pulled back the vent cover. I clicked on the pen light and stuck it in my mouth so I could see while lowering myself into his office. I had to drop down, but it was a short drop, and I came down silently.

A sense of hope washed over me as I focused the light on the doorknob and saw that it could be opened without a key. I pressed my ear to the door and listened for footsteps, and then dropped to the floor to look through the tiny gap at the bottom. It was dimly lit in the corridor, completely silent. No one passed by. I stood back up and turned the lock on the knob with sweaty fingers.

My heart was pounding, but when I closed my eyes and took a calming breath, it slowed down. I turned the knob, the gears and springs inside quietly groaning, and cracked the door open. In the distance, a door slammed shut. A car started, the engine revved, and then the noises faded. It must have been Dr. Sawyer going home. I opened the door all the way, stepped into the corridor and quietly closed the door behind me.

Charlie was outside smoking, but I had no idea if James or the other orderlies were still on site or where they'd be if they were. To my right was the hallway that led to the smoking area. Straight ahead was a hallway I hadn't been down before, but there was a light on at the far end and I decided to take the hallway to my left, which was completely dark.

There was nothing in the hall for the longest time, but then I came to a door that was cracked open. I turned off the flashlight and listened, there was nothing. I turned the light back on and shined it on the door, then pushed it open slowly. The hinges cried out and my whole body tensed. It was the Thinking Room; empty and dark. I closed the door and was starting to calm down when another door opened. From the direction of the sound, it was probably Charlie coming back inside from the smoking area. I turned off my flashlight and pressed my body against the wall, tried to sink into it, become invisible. His footsteps faded into the distance.

With the light still off, I slowly shuffled down the hallway. My breathing was shallow and my skin prickled. All my attention was focused on staying quiet and listening for any signs of activity. My feet were cold and clammy. I turned on the flashlight and immediately spotted a door at the end of the hallway, just a few feet away. It was a security door that would require a key. I tried opening the door anyway, but it was locked. I turned the light back off and slowly shuffled back toward the main corridor. As I approached, the light from the moon spilling in through the windows illuminated my path.

I stepped into the corridor and started walking down the only hallway remaining that could lead to an exit. My heart was racing, and I had to keep wiping sweat from my face. I passed a door secured with chains and a padlock. The lights overhead flickered momentarily, giving the hallway a sickening strobe light effect, and I continued.

There were four more chained doors, two on each side of the hallway. The hall I was in branched off left and right. There was a security door straight ahead that required a key.

I wasn't sure how long it would be until the next bed check, but I'd been off the ward long enough to realize that my time was running out. If I didn't find something soon, I'd have to hurry back to the ward.

The next door I came to had glass panels, and the room on the other side was dimly lit. The door wasn't chained, but it was locked. Looking in, I could see there was no exit. It must have been the lab Dr. Sawyer referred to. The room was filled with stainless steel drums and tables, what looked like a small conveyor belt, and cabinets with glass doors that had beakers and vials inside. There were rubber gloves and masks. Hanging on the wall were white coveralls.

Down the hallway in the other direction, someone sneezed, a chair squeaked, and I heard approaching footsteps.

"Fuck." My time was out. I turned and ran, careful to only come down on the balls of my feet hoping I was being quiet enough to go unnoticed. I slipped back into Dr. Sawyer's office and locked the door, pulled myself into the vent, replaced the cover and started crawling back to the ward.

I'd narrowed down the areas that could potentially lead to an exit and could focus future attempts on those areas. With Ava supposedly getting released from her own cell the next day, maybe I could find her and form some kind of an alliance that could get me, maybe get us all, out of White Oaks. Of course, I knew nothing about her, whether she'd be willing to help, or if she would immediately notify the staff if we ever did end up crossing paths.

CHAPTER 11

Eventually, after Charlie did a bed check, I was able to fall asleep. The nightmares started immediately.

In the dream, my father was angry with me for joining the Army. He knew it was a just cause, or so we all thought after 9/11, but he shouted in a low-pitched buzz that my mom needed me. That new buzz in his voice made him sound like Charlie.

My dad accused me of abandoning my mom when she needed me the most. When he needed me to be around to help keep an eye on her. His eyes were wide, and his neck veins swelled as he hollered at me to stay, but then his voice reduced to echoes across the mountains of Afghanistan. I looked around, confused, and before I had time to realize where I was, a mortar round whistled in the air above me and the entire platoon dropped. The explosion was close, but no one was hit. Then there was another whistle and a boom, then another whistle, another boom. The rounds got closer. They were adjusting coordinates.

It was my first week in the Korengal and we'd made the mistake of travelling during the day in a spot that was an insurgent's dream for an ambush scenario.

Stacked in hasty piles about twenty yards from our position were mounds of logs, which had been abandoned by the local timber smugglers when we arrived. There had been a huge market for it before the war, smuggling timber into Pakistan. Why trees had to be smuggled anywhere, I didn't know, but I'd noticed the timber piles on my first long march outside the camp's perimeter and that's what the Platoon Sergeant told me.

The mortars got closer. Everyone was shouting and pointing, and the air filled with the rip and hiss of passing bullets. One snapped the ground next to me and sent scattered rock fragments into my cheek. We all ran for the timber. It was the only cover available. Machine gun fire was coming from every direction. The man beside me screamed into a radio. There was a pause in the mortar fire as they adjusted coordinates again.

We were pinned down so completely that there were few opportunities to return fire. The one soldier I saw exposing his position long enough to do so had no face, no features, no eyes. Just smooth skin surrounding a screaming mouth and holes where his teeth should have been. He looked down at me and smiled, then his head vanished in a cloud of red mist and something wet and hot landed on my face.

***

I sat up in bed, shuddered, and mopped the sweat from my head with a sleeve. Only broken scenes of the dream remained clear, but it was enough to make me wary of trying to get back to sleep. My dad's accusations were the only thing to linger with any real clarity, and though the details were off in the dream, the actual situation that spawned them were close enough.

Unlike the father in my dream, my real father never shouted for me to stay home and help him keep an eye on my mom. He didn't accuse me of abandoning her to guilt me into staying home, though the accusations came later.

My parents had quietly accepted my enlistment. Having both served themselves, it came as no surprise, especially after 9/11. When I left, it was clear something was bothering my dad, but he said it was nothing and told me to focus on the task at hand. His interactions with my mom before I left were cold, and I sometimes heard whispered arguments in the other room, but by that point I didn't have much of a relationship with either one of them and was as ready to leave as they were to get rid of me.

I didn't know until much later, but when I left for the Army, my mom was struggling with her own substance abuse. That's what was bothering my dad and why I heard muffled arguments between them. It wasn't until I returned home from my last deployment that she cleaned up. She had just barely escaped dying after an overdose. That experience, coupled with my near death in Afghanistan, caused her to turn back into the bad ass woman I'd grown up loving. She helped get my disability set up with the VA. She took me to physical therapy and treatment appointments. She did everything to make up for lost time that I didn't even realize was missing.

A couple years after returning home for good, my own drug issues surfaced. I was able to keep it under wraps for a while, but eventually they realized I was in a downward spiral. My dad said it was my using that caused her to relapse. I didn't want to believe that but couldn't refute it either. My abuse caused her old hunger to resurface.

Just one shot of heroin cut with fentanyl and she was gone.

At the viewing, before the burial, he was inconsolable. I'd never seen him cry before that day. Family members I'd never even met before formed a line and one by one told us how sorry they were for our loss. In between Aunt Joy's warm smile and Uncle Walter's salt-and-pepper beard, my dad grabbed my damaged hand and squeezed it hard enough to hurt.

"You did this," he said through clenched teeth and squeezed my hand harder. Sensing the coming emotional IED, the family members in line took a step back. He glanced at my mom, looking serene and plastic in her coffin, and his face contorted. Between sobs he said, "She had been clean for years. She's dead because of you." He finally released my hand and stormed out of the room. There was a long silence, and the line of people offering condolences scattered, leaving me alone in the room with my mom.

I couldn't even look at her.

***

As the ward bustled with activity around me, I stared out the window thinking of the last time I'd been to Colorado. We lived there for the last few years of my dad's time in the Army. First at Fort Carson in Colorado Springs, then when he was a recruiter in Lakewood, a suburb of Denver.

After my second overdose that required medical intervention, my dad refused to see me and wouldn't return my calls. It was almost the third anniversary of my mom's death. I was feeling nostalgic and wanted to get out of town for a while. Even though we only lived in Colorado for a few years, it had always been my favorite place.

I had no real plans and no one to visit. I just packed a bag, got in the car, and started driving west. When crossing through the rolling plains with the mountains in the distance, I started to feel at home, but the feeling didn't last.

As I drove through the towns we used to live in, I barely recognized either place. Everything was different. The Colorado I spent my best years in was open, empty, and quiet. By then it was nothing but traffic and noise. The hills and fields I wandered as a kid were gone. In their place was an endless expanse of subdivisions and shopping complexes, each one a copy of the last. The only hint of wilderness was the occasional coyote or bear that wandered into a neighborhood following the smell of wasted food in lines of blue trash bins. Every road was nothing but brake lights. Every lake and river was crowded by swimmers, boaters, and fishermen. Every trail was torn up with overlapped footprints.

I went back to feel my mom's presence again, but there was not even the slightest trace of what we once had or who we once were, and I wanted to leave almost as soon as I arrived.

After that, I drove to Montana. I'd never been there and always wanted to visit Missoula, the town the movie *A River Runs Through It* was based in.

Being in Missoula was like travelling back in time to the Colorado I grew up in. It was open, vast, and quiet. The whole state was that way. Every town was small and slow with polite nods from strangers on uncrowded sidewalks.

My last stop in Montana was at Glacier National Park. The lake at the entrance of the park was the loveliest place I'd ever been.

A barely visible path off the main road led to the lake. The beach wasn't sand, but pebbles the size of corn kernels, smooth as glass. Where the pebbles ended, the mirror began. Two rows of evergreens, two stacks of mountains, two rows of clouds rolling across two skies. I sat on the beach and mirrored the scene in my own way, with silence.

Then my cell phone rang. It was my dad. He wasted no time with pleasantries. "Three-year anniversary is next week," he said.

"I know."

"Still using?"

I sighed but said nothing.

"That's what I thought."

"What do you want, Dad? I'm kind of busy right now."

"Where are you?"

"Montana."

"What are you doing there?"

"Right now, I'm sitting on a beach by a lake. I'm actually surprised I get service up here."

"Surprised or disappointed?"

I scoffed. "Did you just call to pick a fight?"

"No. I want you to come by the house on the anniversary. You going to be back in town by then?"

"I can be. What's this about?"

"There's something I want to show you. Be here at noon. Don't be late."

He hung up before I could respond. I didn't know it at the time, but it was the last conversation we'd ever have.

***

A hand dropped on my shoulder. It was Michael. "You okay?" he asked. "You've been standing here a long time."

"I'm all right," I said. "Just thinking."

I folded my arms, leaned up against the wall, and looked back out the window. "Maybe I should be here," I said. "Maybe I deserve it."

Michael grabbed both of my shoulders and I looked at him. He never appeared more sane or serious. "None of us should be here, Jason. None of us."

Stephen was sitting on the floor, facing the corner, rocking back and forth, and mumbling to himself. Whatever he was saying, it wasn't happy. The end of each incoherent sentence was emphasized with an aggressive low growl.

"Okay," Michael said. "Maybe Stephen should be here."

We both chuckled.

"Seriously, though, no one is getting better. Kevin might be re-growing some hair but that's the first decent thing that's happened in the time I've been here." He looked around the ward. "Patients have left the ward before." He lowered his voice before continuing. "I mean left and never came back, but only the really sick ones, and if you ask me," he said, crossed his arms, hugged himself and looked around the room again. "They might have left the ward, but I don't think they ever left the hospital grounds."

"What do you mean? You think there are patients on another ward somewhere in the hospital?"

He shook his head. "No, I don't. That's why they don't have cameras anywhere. Have you noticed that?"

"Actually, yeah."

"They don't want any record of what's going on here."

He was making some good points. The lack of cameras anywhere was unusual. He sounded a little paranoid, but I knew it wasn't misplaced. If he'd overheard that conversation between Charlie and Dr. Sawyer, his paranoia would be on overdrive. Still, I wasn't really sure what was going on, and didn't want to feed his paranoia because it might just put the staff on higher alert. Besides, what if I told Michael what they said and he lost it and panicked?

"I don't know, man," I said. He frowned at me.

A low moan came from across the room. It was CJ. He cried out and was reaching into the air, grasping at nothing. His voice was full of panic. We both ran over to him. I knelt down and put a hand on his chest.

"CJ, what's wrong?"

His eyes were milky and jumped from one spot to another, like he was looking for something to focus on but couldn't find anything.

"Can't see," he cried out, his breaths fast and raspy.

"It's okay," I said, trying, yet failing, to soothe him. "We'll get you some help."

Everyone, except Stephen, was looking at CJ, all of them silent and dismayed. Stephen was still sitting in the corner, only then he was pressing his hands against his ears. Leonard started to cry and covered his face.

I turned to Michael. "Get help," I said, but he didn't budge. "Michael," I snapped, and he finally looked at me. I gestured toward the door with bulging eyes. He ran and started banging on the door, screaming for someone to come help.

CJ's face contorted. He let out a series of harsh barking coughs, and speckles of blood hit my shirt. I pushed the hair out of his face. The door burst open, knocking Michael to the floor. Randall pushed me out of the way, picked up CJ, and ran out of the ward. James looked around the room at all of us, slammed the door and locked it.

***

Hours later, the ward was roaring with overlapping conversations as we set up the chairs for that evening's group session. With the exception of Stephen, who seemed indifferent to just about everything, we were all scared and worried about CJ.

Dr. Sawyer barely made it through the main door before we were all questioning him.

"Where's CJ?" Leonard asked. He was mashing and twisting his hands together so aggressively that they were a mix of dark red and stark white. "What'd you do to him?"

"Is he okay?" Michael asked.

Dr. Sawyer held up his hands to quiet us. Before he could speak, Leonard screamed, "Where is he, you bastard?"

James and Charlie rushed over and forced Leonard to sit in one of the folding chairs that formed the ragged circle. He tried to cover his face, but the two guards each held an arm down.

"Everyone just needs to calm down," Dr. Sawyer said in a soothing voice. "Please take your seats, and we'll talk."

Kevin put an arm around Michael, who was visibly shaking. "Come on, Michael," he said, and I followed them. We all sat next to each other and leaned forward in anticipation of Dr. Sawyer's explanation.

"CJ is fine," he said. "He's in the infirmary and has been stabilized."

"What do you mean, he's fine?" I asked.

"You don't have any business questioning the doc," James snapped.

"Doc says he's fine, that means he's fine."

"Fuck you, hillbilly," I said without looking at him.

Dr. Sawyer raised his hands again in an attempt to quiet us both. "It's all right, James. CJ is well liked on the ward and it's normal for them to be concerned."

"Let me go," Leonard whined, and tried to squirm out of their grasp.

"Only if you calm yourself," Dr. Sawyer said. Leonard stopped squirming and let out a long uneven breath. He nodded at the doc, who did the same to James and Charlie. They released him and Leonard rubbed his arms where they'd been gripping him.

"We are concerned," Kevin said. It wasn't just the extra hair that improved Kevin's appearance. For the last few days his complexion had cleared. He fidgeted less and maintained eye contact for longer periods of time. He sat up straighter and just appeared all around healthier and more confident. I didn't know what the doc was giving him, but I found myself suddenly jealous of whatever it was. "We're worried about our friend."

"How exactly is he fine?" I asked. "Just in the last couple weeks he's had at least one seizure that we know of, he's sneezed out a tooth and lost others in his sleep and gone blind. That's only the big stuff."

"What did you do?" Leonard almost growled.

"That's the last one," Dr. Sawyer said, an outstretched finger targeting Leonard. His tone quickly shifted from soothing to threatening. "Another outburst and you will be removed from the ward."

Leonard's head sunk toward his shoulders, like a human turtle retreating into its shell, and his eyes dropped to the floor.

"All we know about CJ's health history," Kevin said. "All we've ever known, is that he has OCD. None of what's been going on makes any sense for someone with OCD."

Dr. Sawyer didn't respond quickly enough for my liking. "This is bullshit." I said. "Start talking."

Michael spoke up. Kevin still had an arm around him. "Please, Dr. Sawyer. Please, we're just really worried."

"People don't just suddenly go blind without a reason," I said.

"That's true," Dr. Sawyer said. "They don't. First of all, Leonard, I can assure you that we haven't done anything but try to help CJ. His blindness was temporary. His vision has been restored."

"How?" I said, a little louder than intended, and it was obvious Dr. Sawyer was losing his patience with me.

"Have you ever heard of conversion disorder?" he asked.

"No," I said, and no one else in the room said anything different.

"It used to be referred to as hysterical blindness. It's a temporary side effect of the disorder. It also explains the seizure."

"What about the sudden tooth loss, or any of the other issues he's been having lately?" I asked.

"CJ's entire medical history is not your business or concern. All that should matter to you is that we've stabilized him and everything is under control."

"That's not all that matters to me, and I don't trust you, any of you, to take care of CJ."

"Jason," Kevin said, and I turned to face him.

"No, Kevin, fuck this. They're not telling us something." I turned back to Dr. Sawyer. "CJ had been complaining about the medication he was on. He complained to Craig the other day, and Craig promised to talk to you about it. Did he?"

Dr. Sawyer didn't respond. He shifted in his chair and adjusted his lab coat, then folded his hands and rested them in his lap.

"You did something to him," I said, stabbing the air with one pointing finger to emphasize each angry accusatory word. I was angry, but also afraid. I knew from overhearing their conversation that they were holding an employee against her will after she apparently rebelled against Dr. Sawyer on the night of my admission. What exactly she was rebelling against, I had no idea, but the fact that she had, and that Dr. Sawyer's response was to imprison her, put everything about White Oaks into question. My worry for CJ made me lose sight of what was the smartest thing to do. I couldn't control that worry and fear and was lashing out when I should have been focused on finding Ava and getting the hell out of there.

Dr. Sawyer's eyes flicked over to Charlie, who immediately left Leonard's side. He walked to the pharmacy door and knocked four times, in what appeared to be code of some kind. Knock, knock – rapid, one right after the other – then a long pause followed by two slower ones;

Knock…

…knock.

The room had gone silent. My hand was still in the air, my finger still pointed at Dr. Sawyer, but no one moved. Seconds later, the pharmacy door opened, Randall and Lee stepped out. Randall handed a syringe to Charlie, and they walked toward me. I slowly dropped my hand and let out a long breath, feigning resignation, and then lunged at Dr. Sawyer.

Randall and Lee each grabbed an arm and held me back. They seemed to have no issue with it at first, but when Charlie stepped toward me with the syringe, I kicked at the air in front of him, flailing wildly, trying to break their grasp.

Lee knocked my legs out from under me and they slammed me to the ground. The force of it drove the air out of my lungs. One of them dug a knee into my reeling back and pulled my pajama pants down. There was a sting in my butt cheek as Charlie injected me with whatever.

I continued to struggle, but with little air in my lungs and some new drug pouring into my body, it wasn't much of a struggle. I looked up to where Kevin and Michael were sitting. Michael was turned away from me, his face buried in Kevin's shoulder. Kevin watched me with unmasked disappointment.

Next to them, Stephen looked euphoric, and though I couldn't swear to it, his pajama pants appeared to be tented at the crotch. Whether that was the case or not, the bright excitement in his eyes made it clear that he was enjoying the festivities.

Within a few minutes, I'd stopped struggling. Not by choice, but because I couldn't move, and could barely even feel my body in any tangible way. I tried to speak but couldn't.

The three of them pulled me up off the floor and put me back in the chair. My head dropped and I almost fell to the floor again, but Randall steadied me.

Dr. Sawyer looked at his clipboard, made a few notes and crossed his legs. "As I said before, CJ is stable and doing fine. That's all you need to know, and all I'm going to say on the matter." He wiped crud from one eye and pushed his hair out of his face. "Now, Clint," he said. Clint sat up and rubbed his hands on his thighs. "Would you like to share anything tonight?"

Randall turned my head to face Clint, and I had to sit there in motionless silence and listen to him drone on about his alien experiences explaining how he had figured out their invasion plot. How he'd managed to overpower a seemingly indestructible alien and escape. How he'd saved me, and scores of others trapped on the alien mothership. How I lied about my military service because of the shameful cowardice I'd exhibited on the alien mothership and wanted to make myself look like the hero Clint truly was. How he was biding his time at White Oaks until they tried to invade again when he would save us all.

When it was finally over, Randall carried me over to my bed and set me down on the mattress. James was close behind him. He straightened me out on the bed and propped my head up on the pillow so I wouldn't choke on my own spit. He fixed my shirt, and pulled the covers up to my chin, like he was putting a little kid to bed.

"Call me a hillbilly, you punk," he said in a low voice through clenched teeth and looked around the room. His face was red and sweaty. When he confirmed that no one was watching, he snapped a backhand into my crotch. I couldn't move or react in any way to the pain that exploded from my balls up into my stomach.

He put his face right in front of mine. A bead of sweat dropped from his forehead onto my cheek and slid down to the back of my neck. "That stuff won't wear off for a few more hours," he whispered. His acrid breath burned my nostrils. "Maybe I'll come back after everyone's asleep and have my way with you."

I stared at him as he continued to pant in my face.

"Hey, tough guy, do something for me. If you want me to come back later so me and the other boys can run a train on you, just lay there still and don't say a word."

I tried to move, and he seemed to be able to tell just by the look in my eyes that I was doing everything in my power to move. He smiled, and then laughed, a harsh barking laugh that stopped almost as soon as it came out of his mouth.

"I'm just messin' with you, man," he said and stood up. "You have yourself a good night, now."

At least they hadn't tossed me into the Thinking Room again, but they'd managed to take away any chance I had of attempting escape or finding Ava that night. I had to keep my cool from now on, but they made it so hard.

I lay there half the night, cursing myself, cursing them, and staring at the vent.

CHAPTER 12

The next morning, everything ached, and when I tried to stand up, I wavered and had to sit back down.

After medication and breakfast, I started to feel better and went over to the TV area to burn a few of the boring hours away with cartoons and crime dramas.

I was angry, worried about CJ, and didn't believe Dr. Sawyer when he said CJ was fine. I missed big picture stuff like the freedom to do whatever I wanted and not having to worry about people drugging and threatening to rape me in the dead of night, but I also missed normal things like music, the pizza place down the street from my apartment, and the mind-numbing qualities of marijuana.

Every single day at White Oaks was the same drawn-out boredom and schedule inflexibility, and I just wanted something, anything, to be different.

Kevin sat down next to me and let out a long breath. "You shouldn't have done that," he said.

"Aren't you worried about CJ?" I asked.

"You know I am, but lashing out at them and getting yourself drugged for your troubles doesn't help CJ. Or you."

I rubbed my face and sighed. "What am I supposed to do?"

"Just don't give them cause. That's all I'm saying."

"So just take it, accept whatever they decide to do?" I asked and finally turned my attention away from the TV to him. "Half the time it's arbitrary, like they're just itching to mess with us."

He nodded. "I know."

"Do you really think CJ is okay?"

He shook his head and looked at me. "No, I don't."

On the other side of the room, James was playing spades with Leonard, Michael, and Clint. James' tongue was sticking out of the side of his mouth, and for a second my attention was pulled away from the conversation with Kevin. I wanted to sneak up behind James and smack the bottom of his chin so hard that it'd clip off the tip of his tongue. James looked over at me and frowned, like he could feel the hostility radiating off me.

As we watched TV, the game of spades got louder, and James was getting aggressive and angry with his partner, Clint.

"You stupid son of a bitch," James yelled at Clint. "Are you kidding me? You had three guaranteed tricks and you only bet two. That's the third time you underbid, and it just cost us a hundred points."

Michael gathered the cards and started to organize and shuffle them. "Come on, James," he said. "Relax. It's just a game." James glared at Michael but didn't respond. Michael refocused his attention on shuffling.

"It's like playing with a bunch of kids." James' face was getting red. Clint opened his mouth to say something, but James cut him off. "Shut up."

Michael sighed loudly.

"You got a problem?" James asked.

"I'm not the one with the problem," Michael said and continued to shuffle.

James swatted at Michael and the deck of cards exploded in his face. Michael tumbled backward out of his chair and hit the back of his head on the floor.

Without even thinking about it, I was out of my seat.

"No!" Kevin shouted at me, but I ran right through his outstretched hand and rushed over to the table. As James started to get up, I shoved him hard. His foot clipped one of the beds; he tumbled over it and went sprawling on the ground.

I leaned down to check on Michael. He seemed fine and was rubbing the back of his head. "You all right?"

"I'm fine," he said. "You shouldn't have pushed him, Jason, he just startled me."

Kevin was standing beside the couch watching the scene unfold. He threw his arms up and shook his head at me. "Unbelievable," he said. "What'd we just talk about?"

The main door opened. Lee and Randall rushed into the room. Kevin held out one arm in their direction to emphasize his point.

As much as I wanted to fight them off, it would only worsen the situation. I stepped away from Michael and held my hands up.

"James attacked Michael."

Neither of them responded and didn't slow their approach. Randall got there first. He spun me around to face the wall, and then slammed me against it with enough force to split open my eyebrow. The blood ran, hot and sticky, down the side of my face. They pinned me against the wall, each of them digging into different pressure points.

Lee twisted my right arm back and up between my shoulder blades and pressed his forearm against the base of my skull. There was a loud pop in my neck and a rush of hot needles shot through my skull and into my eye. I cried out, and then felt a small pinch in my butt cheek.

***

When I woke up, I was sprawled out on the floor of the Thinking Room, naked and shivering from the cold. There was a small pool of blood under my face. I tried to sit up, but my back and neck would have none of it at first. With a great deal of effort and careful, slow movements, I was finally able to sit up.

The base of my skull throbbed and my vision blurred. In the spot between my shoulder blades, something was wrong. The discs were over-inflated balloons impinging on nerves. My right hand was numb and in bursts would come back to life just long enough to burn. I slid myself up against the wall and slowly lay back down on the hard concrete floor.

The Thinking Room was cold, but only enough to make it miserable, not so cold that it was dangerous, and I lay there shaking. With every single movement and shiver the muscles in my back got tighter. I didn't even have a rag to wipe the blood off my face with.

The hours passed slow and sharp. Everything had teeth. If I'd been sitting on the bed in my apartment, I could have reached into the nightstand drawer and grabbed the loaded pistol that I never had the guts to use. I thought of that nightstand for a long time. The wood grain and circular stains left from glasses never set on coasters. More than anything, I wanted that nightstand next to me so I could slide the drawer open and finally get some rest.

Instead, I slowly scooted myself over to the drain in the middle of the floor, emptied my bladder without standing up, and scooted back up against the wall.

The lights overhead flickered and then came back on. In the distance I could hear loud voices but couldn't make anything out. It had started to rain and on the far wall a thin line of water zigzagged down to the floor. The puddle got taller and wider, until it finally slid across the floor to the drain.

The lights went out again. After a minute, there was a flash of light coming through the small window in the door and in the distance the slow roll of thunder, and then the lights came back on.

I lay down, resting my head on an arm pillow, closed my eyes, and listened to the rain. After a while, I was about to drift off to sleep, and then heard someone else in the room. Heard their breathing. In and out, slow and long. Sitting cross legged on the floor, leaning against the wall, was Tony. I sat up fast and let out a scream. Not because he frightened me, but because of the jagged bolt of fire that went from the center of my back into my eye.

He didn't say anything, just tilted his head with a little smirk surfacing on one side of his mouth and breathed slowly, in and out. His eyes, the part that had been green before I choked the life from them, were black like he had nothing but giant pupils.

The smirk widened into a smile in slow jerking unnatural movements. When his lips parted to expose teeth, they were veined with black syrupy goo. The smile got wider, and he started to laugh. Long wracking all wrong sounds. His shoulders shook and his chest heaved as his laughter got louder and filled the room.

My ears started to ring, and I could hear his rumbling laugh, not only with my ears, but with something inside.

His laughter stopped abruptly. He gasped for breath and his eyes bulged. Sand started pouring out of his mouth into a pile in his lap, and the gagging sound he was making was going to drive me all the way insane. I covered my ears, but it didn't dampen the noise at all.

With the back pain temporarily drowned out by adrenaline, I made the first move toward him, and then the gagging stopped, and he stilled. My hand was reaching out to him, and then he dissolved, mixed with the sand, and went down the drain.

I crumpled onto the floor hugging myself and crying until finally, mercifully, I fell into a dreamless sleep.

CHAPTER 13

"Wake up," Charlie buzzed and nudged me with his foot. "Come on, Jason."

"I'm up," I said, pushing myself off the floor and against the wall. He looked me up and down, unable to hide the disgust in his expression. I didn't even bother covering myself in any way. They'd seen some of the worst parts of me already, things much more embarrassing and shameful than a set of dangling balls.

"Get much sleep?" he asked.

"Oh yeah, slept like a baby," I said. "There's just something about the ambiance of this room."

"How's the pain?"

"Considering what Lee and Randall did to me, it's actually better than expected."

"And whose fault was that?"

"What do you want, Charlie? Come to check my prostate?"

He chuckled. "Not in my job description. Just need to get an update on any side effects you might be experiencing."

"But not to let me out?"

"Are you..." he started, but I interrupted him.

"Ready to get out of here?" I asked. "Yes, Charlie, sure am."

"How's your mom doing?"

"She's still dead, thanks for asking."

"No more visits?"

I shook my head, rubbed my face to clear the morning fog, and ran my hands through greasy hair.

"Any other hallucinations? Any other side effects at all?"

I thought of Tony dissolving and rolling down the drain and shook my head.

He raised his eyebrows in a look of pleasant surprise. "Great," he said and jotted some notes on a clipboard. "That's very good news."

I didn't know why that was good news and was pretty sure I didn't want to know. I lied about my symptoms because I didn't trust him. I had no idea if telling anyone the truth would make things better or worse.

When he walked out of the Thinking Room, he left the door open. For a long hopeful moment, it seemed I was going to be able to get back to the ward, but right as I was about to stand up, he came back in with a black five-gallon bucket in one hand and set it in the corner.

"Toilet," he said, walked out the open door again, and came back with another bucket and a rag. "Here, get cleaned up. You stink." He tossed me the rag and then set the bucket full of steaming soapy water in front of me.

"I'm no legal expert," I said. "But this being left naked and drugged in solitary confinement bullshit has to go against some kind of regulations."

"You're already going to spend a couple days in here," he buzzed. "Starting something else is only going to extend that stay."

"What do you expect to gain from putting me in here? What kind of help is this supposed to be providing?"

"It's to emphasize that you need to do is what you're told and keep your hands to yourself."

"I got my fill of that do-whatever-you're-told bullshit in the Army, and I'll keep my hands to myself when you and the other guards do the same."

"That water's going to get cold," he said with a little smile touching one side of his mouth. "I'll be outside."

I dunked the rag into the water, wrung it out, and slowly cleaned the cut on my eyebrow first. I wiped down every inch of my body and enjoyed the warmth of the water for as long as I could.

"You almost done?" His buzz echoed in the corridor outside the Thinking Room.

"Done."

"Dump the water down the drain."

I did as instructed and silently apologized to Tony for washing him even farther down the drain.

"Do you have a towel?"

One arm poked through the door, and he blindly tossed me a towel. I dried off slowly, making sure to get my hair as dry as possible. I'd catch something with a wet head and no clothes in the freezing room.

Charlie came back with a fresh set of White Oaks issue pajamas, handed them to me, took the towel and bucket, and left without another word. The door slammed loudly behind him and the lock sliding home echoed.

I spent the next several hours trying to count the cinder blocks in every wall, but kept losing track, and got tired of starting over. Some of the old mortar was dark from the moisture, other areas were dry and crumbling.

The lone small window on the door had been covered. It was their way of stealing away time as well as light. I missed the sun right away.

Growing up, I used to sit in the sun with my mom. She said the rays passing through windows were filtered so only the bad UV rays got through. To get the right rays with the right vitamin D, she'd often force me to go outside with her. Even though many of those sessions went on in silence, some of the best conversations we had were when it was just the two of us sitting outside, soaking in the right kinds of rays.

I sat upright against the wall of the Thinking Room with my palms facing up, closed my eyes, and remembered those days, while pretending the scant heat from the artificial light above me was coming from the sun. I thought if I could feel the sun again, maybe I could smell the lilac bushes she planted on the side of our house and hear her breathing there next to me. Right when I started to believe it, that I was outside soaking up the sun with my mom, the light blinked off and didn't come back on.

Being in the dark all the time was disorienting in a way I couldn't even describe; it was so foreign. I didn't know when to be tired or awake and had to guess at everything. Even though I could still hear some of the activity on the ward, I stopped trusting it, thinking the staff was changing up the schedule just to mess with me. Your eyes never adjust to complete darkness. After a while, I started to see temperature changes as vibrations of color.

At some point, probably days later, the world tilted, and I lost focus on reality. It was a full on out-of-body experience. I felt myself condensed down to the size of a peanut to become only a passenger in my own eyes as I shouted insults at the guards and shrieked about the dead things. Eventually, they stormed in and restrained me.

When the door opened again Dr. Sawyer came in. He knelt down beside me and slowly removed the muzzle one of the guards had secured around my head and face, like they thought I was Hannibal Lecter.

"If I remove the restraints, are you going to behave?"

I nodded, but said nothing, and he freed me. I sat up and pushed myself away from him against the wall. I rubbed my wrists and ankles and waited for him to let me out or at least give me some kind of indication of how much longer my stay would be.

"We spoke before about you not attacking any more guards," he said.

"James attacked Michael first. I'm not just going to stand there and watch your employees brutalize the patients."

He stood up and brushed at his lab coat. "I don't believe you, Jason. The guards are here to help."

"Do you believe the cut over my eye, or the restraints?"

He shrugged. "The cut wasn't intentional. You attacked a guard, and the others were trying to protect themselves, and you. You wouldn't have that cut, wouldn't have been restrained and wouldn't have been moved to the Thinking Room if you'd left James alone."

"I already told you, James attacked Michael. I wouldn't have touched James otherwise."

"James knocked a deck of cards out of Michael's hands, and he's been reprimanded." He paused and studied me before adding. "You're making excuses to justify your violent nature. Frankly, Jason, I don't think you realize how sick you are. You may not agree with our methods, but we really do want to help. You've attacked two guards, been hostile towards other patients, especially Clint, and have been experiencing severe visual and auditory hallucinations."

Maybe James really did only hit the cards and I'd overreacted. Could I have been imagining things, exaggerating things to take the spotlight off me? I knew he was right about one thing for sure, the hallucinations had been severe. Realizing that made me suddenly question everything. Maybe I'd even imagined the conversation I heard between Charlie and Dr. Sawyer. Maybe there was no Ava at all, or I'd just misconstrued what her situation was.

"What reason do I have to let you out if you're just going to assault someone again?"

I sighed and dropped my head. "I won't."

He nodded and stroked his beard. "What's more important right now is that you properly report any side effects you're experiencing from your medication."

"What do you mean?"

"You told Charlie you didn't experience any other hallucinations after seeing your mother on the ward the other night. Obviously, that's not true."

"What about CJ?" I changed the subject to avoid what was obviously true.

"What about him?"

"He reported his side effects to Craig but was still forced to take his medication."

"CJ's case was an unfortunate one. We were working on something to fix his meds."

"Are you working on something to fix his teeth?" I asked, and then wondered if I'd really heard him refer to CJ in the past tense.

He sighed and dragged an almost imperceptibly shaking hand down his face. "Come on, Jason. Give me a break."

I said nothing.

"Need a blood sample," he said and pulled the equipment out of his lab coat. "May I?"

"What for?"

"To see if there are any abnormalities. Just want to make sure we get you on the best possible meds. I think we're headed in the right direction, but the hallucinations won't do."

"All right," I said and held out an arm. Just like the other shit that came out of his mouth, I didn't know whether or not to believe him but didn't know what else to do. I could fight him off and it would accomplish what exactly? It'd just result in more time in the Thinking Room and another beating before they took whatever blood, stool, or hope they needed. My mom told me all my life to pick my battles, and I decided to listen to her advice for once.

After finishing, he left the room without closing the door, reached around the corner and picked up a plate of food. It was more than the standard plain bread or oatmeal. It was a big sandwich with a bag of potato chips and an apple. They were all gone in about ninety seconds, and I chased it with a large glass of water the doc gave me.

"I guess that means you're not letting me out yet?"

"Not quite," he said. "No meds tonight. Give me a little time to figure out the right thing for you, and then maybe you can go back to the ward."

"I might actually believe your claims of wanting to help if you at least had a bed in here. You're not helping anything by making me physically uncomfortable."

He seemed to consider that for a long moment. "Fair point," he said and left the room.

Although pretending the artificial light was the sun didn't work, I tried to picture myself on the shore of that lake in Montana. The one my dad called me home from right before the third anniversary of my mom's death. I could remember the quiet at the lake and how fresh the air was, but couldn't remember the smell of it anymore. By that point I was so consumed by the pain, very little of the beauty and tranquility of that half-remembered lake seeped through my scattered frantic thoughts. There was nothing to read or draw with, no games or activities of any kind. There was nothing to do but sit there.

I wanted to see Tony again, but at the same time, I didn't. I never had real brothers, but what I had with the other guys in the Army was deeper than that, especially with Tony. We hit it off from the first day, right after a whizzing piece of shrapnel sent by a sniper's shot about ten minutes after my arrival in the Korengal hit my cheek. He knocked me down behind a barrier, made sure the wound was superficial, and started laughing. In the meantime, the others had opened up on the hillside the shot came from and they either hit the sniper or scared him off.

The welcoming shot could have sent me in the wrong direction mentally. Some guys would have been rattled a little too hard to recover from that shot effectively, but Tony's laughter made it seem like a joke that was prearranged between the two sides to defuse any built-up tension I may have brought with me.

It wasn't until that moment, sitting alone in an inescapable room, that I realized I never thanked him for that.

CHAPTER 14

The last couple days spent in the Thinking Room – or maybe it was just the final five minutes, that's how slow time passed – they kept the lights off. The pain had returned since I wasn't taking Dr. Sawyer's medication anymore, but it wasn't completely out of my system because the hallucinations lingered.

I sat in complete darkness and tried to convince myself I was alone in the room. Seeing the dead from my past was bad enough, but knowing they were in that cramped dank room with me and not being able to see them was somehow worse. More than anything, it was their breathing. It bounced off the walls, making them sound everywhere, and yet, just out of reach.

Acclimated to the dark, my pupils must have shrunk down to the size of the tip of a needle. When the door shot open, Dr. Sawyer's silhouette was in the doorway. I squinted and held up a hand to cover my eyes, but the light penetrated everything and burned into my brain. Feeling the sensation of its warmth after such a lengthy absence was intoxicating, despite the pounding headache the sudden burst of light created.

Dr. Sawyer looked like a wobbling stick figure outline of a person kneeling down in front of me. "Mr. Miller," he said and fussed with his lab coat. "We take your care very seriously. That's why it's important that you tell us everything that's going on, no matter how strange or frustrating it may be. It's all to help you."

"You're saying this to the guy you locked in solitary for days, but I get the picture, go along to get along. I'll be a good boy."

He straightened up. "I'm glad to hear that, Jason." Since I was cooperating, or he believed I was, he dropped the formality and went with my first name. *What a pal.*

I didn't respond, just let my eyes adjust and allow his form to take shape. He stood up.

"So," I said. "About letting me out."

"Yes, I suppose it's time."

"Go along to get along," I repeated.

"Indeed," he said. "And all for your own benefit." He adjusted his coat once more and walked out of the room. I didn't want to give him the chance to change his mind about letting me out, so I followed soon after.

"You might want to take a shower before reintegrating," Dr. Sawyer said before unlocking the ward.

"You think?" I said in a mocking tone, and he frowned at me.

That's exactly what I did. No hellos, handshakes, or eye contact with anyone, just straight to the shower I went and didn't come out until I was waterlogged and wrinkly. I decided to keep the beard and see where it went. It was something to do.

The first person to approach me when I came out of the bathroom was Michael. He'd been waiting. "Are you okay?" he asked.

"I'm fine. Has CJ been back on the ward at all?"

Michael shook his head. "No."

"How are you?"

"I'm all right," he said. "It's been a little tense lately."

"Well, we're going to tone it down for a while, okay?" That was my big plan at the moment. Rest, recover, and figure out what was next. I'd considered trying to sneak out again and continue looking for an exit that didn't require a key, or look for Ava to see if she could help, but I was so uncertain of myself and what was or wasn't real. I believed the staff at White Oaks meant us harm, but didn't really know how and had no direct evidence to support it. I also believed Ava was real and that the conversation I'd overheard Charlie and Dr. Sawyer have in his office while spying on them from the vent really happened. However, I was afraid of finding out that she wasn't real and that I was really as sick as Dr. Sawyer claimed. It seemed like every option in front of me was bad, and I didn't know what to do, so my plan at that point was just to do nothing.

Mentally and emotionally, my plate was already full. I'd been thrown further off balance by being at White Oaks longer than I ever imagined possible and had never been more uncertain of myself. That uncertainty was compounded by Dr. Sawyer's attempts to convince me that he was there to help me, help us all.

"Tone it down," Michael said and smiled. "Sounds like a good idea."

Kevin walked over. "Hey, Jason."

"Hey, man." I shook his hand. His hair had filled in more in my absence.

Michael turned to Kevin. "Jason said we're going to tone it down for a while." His smile was even bigger.

"Sounds good," Kevin said.

"That's exactly what I said." Michael was beaming.

"Right now, fellas," I said. "I just want to sit down somewhere comfortable." I walked over to the TV area and sat at the end of the couch so I could rest against the arm. They both sat down, and we all sank into the couch, not talking.

After a while, the medication cart came around and there was something new for me from Dr. Sawyer, with compliments. I swallowed it without question.

The pain in my back and neck had previously hammered itself into permanent memory but was fading within a few hours of receiving the new gift from Dr. Sawyer. It was a welcomed surprise.

The others were happy to see me as well. I talked to everyone except Clint and Stephen. We played games and sat with each other whispering stories about nothing. It was a slow, recuperative day leading up to the evening group therapy session. Throughout the day, waiting for that session to begin, I went outside with every group, smoked two cigarettes at least during each of those breaks, watched the trees, and drank in their scent.

Then, at the session, we set up the chairs in the same circle as always and everyone sat in the same seats as always. Any deviation from the unwritten seating chart would cause cat fights, and no one was interested.

Dr. Sawyer came onto the ward, cleared his throat, and sat down among us. "We're all happy to see you back with us, Jason."

I smiled thinly but said nothing in response.

"Well then," Dr. Sawyer said. "I believe it's your turn to share, Leonard, if you want to."

Leonard nodded a few times and wiped his hands on his pants. "Yeah, okay." There was a long pause as he slowly looked around the circle at each of us, his expression transmitting nothing. He nodded again and began.

"My wife and I were good companion depressives. We both went through spells, but they were usually on different schedules, so the other could help out and be helped out when it was their turn."

He paused and the room was silent, expectant. Water dripped in a corner somewhere behind me and the wind licked the walls with enough force to cause the building to creak.

"We were together twenty-five years. I don't think there was a day in that time that we didn't see, or at least speak, to each other." He smiled at the memory of it, but there was pain behind the smile. "She battled the cancer really hard for a long time. I was there every day. I was there every day," he repeated. "But couldn't be there at the end." He looked around the room and it was clear the memory burned. It was hard to watch.

"Such a stupid thing too. I'd gone to the cafeteria to get lunch. I don't even remember what it was anymore. Whatever it was, it didn't sit well. I spent some time in the bathroom attached to her room and was making a foul stench. I kept apologizing to her for stinking up the place. I washed my hands, went back out still apologizing and she was gone. After all the years together," he said and sucked in a quick breath. "And she died smelling my shit and listening to me sheepishly apologize for it."

The room was silent, soaking in his words. He almost chuckled, then wiped absently at his cheeks and added, "It's actually kind of funny, when you think about it."

There were a couple uncomfortable chuckles. I coughed and cleared my throat. Leonard covered his eyes and shook his head.

The others in the circle shared experiences and what they had been thinking about recently. When it was my turn, I just mentioned that being in the Thinking Room for too long only reminded me of a desire to get healthy. The others smiled, and Doctor Sawyer nodded. Then the session continued until everyone had a turn to participate.

"I think that's enough for tonight, gentlemen," Dr. Sawyer said. "I know it's a bit early, but we've had a long day, and I'm ready to turn in."

There was a low murmur of approval.

"All right then," he said and stood up. "Just leave the chairs out for tomorrow."

***

Despite being in a bed for the first time in days, I couldn't sleep and lay there thinking about my time in Afghanistan.

I had been in the Korengal for a year and was slated to go home, but our orders were changed at the last minute, and our tour was extended.

Everyone and everything in the valley seemed to want us gone. The mountains crumbled underfoot, sending jagged rocks down to meet unsuspecting friends below. Monkeys came from nowhere at night and would screech at us around the perimeter of the outpost. I didn't even know monkeys lived in such places, which only made their midnight sessions more disturbing. Some of the villagers set us up for ambush after ambush. Of course, the Taliban, and whoever else, was always hitting us with mortars and small arms fire. RPG explosions turned the air to dust that constantly jammed our weapons.

About a week after our time there was extended, the IED ended my Army career, and I was in a hospital bed in Landstuhl, Germany full of the drugs that would hold sway over my life for the next decade and beyond.

The sky was starting to change color when I closed my eyes for good. It couldn't have been more than an hour before Charlie burst in to buzz us all awake.

That night was going to be a first for Michael, who was the foodie of the group, and who always suffered greatly at the expense of our cafeteria's menu. Jalapeno cornbread. Chili with jalapeno cornbread. Supposedly, butter would also be part of the deal. Michael was ecstatic. It seemed odd to me that he'd never had cornbread in his life, but he'd been institutionalized since he was a teenager and if the standard menu at White Oaks was any indication of the norm, he'd probably missed out on a great many foods.

There was butter, and both the chili and cornbread were homemade in cast iron skillets. The chili had chunks of onion, green pepper, green chiles, and a fresh green onion garnish. There were dollops of sour cream. It was the finest meal any of us had had in a while and we were glad of it, Michael in particular. He raved about the cornbread, perhaps a little loudly but not so loud anyone needed to intervene.

Without warning, James came up behind an exclaiming Michael and dug under his arms. Michael cried out in surprise, and James put him in a headlock, yanking him up. Cornbread flew out of Michael's hand. He cried out again, and James pulled him over the bench seat, his heels flopping on the linoleum on the other side. Michael relaxed his body, James carried him away, and we all sat there wondering what in the hell just happened. Michael hadn't done anything wrong. There was no reason for James to react that way. We were all shocked and angry and bewildered by the whole thing. For the first time in days we were actually enjoying ourselves, as well as our food, and James had ripped it away for no reason. That's often how they operated; it was like they never wanted us to feel safe or content, even for a moment.

The scene did nothing to quiet the battle inside my head. I'd gone from being certain that White Oaks was a sinister hell hole and the staff being intent on hurting us, to being completely uncertain of my own sanity and thinking that maybe I was the problem and not them. Then James went after Michael for no reason, and I was back to questioning everything. The one thing I was really certain of was that I needed a break from the Thinking Room and some time to figure out the best course of action before making any other drastic moves.

***

Michael was brought back onto the ward first thing the next morning, looking haggard and weak, like he'd spent a month in the Thinking Room instead of just a few hours. He went right for his bed, nodding to us along the way. He pulled back the covers and then froze there looking at the mattress.

After he was taken from the cafeteria, I talked to the others, and we gathered all the untouched cornbread in napkins. It was a risk to sneak food out of the cafeteria, but Michael had done nothing wrong, only expressed joy and happiness about something new. I convinced them all to carry out one piece each. We all liked Michael, so it didn't take much convincing. All the pieces were neatly stacked on Michael's bed, hidden under the covers, individually wrapped in napkins. After he pulled back the covers, he laughed quietly, just a short burst of air through the nostrils, and picked up one of the napkins. He unwrapped it, ate the cornbread in two quick bites and grabbed another one. He unwrapped that, ate it in two more quick bites, then looked around the room with a big cornbread infused grin on his face.

"Thanks," he said. "You guys are the best."

CHAPTER 15

Before Charlie had the opportunity to buzz us awake, I opened my eyes to see Michael sitting on the floor next to my bed, picking at his fingernails and cuticles.

After squinting at the light and rubbing my face, I asked, "What's up, man?"

He looked up at me and offered an apologetic half smile. "Sorry, I just wanted to tell you that I don't want to change the plan."

"What plan?"

"The plan to cool things off on the ward. I just wanted to make sure you weren't mad about them putting me in the Thinking Room the other night."

"Of course I'm mad. But I didn't do anything about it, and need a breather from their bullshit and that damn room. I won't do anything to get myself, or anyone else, into trouble." I sat up and looked around the still, quiet room. "For a while anyway." I added and smiled.

"Good," he said and stood up. He went back to his bed and slowly pulled the covers over himself. A few minutes later, Charlie came thundering onto the ward. The door flew open and before it had even smacked against the wall, he was banging his flashlight on the inside of the metal trash can. When he crossed the threshold, he tossed the can. It bounced around the room and fell silent next to Leonard's bed. He rose, frowned at the trashcan, and rubbed the sleep from his eyes.

I sat on my bed and waited for the medication cart. When it came, I swallowed my pills without argument, and James rolled the cart to the next bed. I stared at the ventilation shaft and thought of the pharmacy with a familiar hunger. The right thing to do was what I had told Michael, and let things cool down. Another trip to the pharmacy would only make things worse. Still, that hunger yapped in the background of my mind and it wasn't silenced until someone on the ward, I'm not even sure who, laughed the same way my Uncle Alex used to.

Uncle Alex had been an Army Captain in Vietnam where he had called in so many airstrikes that his troops started calling him Captain Jupiter, the one who always called down the thunder. He didn't like being called that after the war and every time my dad did, Uncle Alex would give him sideways glances full of fire.

A few months before my dad called me home from the shore of the lake in Montana, I had gone to visit my Uncle Alex up near Cleveland. It'd been years, and he was surprised by the visit. In truth, I had only gone up there because he was a fellow chronic pain sufferer and would have drugs somewhere in the house. I'd swallowed up my own prescriptions too quickly and was almost out of all pills. It didn't matter that I had multiple prescriptions from multiple doctors, my supply was nearly exhausted in less than two weeks. My only shot at getting drugs, other than off the street, and that wasn't exactly my field of expertise, was to score them off Uncle Alex.

We had a good, though awkward, visit. The first morning there, I opened the cupboard to get a coffee cup, but opened the wrong door. Inside the cupboard were rows and stacks of orange pill bottles. I only needed to glance at them to recognize the familiar names: Tramadol, Percocet, Vicodin, Cyclobenzaprine.

That night I sneaked out of my bedroom in the middle of the night and helped myself to hundreds of pills. Some were in expired bottles but were still full. As far as I could tell, he filled up all kinds of stuff he never got around to using. He wouldn't miss them. The day after I got back home, he called me.

"Hey, I just wanted to make sure you made it home all right."

"Yeah," I said. "Thanks for checking. Should have let you know."

There was a long silence on the line. "Well," I started, but he interrupted me.

"Is there anything you need to tell me?"

At first the question confused me, then my stomach got all hollow and my heart started to thud. "I don't think so. Why?"

He sighed. "It's probably me anyway. Memory isn't so good anymore."

"What is it?"

"Well, it's just," he said, paused and sighed. "I'm missing some pills. A lot of pills. And, well, your dad has talked to me about some of your issues with that."

"I'll have to thank him next time we talk," I said.

"No, Jason. Come on now; don't say anything to your dad. He'd probably be mad I said something to you."

"I didn't take your pills."

"Figured," he said, and there was another long pause. "Hell, Jason. I'm sorry. I shouldn't have accused you." I had to pull the phone away from my ear because he started coughing. "Sorry," he said. "My daughter was just here the other day. She's no angel herself. Or maybe I just forgot. A lot of times I fill up my scripts before I'm out, so I'll just dump the new pills into old bottles. Maybe I thought some were expired and tossed them."

"No worries," I said and hated the sound of the words, but continued. "I'm just glad we got to hang out."

"Yeah, me too."

"Well," I said. "I'm about to hop in the shower, so I'll talk to you later."

"Yeah, okay. Love you, kiddo."

"Love you too," I said and hoped my voice didn't sound strained because my throat was burning and trying to tell the truth on my behalf.

After hanging up the phone, I sat on the floor and covered my face with my hands. Uncle Alex was a good dude. He welcomed me into his home. As thanks for his hospitality, I stole from him, and then lied about it. I thought of him accusing my cousin and though we barely knew each other, the idea made me sick. Then I thought of him beating himself up over the missing pills, thinking he'd done it himself. Twenty minutes later, I called him back.

"Hello?"

At first, I couldn't say anything. As much as I wanted to tell him the truth, something inside me had mutinied.

"Jason?"

"Hey, Uncle Alex."

There was a drawn-out silence interrupted by another bout of coughing from him.

I took a deep breath and let it out. "I took the pills."

"Oh," he said and paused. "Okay."

"There's no excuse for my behavior. You welcomed me into your home, and I stole from you. I am so sorry." The last couple words came out sideways and I took another breath to still my pounding heart.

"Listen to me, Jason."

"Yes, sir."

"I don't want you beating yourself up about this. We have different problems, but I know what you're going through. I've had chronic pain for years and sometimes, no matter how strong you try to be, no matter how much you try to convince yourself you're stronger than the pain, sometimes that voice inside just takes hold and won't let go. It can make you do things you aren't proud of."

At first, I couldn't say anything. Tears were streaming down my face, and his understanding only made what I'd done hurt more.

"But," I started.

"But nothing," he said. "I have more than enough pills to hold me over."

"I'm so sorry. All I can do is ask for your forgiveness."

"I know you're sorry. I can hear the hurt in your voice and can't stand to hear it anymore." He paused and took a deep breath. He was crying too, and that hurt worst of all. "This don't change anything between us. Just promise me it won't happen again."

"I swear to God, it will never happen again."

"All right," he said. "That's good enough for me. You're welcome back here any time, okay?"

After shaking off another wave of tears threatening to spill out, I cleared my throat. "Okay."

"I love you, kiddo."

"I love you, too."

"Don't beat yourself up over this, you hear? Promise me that."

One last time, I lied to him. "I promise."

"All right. We'll talk again soon."

"Sounds good," I said, and we hung up.

He was dead a few weeks later. I'd known he was sick, but not the extent of it. Shame washed over me like a sickness after remembering that phone call.

Hearing that laugh and being reminded of Uncle Alex was all I needed to move my greedy thoughts away from the pharmacy. I was determined to never be that person again.

CHAPTER 16

A month passed by slowly like years. Time was dragging, but I'd decided to wait things out and see what happened before attempting another escape. I was also afraid if I got back into the vent again that my hunger for the pharmacy would be too strong to overcome and I wanted to see if the medication Dr. Sawyer had me on might work enough to be able to permanently replace opioids. With everything that'd happened, I simply wasn't sure enough of myself to take any more risks and thought if I just cooperated for a while, they might see the changes, and finally let me out.

Leonard started taking a new medication for his depression and within a week his hand started shaking and wouldn't stop. They switched his meds again, but that hand kept moving.

Michael's delusions about men in suits and various other things, even about White Oaks, slowed, and then stopped all together. His complexion cleared and he started to gain a little bit of muscle, despite the lack of activity or work out room. He wasn't jacked; just stopped looking like a stiff breeze might blow him over.

CJ never came back to the ward. Dr. Sawyer finally claimed, after being asked for weeks and brushing off the questions, that CJ had been moved to another facility and was doing fine.

Stephen spent the better part of that month staring at nothing and saying nothing. It was nice to not have him belittling the other patients or getting a boner when one of us was being assaulted by the staff, but it was also creepy enough to outweigh the benefits. Being in the same room as Staring Stephen was like being locked in a room with a mannequin that you could swear was alive but only when you weren't looking.

Clint suffered from a bout of anal bleeding so severe that the staff gave him diapers, but he bled through those. They switched his meds and he was back to just being an asshole after that.

Kevin had more hair than he'd had in his twenties, and, like Michael, put on some muscle. Unlike Michael, Kevin was pretty jacked and spent at least an hour of every day doing push-ups; dozens of them like it was nothing. However, in the last week or so of the slow time, his workout times lessened and he had dark patches under his eyes that made him look tired and sick most of the time. My own medication had been switched again and the hallucinations finally stopped.

All things considered, it had been a quiet month. There were some mixed results with medications, but the staff hadn't been as hostile toward us and no one was sent to the Thinking Room the entire time. I was finally convinced that I'd made the right decision to stay on the ward when things suddenly got much worse.

***

I was sitting on my bed, leaning up against the wall under the small window. There was a little bit of cool air coming in through the old poorly sealed window, and I could hear the breeze outside. Leonard walked out of the bathroom massaging his shaky right hand.

From across the room, speaking for the first time in weeks, Stephen shouted, "Hey, Leonard, if I can smell your shit from all the way over here, I wonder if your wife didn't die from cancer."

Leonard stopped in the middle of the room and looked at Stephen. "What'd you say?"

"Maybe she just choked on the stench is all I'm sayin'."

"Stephen, really, what the fuck?" I said, but he didn't acknowledge me. He just sat there staring at Leonard with a big grin on his face.

Stephen pinched his nose, made a gagging face, and then laughed. Leonard, saying nothing, just lowered his head and shuffled over to the TV area. He sat down, looked at Stephen, then at me and then gave his full attention to Drew Carey on *The Price is Right.*

I was about to say something to Stephen when there was a low groan from across the room. Kevin was buckled over and holding the back of his head. I sat up.

"Kevin?"

He stood up straight, dropped his hands to his sides, and looked at me. A single line of blood ran from his right nostril. At first his expression was blank, but then his brow furrowed, he reached up with both hands to hold his head and started shrieking. I jumped out of bed and started to move in his direction, but then the shrieking stopped, he dropped his hands and returned his blank gaze to me. Then his eyes rolled up and he collapsed. He was too far away to catch, and his head smacked off the floor.

Running past Kevin, I started banging on the pharmacy one way glass and yelled for help. When none came, I ran to the main door and did the same. Charlie, James, Randall, and Lee all ran onto the ward. James was last and he pushed a gurney. They each grabbed a limb, counted to three and lifted Kevin onto the gurney, and then they were gone.

I stood in that spot by the door, hands on hips, trying to catch my breath, when there was a muffled gagging noise behind me. I turned around and saw Leonard lying flat on his back. Stephen was on top of him. He had each of Leonards' arms pinned under a knee and was choking him. Leonard's face was a disturbing shade of red.

I ran over to them. I didn't bother to struggle with Stephen, and he was so transfixed with strangling Leonard that he never saw me coming. I lowered a shoulder and ran full speed into him. He flew off Leonard and smacked into a nearby wall. Leonard was coughing and gasping for air. I recovered from my tackle and grabbed Leonard under his arms, dragging him backward and up against another wall. His eyes were full of broken blood vessels.

Again, I went over to the main door and started banging. The door flew open, almost knocking me over. Randall, Lee, and James burst into the room looking around with bulging eyes.

"What the fuck is it now?" James hollered.

"Stephen was choking Leonard."

They all looked over at Leonard. He raised a hand to indicate that he was all right. Stephen shifted on the ground and slowly stood up. The side of his head and face were covered with blood. He touched the wound, examined his fingers, then looked up at me, and smiled.

The three guards all started approaching Stephen. They spread out as they got closer, and Stephen's smile widened.

"Come on, Stephen," Lee said.

Stephen responded by kicking Lee in the groin. He let out a high-pitched cry, grabbed his balls, and dropped to the floor. James and Randall rushed in. Randall was in front of Stephen, James behind him.

James grabbed Stephen around his mid-section, trapping both arms. Stephen pushed back against him as Randall rushed toward his front. I considered helping them, but didn't want my involvement to be misconstrued, and stayed out of it. Stephen jumped up, being supported by James, and drove both feet into Randall's chest. He stumbled backward, tripped over his own feet, and went down hard. Lee was still holding his balls and moaning, but he'd moved some and was trying to stand up. Stephen leaned his head forward and then threw it back, crushing James' nose. James fell back, and Stephen landed on top of him. Stephen turned and started strangling James just like he'd done to Leonard.

Finally, back in the fight, Lee rushed over and connected with Stephen's ribs with a sweeping kick. There was a small crunch and the air escaped Stephen's mouth, but he didn't stop strangling James. Randall grabbed Stephen from behind in a headlock.

"Let go of him, Stephen," he yelled.

Lee dropped to the ground beside them and started to pry Stephen's fingers from James' throat. "Let go damnit."

James kicked and flailed his feet around and joined Lee's efforts to pry Stephen's hands off his throat. Randall yanked back on Stephen's head, and that finally got him to release James. His face was the same mix of red that Leonard's face had been as Randall continued choking him out, but the expression on his face was that of defiance and maybe even a little relief. Stephen looked over at me and winked, then he went limp. The three guards hoisted Stephen and carried him off the ward.

As soon as the door closed and was locked behind them, there was a loud grunt and a crash. I stepped closer to the door to hear better. There was an ensuing struggle, and I wasn't sure if Stephen was fighting back again or if the guards just couldn't wait any longer to start beating him.

"No," James yelled.

After another loud crash and series of grunts, there were several long, pained screams, some from Randall, and some from Lee. Indistinguishable yelling overlapped the sound of running footsteps, probably Dr. Sawyer, coming from wherever. There was a loud snap, clearly a bone belonging to someone breaking, a high-pitched scream that I couldn't attribute to anyone in particular, and then silence.

No one came back onto the ward that day, not for meals or smoke breaks or anything. Around the normal time for medication dispensation, the lights flicked on under the pharmacy door and we were each called by name, one by one over the loudspeaker, to come to the one-way window and get our meds through a shoot.

CHAPTER 17

The next morning Dr. Sawyer and Charlie came onto the ward together at lights on and gave everyone their medication first thing. We were granted a one day reprieve from being woken up by Charlie's trash can. Dr. Sawyer asked us all to gather around.

"I do apologize that the schedule was so disrupted yesterday. After being removed from the ward, Stephen attacked James, Randall, and Lee. James' arm was broken, and he'll be taking a couple days off. Randall and Lee both suffered more significant injuries. They're fine, but they'll both be on a slightly longer leave of absence. Stephen is being confined in another area of the hospital and he will not be returning. His violent tendencies are too much of a risk to all of us. For now, we're going to be a little understaffed, so please do your best to make things a little easier on Charlie, Craig and myself."

***

Later that afternoon I had a one-on-one session with Dr. Sawyer and asked outright when I'd be released. I reminded him of my cooperation, lack of disciplinary problems, that I wasn't suffering from hallucinations anymore, and was ready to move on with my life. He didn't agree, insisting that there was still a long way to go with my treatment. As soon as he said that I started thinking about trying the vent again. I'd already been there for months and *a long way to go* sounded like additional months I couldn't deal with.

At the start of the evening group session, before Dr. Sawyer sat down, really before anyone sat down, I asked about Kevin.

"He's fine," he said dismissively.

"In the same way CJ was fine?"

He didn't respond to that at first, just stared at me and then finally said, "Kevin will be back on the ward very soon. That I promise you."

It seemed sincere. He'd get the benefit of the doubt for a day, maybe two, that was it. "Okay." There was more to say that night, but I chose to pick my battles carefully. For once, I actually believed Dr. Sawyer was telling the truth, that Kevin was fine and would be right back to us.

He looked at his clipboard and then back to me. "It's your turn to share tonight, Jason."

"Great," I said, sitting back and my arms folded. I didn't want to share. The first thing that popped into my head was my dad, but I wasn't going to talk about him.

It was always cold on the ward. The pajamas came thin and wore fast. The air was often sharp in that room. Before starting to share, a shiver ran up my spine.

I decided that the best course of action was to be a smart ass.

"I had this friend, Eric. This was when I was like, I don't know." I scratched my beard, which was coming in nicely; I'd never tried to grow one before. "Maybe ten years old? We lived on base at Fort Irwin in the middle of the Mojave Desert. This wasn't long before we moved to Colorado. There were pools everywhere and the swimming season was long. Anyway, my friend Eric came over and we were swimming for like five minutes and the guy throws up in the pool."

Dr. Sawyer stared at me with unmasked irritation.

"That was bad enough, but what was worse was that he'd just eaten a hot dog and floating in the pool was half of an unchewed undigested hot dog. I never got mad at my mom for telling me to properly chew my food again."

"That's gross, dude," Michael said under his breath, but he was smiling a little. He looked up to Dr. Sawyer, then started biting his fingernails and looked at the ground. Dr. Sawyer was still staring at me, a blank expression on his face.

"That's what you wanted to share, Jason?"

"Yeah," I said and let out a breath. "Feels good to get that off my chest."

There were a couple chuckles around the circle. Dr. Sawyer quickly glanced at everyone and then returned his gaze to me. I threw up my hands and laughed. "I'm just messing with you, Doc, calm down."

"Do you have anything legitimate you'd like to share?"

What could have been discussed, if I was being treated by a respectable professional, was my dad. My mom's drug problems had their influence, but I never really knew for sure what was going on with her until it was too late.

I thought of the lake in Montana and the phone call from my dad, which essentially ended that trip. I didn't have anything else planned, not specifically, but there wasn't much to return to. Still, my dad had said he wanted to see me on the third anniversary of my mom's death.

***

When I got back to my hotel room after taking in the stunning beauty of Glacier National Park, I packed my bags and the next morning was on the road back to Ohio.

Driving under the blue arch across the highway and the *Ohio: Find it Here* sign felt a lot more like coming home than going back to Colorado, the first leg of the trip before Montana.

I had only been away from Ohio a couple weeks, but the trees and rows of crops were a welcomed sight. When I pulled into the gravel drive of my parents' house, the one with the black walnut tree on one side, the sun was starting to set, turning the vibrant green rows of corn into purple with flaming orange tops.

As soon as I opened the car door and stepped out, everything felt wrong. It was too quiet. I closed the car door behind me and took a few steps forward until the front door came into view, it was a faded relic that my mom had painted yellow. A note with my name on it was taped to the stained-glass part of the door.

"There's something I want to show you," my dad had said when he called me a couple of days before when I was at the lake. "Be here at noon, don't be late."

I was late.

I was always late to everything; even the Army never cured me of that. What could he have wanted to show me? And if he was showing me something, why the note? I didn't want to know the answer to either one of those questions, but couldn't just stand there. I pulled the note off the glass. It was short, like most things my dad had to say.

Late as usual, right? I can't just sit here and watch you throw your life away the same way your mom did. If this doesn't wake you up, what hope do you have?
Dad

Slowly, I folded the note, put it in my back pocket and listened to my heart thud in my ears. I turned the doorknob and stepped inside.

"Dad?"

There was no response. I searched the house, every room, but he was nowhere to be found. Everything was clean, neat, and orderly.

I walked over to the side door, flipped on the switch for the light on the porch and stepped outside. Thirty or so feet from the door stood the lanky black walnut tree. Nuts were scattered all around the base, now that my mom was no longer there to collect them for batches of ice cream. Even the squirrels seemed to stay away.

My dad was sitting on the ground at the base of the tree. He was leaning against it, facing the house. His head drooped to one side. The pistol was still clutched in his hand, though it was at an odd angle with the barrel in the dirt. My knees loosened and I wavered, sitting down hard on the steps. For a time, I stared at him, hurt by the act, but more than anything, confused at how he'd placed it all on me.

After a while, I went back inside, took out my cell phone, and called the police. I didn't show them the note. It was a private devastation never to be discussed with anyone. Both my parents were dead because of me. If only I'd been a few feet closer to the IED, then they'd both still be alive.

He'd asked what hope I'd have if his suicide, and the reasoning behind it, didn't cause me to quit abusing drugs and risking my life on an almost daily basis. However, I refused to accept that he was right about me. Despite everything that'd happened, I still felt like there was hope for me to turn things around.

What I wanted more than anything was to prove him wrong.

***

"I'm sorry, Dr. Sawyer," I said and shrugged my shoulders. "But I really don't have anything to share tonight. Maybe next time." Not for the first time, my time at White Oaks felt like penance. Something I deserved.

He sighed and scribbled something on his clipboard. "Okay," he said. "On to you, Clint, if you're willing."

There was a momentary pause in the conversation. Outside a bird whistled. Its call was answered and then both voices flew away and vanished into the distance.

"What really happened to Kevin?" Clint asked.

"What?"

Clint sat up slowly and straightened out his pants. "Did they need a specimen?"

"Ah, for crying out loud. Here we go again," Michael said.

Dr. Sawyer said nothing.

"Are you working with them?"

"The aliens you mean?" he asked, immediately bored.

"The aliens, Dr. Sawyer. The aliens. You know that's who I mean." Clint sat forward and pointed at the doc. "I know what you're doing."

"All right," Dr. Sawyer said, his voice rising. "No one is working for anyone. Kevin is in the infirmary. I'm tired of this and don't want to deal with this anymore." He stood up and rushed out of the room. The lock hammering home echoed throughout the ward.

We sat there staring at each other until the lights went out a few seconds later.

***

Dr. Sawyer didn't come onto the ward at all for another two days. We weren't allowed smoke breaks for that time, and weren't even taken to the cafeteria for meals. The only person we saw was Charlie, when he brought us pre-packed meals to eat on the ward. We still got our medication, but only through the shoot in the pharmacy window.

By the end of those two days, I made up my mind that no matter the cost, I was getting out of there. I would find a way out and prove my dad wrong; prove that there was still hope.

When the remaining staff did return to the ward, they brought Kevin with them, a peace offering, though not much of one. He looked like he'd undergone a year of chemotherapy in the three days he was gone and his previously thick hair had thinned a bit. There were a couple small patches missing entirely on one side of his head. He had dark circles around his eyes and was hunched over like he couldn't even hold his own weight.

"I look worse than I feel," Kevin said when he got to the huddle of patients. "Really," he said and looked at me. "I'm fine."

I opened my mouth to question him, but couldn't come up with anything to say, so I closed it and simply shook my head.

"Did they tell you what happened with Stephen?" Leonard asked.

Kevin nodded and tried to stand up straight but winced at the effort and stopped.

We got meals and smoke breaks, but no group therapy session and none of the staff said more than five words to any of us throughout the day. Any questions that were asked went unanswered as they tried to navigate around us all. Kevin stayed in bed the whole day.

***

That night, after everyone was asleep, I climbed into the vent again. Instead of turning right at the first break to get to the pharmacy, I continued straight until reaching the opening leading into Dr. Sawyer's office. I eased myself out of the vent.

I'd already eliminated several potential exits and could focus my attention on the areas of the building I hadn't checked yet. Charlie was the only guard in the facility that night, with James, Randall, and Lee temporarily absent. I found three other doors that weren't secured with chains and padlocks, but they all required keys.

On one side of the building there were a few rooms that were open but had no exits. There was a break room with a fridge and coffee maker, some scattered tables and chairs. There was an office with counters, cabinets, steel tables, and a copier. In the back of that room was a small bedroom with stacks of books on the floor, a twin-size bed that was unmade, a small vanity with some lotion, and miscellaneous make-up products and a small dresser with women's clothes inside. I convinced myself that it must have been Ava's room, but she wasn't around to validate that.

On the other side of the building, I almost got caught when Charlie walked around the corner on his way to the exit leading to the smoking area, but he didn't see me. As soon as he went out that exit, I checked the room he just left, but it was just a standard breakroom. A couple old couches, tables and chairs, a fridge, and coffee maker. A couple of the cabinets by the fridge had locks on them.

As soon as I'd confirmed that there was no way out of the facility without a key, I started heading back toward Dr. Sawyer's office. The lab was the first thing I had passed by when I left Dr. Sawyer's office at the beginning of my trek through White Oaks, and when I did go by it was empty. When I approached it on my way back into Dr. Sawyer's office, the lights were on. Ava must have made her way there when I was searching other parts of the building.

Slowly, I glanced into the room through the glass panel on the door. Working inside the lab was a woman. I assumed it had to be Ava. Some of the equipment was running. There were circular white pills rolling along the conveyor belt and she was leaning over it, inspecting them.

Now I knew the possibility of having heard a woman may not have been a figment of my imagination. I also had concluded that there was no way out of White Oaks without a key, so it was clear, she was my only hope of escape. Of course, I was assuming and projecting a scenario in which she wouldn't just turn me in as soon as I made contact.

The lab was very close to the exit leading to the smoking area where Charlie was and there was no way to know when he'd come back inside. I knelt down and passed by the lab doors so she wouldn't be able to see me. Again, I considered making contact, but it was too risky with Charlie so close by.

As soon as I turned the doorknob to go back into Dr. Sawyer's office, a key slid into the lock from outside, and Charlie came back into the building. I slipped into Dr. Sawyer's office, quietly closed and locked the door behind me, and stood still, my heart pounding. When his footsteps receded into the distance, I took a deep breath and started to calm down.

I hadn't noticed until then, but Dr. Sawyer didn't have a computer in his office. He didn't even have a landline. In fact, I hadn't seen a computer or phone anywhere since arriving at White Oaks. Michael had brought up the lack of cameras at the facility and how they didn't want any record of what went on there. Adding that information to the lack of computers and phones made Michael's claim sound more legitimate. As far as the cameras, maybe there were some privacy laws I wasn't familiar with regarding facilities like White Oaks. However, the lack of computers and phones made no sense.

What the Doc did have were filing cabinets along one wall. I shined my penlight on those. Each drawer was labeled alphabetically. In the first one were patient files and treatment records. There was nothing alarming, at a glance, in any of the folders, including my own. My curiosity peaked, though I didn't understand most of the entries in my file. There was a lot of shorthand and what looked like code. The only thing that bothered me was in the list of my medications. There were no names, just batch numbers and dates. Batch 4-A was the first. A more recent entry showed I was on batch 9-C. They must have been manufacturing their own medications to give to us, hence the lab and batch numbers. I didn't know much about the pharmaceutical industry, but that didn't seem like something that would be allowed. What in the hell is this place, I wondered.

The last cabinet drawer on the bottom had no label. There were four files inside. Two red, two blue. The blue file folders belonged to Lee and Randall and contained nothing of particular interest. Both had been stamped *Permanent record: Employee Archive* on the outside cover.

The two red file folders belonged to CJ and Stephen, and both had been stamped *Permanent record: Patient Archive.*

I opened CJ's file, and it was much like my own, except for the final entry, which was dated around the same time he was taken off the ward for the last time. The date and the words had been rubber-stamped into the file without any care – crooked ink entries, a little smeared – without any sign of professional etiquette, sympathy, or concern. But the words themselves had meaning that struck me with disbelief bordering on panic. Shocked, I stared at the two-word entry while scenes of CJ flashed through my head. Then, breathing heavily and feeling nauseous, my body slid down the side of the cabinet where I sat on the floor. I closed CJ's file and opened Stephen's. The last entry was the same.

Patient Deceased.

CHAPTER 18

In the morning, Michael came and sat on my bed. We didn't say anything to each other at first. I got out a deck of cards and started dealing. I didn't ask what he wanted to play, and he didn't ask me. I stopped at ten cards each and we arranged our hands.

"You first," I said.

He dropped a seven of spades.

"Does it have to be in the same suit?"

He shrugged his shoulders. "I don't care. Just the higher card. Any suit."

"Okay." I dropped an eight of diamonds, picked the cards up and started a pile.

I couldn't decide whether to tell him about CJ and Stephen. I didn't know what to think about Randall or Lee either. Maybe Stephen killed them both, or they were injured badly enough that they'd never be coming back to work. If they were coming back, why would their personnel files be going into some archive? I didn't really care about them, at least not as much as I cared about CJ and Stephen. Dr. Sawyer told us CJ had been moved to another facility, and that Stephen was being held in another area of White Oaks, permanently segregated from the rest of us

There was no longer any uncertainty about the kind of situation that we were all in. I didn't know all the details about what they were doing or why, but patients were dying in their custody, and they were covering it up. It seemed clear, given the lab and batch numbers instead of medication names in everyone's files, that they were experimenting on us.

Although my relationships with the other patients, especially Michael, were strengthening, I still wasn't familiar enough with any of them to know how they'd handle information like that. The situation was clearly dangerous for all of us, though to what extent was uncertain, so doing anything even remotely risky was a bad idea. I no longer had any doubts about what I'd overheard Charlie and Dr. Sawyer discussing, which meant that Ava wasn't supportive of what was being done to us. She was being held against her will, and since confirming there was no way out without a key, the best course of action was to find her when Charlie wasn't so close by, and at least attempt to form an alliance with her that could get us all out of White Oaks alive. I decided not to say anything to the other patients, but it would only be a matter of time before they'd all need to know what was going on.

"Have you thought about the last day Stephen was on the ward?" Michael asked. It was almost like he could sense what I was thinking about.

"In what way?"

He sighed and shook his head. "It doesn't matter," he said. "Forget it."

"No, really." I set my cards face down on the mattress. "What's on your mind?"

He shifted and leaned forward, speaking softly. "If Stephen hurt Randall and Lee so bad that they have to be on an extended leave of absence, wouldn't they have called an ambulance?"

"What makes you think they didn't?"

"Did you ever hear any sirens? See any flashing lights? If an ambulance came we would have seen, and heard, it. They probably would've called the cops too, don't you think?"

"We could have just missed it." Obviously, I knew that wasn't true.

"Do you really believe that?"

"We're all a little bit wrong in the head and getting mysterious drugs fed to us. It's possible that we could have missed or forgotten about it."

"What do you mean, mysterious drugs?"

Shit. "I just meant that people have weird side effects, like CJ and Kevin especially." As much as I wanted to tell him just how right he was, it was too soon. I needed to get my head wrapped around the big picture and then we'd talk. If we were going to get out of there, I had to be careful. Soon enough, they would know, but at that point I just wanted time to think.

He didn't seem convinced by that response, but moved on anyway. "I've talked to the other guys," Michael said. "No one saw any lights or heard any sirens. Not one person."

"I don't know what to make of most of the shit they do."

"Do you really think Stephen is still here?"

I shrugged and slipped my hands under my legs. It was cold on the ward and my hands were freezing. "Maybe they just took Randall and Lee to the hospital in a company van or something, I don't know. We can speculate all day, but there is nothing we can do about it."

Michael started to respond, but I stopped him. "Can we just go back to our card game?"

He nodded, but said nothing and played his next card.

***

Later that day, I sat in the TV room not paying attention to the show, but watching Kevin on the other side of the room attempting his daily exercises. His appearance hadn't improved and though he'd been doing dozens of push-ups a day without issue before the incident, he got winded after just a few. He leaned up against the wall, panting. Sweat poured off him. I walked over.

"You up for a game of chess?"

"Sure."

As we set up our pieces, I asked, "How are you feeling?"

"Fine," he said and wiped his nose on the back of his hand.

"Really?"

"Really."

"Because you don't look fine."

"You're just mad because CJ's not around to play you anymore."

I didn't respond, and he looked up at me. "What?" he asked.

"Nothing. I'll tell you another time."

"Okay." He didn't seem satisfied with the response, but looked too exhausted to press the issue.

When the board was set and his first pawn was moved, I asked, "What do you think of this place?"

"You mean other than the mystery drugs with horrific side effects and the random beatings and harassment?"

"Of course."

"Well then, I think White Oaks is a first-class establishment. I'll be sure to do a Yelp review saying as much when I get out."

I laughed, moved a pawn up two squares, and looked around the room. The recently reduced staffing levels made private conversations a lot easier.

"Seriously though," I said. "I don't have any other experience with mental hospitals, but this place has felt wrong from day one." I wasn't going to tell him anything yet, but wanted his impression of our situation.

"There's an understatement," he said and moved a knight.

I studied the board for a long time, and then moved another pawn. Within seconds he'd made his next move.

"Do you ever think about what you'll do when you get out?" I asked and moved a bishop.

"I don't know how I'll ever return to a regular life. Don't know if I ever could. Some baggage is too heavy to carry alone, and places like this can help lighten the load. Besides, I have nothing to go home to."

"We all have baggage," I said. "And there are resources out in the world. Living in a cage isn't the only way to get help."

"Maybe we don't deserve help," he said, his tone and mood darkening.

"What does that mean?"

"Checkmate," he said.

"What?"

"Checkmate, shit head."

"How'd you do that so fast?"

"I had a lot more time at the table with CJ than you."

Him mentioning CJ again caused a flash of anger and hurt.

"We're not hopeless, and we deserve help the same as anyone else." I stood up, knocked over my king and walked away.

***

That night, I opened the vent panel and pulled myself into the duct. What Kevin said about needing help to carry his baggage made sense, we all need help sometimes, but he wasn't receiving the kind of help that would allow him, or anyone else, to feel the weight of that baggage lessen.

Thinking that finding Ava and forming some kind of an alliance with her was my last hope to get out of White Oaks made my heart thud, my breath feel thin and without nutrition and made the ducting sound less forgiving of my movements. After all, she was apparently a prisoner in the same way we were. She might be on our side and willing to do something, but if she couldn't get out either, I didn't know what she'd really be able to do. Still, it was all I had and was going to try.

I lingered over the vent above Dr. Sawyer's empty office long enough to get my breathing and heart rate back under control. There was no light and nothing moved. I pulled up the panel, set it on the other side of the opening, and lowered myself into his office.

I put my ear up to the door and listened for any sign of a wandering staff member in the corridor. There was nothing, but just to make sure, I lay on the floor and looked under the thin opening at the bottom. The hallway was dimly lit. No one passed by.

After standing back up, I grasped the door handle. "Okay," I whispered, turned the knob, and cracked the door open.

The lab was empty, so Ava must have been in her living quarters or the break room nearby it. If Charlie was in the break room on the other side of the building, where I'd almost gotten caught the night before, that would mean he'd be far enough away from us that we might have enough time to talk. All of these were hopes and they swirled with the greatest hope of all – if I found her, I really hoped she wouldn't scream.

While approaching what I started to think of as her side of the building, I heard music, something slow and melancholic. I wasn't close enough to be able to name the song, but it sounded familiar. I froze in the middle of the hallway and listened, then took another hesitant stretch of steps toward the music and paused again.

My heart was pissing me off at that point because it was just jackhammering away. I took another dozen or so steps and waited. The song was getting clearer. Acoustic guitar in the lead. Ten more steps, pause. "*Don't you know that I love you,*" the song was *Angel in the Snow* by Elliot Smith, one of my favorites.

I'd felt sick most of the day, but was so distracted by everything else going on that I'd dismissed it. All of a sudden, I started to feel lightheaded, and my vision got fuzzy. I wavered and clenched my teeth, and that caused a flash of pain in one tooth.

There were black specks across my vision and my stomach clenched. I reached into my mouth and felt the tooth that had flared up; it was loose. My thoughts immediately went to CJ.

On the opposite side of the building, a door slammed shut and it was followed by footsteps. I could barely stand, the hallways started to spin a little, and the sound of the footsteps echoed loudly making it hard to tell where they were coming from.

I stumbled back, away from the music coming from what I hoped would be Ava's living quarters, moving toward the break across from it. The footsteps seemed to get quieter, and another door closed. That's when I bumped into the trash can. For a second, I couldn't move at all and then a sensation of falling in slow motion took over my body. That sensation was replaced by a forceful slam of body and bone onto linoleum.

When I woke up on the floor of the break room, a woman was holding my head in her lap.

CHAPTER 19

I sat up and it startled her. The movement caused my vision to waver again, but I was starting to feel better.

"Are you Ava?"

She pushed ebony hair from her face. "Yes," she said and paused, closely evaluating me. "Who are you, and how do you know my name?"

I didn't respond at first, just looked around the room, trying to remember exactly where I was and how I got there. "What happened?"

"You tell me. I heard something, came in, and you were on the floor."

"I just started feeling really sick all of a sudden."

"You're a patient," she said, more a statement than a question.

I looked at my filthy pajamas and imagined the general crazed expression I must have been wearing and couldn't suppress a smile. "What makes you think that?"

She returned the smile.

"Are you going to tell anyone about this?"

She didn't hesitate. "No. I'm not going to tell anyone, and I'm not going to hurt you. Are you okay?"

"I've never experienced anything like that before," I said. "I felt a little weird all day, but it just hit me like a ton of bricks all of a sudden. I think it's the medicine Dr. Sawyer has me on."

She deflated visibly. Her eyes darted around the room and then back to me. She looked at her watch. "You don't have long. Charlie just came back inside. I think he's in his break room now. How'd you get off the ward? We need to get you back before the next bed check."

"The vents."

She looked at me doubtfully.

"I'm serious. I can access Dr. Sawyer's office through the vents."

She brightened when I mentioned Dr. Sawyer's office. "Were you trying to escape?"

I hesitated and she again said she meant me no harm, so I shook my head. "I've already been everywhere that isn't locked, and there's no way out of here without a key," I said, and she nodded with understanding. "I was actually looking for you."

She frowned. "I don't understand. How do you know about me?"

"I heard them talking about you. Charlie and Dr. Sawyer, I mean."

"What'd they say?"

"Well, when I was first admitted I heard you arguing with Dr. Sawyer. Later, I asked if there were any women at White Oaks and he said no. When I reminded him of that argument, he said it was all in my imagination. One of the first times in the vent, I overheard a conversation between the doc and Charlie. Dr. Sawyer called you an uncooperative little fucker and Charlie said they should have just…" I trailed off.

"Just what?" she asked.

"Gotten rid of you. Those were his exact words. I didn't really know if he meant *get rid* of you," I said with a finger gun pointed at my temple. "Or get rid, like fire you."

"Probably this one," she said, with her own finger gun put into action. She looked at her watch again. "Listen, I'd let you out of here right now if I could, but I can't even get myself out. We have more to talk about, maybe we can help each other, but right now, you need to get back onto the ward before Charlie beats you there. I think you have about ten minutes."

I stood and the rush of blood to my head caused me to waver, but it passed quickly.

"Can you make it?" she asked.

"I think I'm okay. Still feel a little weird, but I can make it."

"Come back as soon as it's safe," she said. "In the meantime, I'll try to figure out our next step. I don't want to be here any more than you do."

I started to leave, but she stopped me. "Wait, what's your name?"

"Jason," I said, and made my way back to Dr. Sawyer's office.

***

When I woke up the next morning, there were a few random numb spots on my face, and a spot in my upper back was so tense the muscle felt like bone. The knotted muscle was strangling a nerve, sending bursts of electrical pain down my right arm.

My back had felt relatively decent for a while, and there hadn't been any episodes in weeks but as soon as I opened my eyes it was clear it was going to be a rough day. I didn't know if the meds they had me on stopped working or if I had an episode triggered by stress and fear. Like every other medication I'd ever been on, nothing worked all the time, nothing stopped episodes like that from happening, and the past few days had been the most stressful of my life, so it was probably just that, but the timing was awful.

Craig was the first person to come onto the ward. The lights overhead blinked on, but Charlie didn't emerge with his trash can. The pharmacy lights turned on. There were a few minutes of tinkering noises behind the closed door's one-way glass, and then he came onto the ward. By the time the cart moved through the doorway, I was already shuffling slowly in that direction.

"Craig, my back is fucked up. Can you give me something for the pain?"

After a theatrical sigh, he muttered under his breath, "God, I can't even start my rounds."

"I'm sorry to inconvenience you with my crippling medical issues."

"Just a minute," he said, smacked the clipboard down on the cart and went back into the pharmacy. When he came back out, he dropped half a dozen one thousand milligram Percocet into my palm.

"I'll give you more later," he said and started to roll the cart away. "If you need it."

"Thanks," I said, tossed one of the pills in my mouth, and then walked to the bathroom for a handful of water to down it with.

Under normal circumstances I probably would've taken two, but since opioids had been out of my system for a while, restraint was exercised for a change. I considered putting the pills in my pillowcase, but took them to the bathroom with me, and wrapped the other five in a piece of toilet paper and stuffed them deep in my pocket.

Charlie came onto the ward and asked if anyone wanted to go out for a smoke with him, and I hollered my intention to join him from the bathroom. While crossing the faded tile floor, I dug into my pocket and grabbed another Percocet. I did this without really thinking about it, my old habits wasting no time to come back to the surface. The action was like blinking or moving my hand away from a fire.

Outside, the smoke billowed all around us and obscured the trees, so I moved off to one side where there was an unobstructed view. It was only Charlie and Clint outside with me anyway, so whatever conversation that might take place wouldn't be of interest.

The limbs of the black walnut trees drooped. The husks resting on the ground had shrunk and blackened from rotting.

I wanted to smoke mainly to calm my nerves. There was no reason to believe Ava notified anyone about my late-night adventure, but it was certainly a possibility. She might rat me out to get back on their good side, for all I knew. None of the other staff had ever displayed even a modicum of humanity or trustworthiness, so my paranoia and worry were completely justified.

The scream from a blue jay filled the air and I turned around just in time to see it land on the highest branch, which drooped and bounced under its arrival. I'd have given anything in that moment to be a bird. To be free of the pain, of White Oaks, and the decades of mounting shame and regret. Watching the beautiful vibrant creature filled me with naked jealousy. It dropped from the branch into the lawn below and started pecking at one of the husks. When it flew away, I continued to watch it until it was just a speck in the distance, and then it vanished.

I finished another smoke, stubbed it out in the dispenser between Charlie and Clint and told them I'd wait for them at the door, neither of them responded.

I wanted to get back onto the ward, see that my concerns about Ava were unfounded, and assure myself no one was waiting for me when we got back inside. Maybe a little breakfast and conversation would do my wracked nerves good now that the Percocet was fully established inside my mind and body.

When they were done, I walked slowly through the door, my heart pounding and my stomach all hollow and wrong feeling. There was mounting dread of finding them all waiting for me, Ava alongside them, my hopes for escape dashed, but the room was clear, and Ava wasn't there to ambush me. I let out a long, unsteady breath. Just getting past that first moment, realizing that maybe she wasn't going to rat me out after all, was enough to get me through the rest of the day in a semi-normal state. Of course, the Percocet added a bit of euphoria to the calm.

I sat on the couch next to Kevin. "Hey, man."

"Hey," he said, but didn't look at me.

"How are you feeling?"

He shrugged. He'd lost a little more of his bulk and looked tired. "I'm okay."

"What's on the tube?" It was a commercial.

He didn't respond at first and I looked at him. He was frowning hard, like some crucial piece of information was on the tip of his tongue. He opened his mouth to speak, closed it again, and shook his head. "I don't remember."

From across the room Craig was asking Leonard what day of the year Christmas was on. Someone sat down on the couch next to me and bumped my leg, but when I looked over no one was there. I stood up fast and backed away from the couch. Kevin was watching me.

"What's wrong?"

Maybe it was just the medication.

"Nothing," I said and sat back down, though cross-legged and a little farther away from Kevin so no one could sit down next to me. The show came back on. It was *Judge Judy*. That was one of a thousand times not having access to the remote control was maddening. Mental patients apparently couldn't be trusted with complex pieces of equipment like remote controls, or maybe withholding it from us was just another way to drive home the idea that we had control over nothing.

"Craig," I shouted. He looked up from his clipboard and walked over.

"Can you change the channel, please?"

"I'm in the middle of something," he said.

"Leonard knows when Christmas is. I don't know what that information is doing for whatever weird study you're conducting, and I cannot sit here and tolerate Judge fucking Judy."

He sighed and crossed his arms.

"We have very little to do," I said and stood up. "I know you're a little overwhelmed with the lack of staff these days." I crossed my arms to match his stance and started slowly walking over toward him. The Percocet had all but silenced my back, but I made a show of hobbling anyway. Mentioning the staffing issue made Craig visibly uncomfortable.

“I’d really appreciate it if you’d change the channel to anything other than that shit.” I jabbed my thumb in the air over my shoulder. “While you’re in there, could you get me some more pills? I’m not out yet, but just to save you an extra trip later.”

Beads of sweat had materialized on his forehead. The room was quiet, save for the judge yapping away behind me.

“Fine,” he said, then turned and walked away. When he got to the pharmacy door, he looked back at me uncertainly. I nodded, then went back and sat next to Kevin.

He smirked at me, and I shrugged, then pulled another Percocet out of my pocket and slid it between my teeth. I had three more, plus whatever Craig brought back. I chewed the pill and swallowed the grainy bits.

There was a piece of the pill stuck between my teeth. When I dislodged it with my tongue, something else came out as well. The tooth that was loose had fallen out. I spit the tooth into my hand and stared at it. Other than the specks of red on the base, the tooth was almost gray. Whatever happened to CJ was starting to happen to me, and I couldn’t become another stamped folder sitting in Dr. Sawyer’s office. I closed my hand around the tooth and squeezed it.

I was going to have to stop taking the mystery drug Dr. Sawyer had concocted. There was obviously a risk in doing that; if they found out they’d just force the matter, probably with me restrained in the Thinking Room. Considering how quickly the pain returned when Dr. Sawyer had me stop taking it while he adjusted the formula, I’d need opioids to function. Crawling through the vents and hatching some kind of escape plan with Ava would be considerably more difficult if I was in constant severe pain. I considered the possibility of making a side trip to the pharmacy when I went into the vents again to meet up with Ava, just in case. There were no better options I could think of.

The TV screen changed to an ad for some kind of new medicine for treating depression. We probably already knew what the side effects of that particular drug could include.

"What's one of your favorite memories from childhood?" Kevin asked me suddenly.

"What?"

"First thing that pops in your head."

"Why?"

He shrugged. "I don't know. Are you busy doing something else?"

"Good point." I sat back and thought but didn't have to think long before a memory I wasn't expecting resurfaced.

"You've got one," Kevin said, pointing at me. "I can tell."

"I do," I said and smiled.

Craig walked back around the corner and held out his hand. "Here you go," he said and wiped the sweat from his brow with his other hand. "No more until tomorrow."

He dropped the pills in my hand. I didn't have to look at them to know how many he'd given me and of what dose. It was the same as the last he'd given me. I added those to the three left in the crumpled toilet paper in my pocket. Craig was halfway across the room before I noticed he'd left.

"Thanks," I called after him, and he held up a hand in response without looking back.

"Well?" Kevin said. "Let's have it. I'm bored. *Magnum, PI* is better than *Judge Judy*, but not by much. Entertain me."

"All right," I said and adjusted my position. "Hold your horses." The wind picked up outside and the branches of nearby trees clapped off each other.

"When I was a kid, we were getting ready to move to Colorado, from Fort Irwin."

"That's in California, right?"

"Yeah, middle of the damn desert. Anyway, I played baseball on a little league team off base. Had been for a while and right before we moved, we had our last game of the year. It was against the in-town rival. We'd never beaten them before. In the three or four years I played on that team, we hadn't beaten them once. Every year a slot for the Little League World Series tournament would be open for a team in the area and every year they beat us out."

"I like where this story is going already."

"Everyone knew it was my last game. I alternated between pitcher and outfielder mostly, and that game, they had me pitch."

Kevin had a big grin on his face. He was leaning forward in anticipation. We'd only known each other a couple months, and under some shitty circumstances, but he seemed to genuinely care. Maybe he was just bored, like he'd said, but the expression on his face read clearly as actual interest, and it suddenly made me love him in a way I hadn't loved since killing Tony. The realization hit me hard and without warning. My expression must have changed because he seemed to notice something and his head cocked to one side.

I offered a little smile and cleared my throat. "I pitched a two-hit shutout. Their best player was their last batter and I struck him out looking. The crowd erupted when that last strike was called. The only thing I remember outside of that with any real clarity is the look on our coach's face. He was a hard man, who rarely smiled or complimented any of us. He was a hell of a coach, but hard to please, and he had the biggest smile," I said and just then noticed the ache in my own cheeks from smiling. "After the game, the whole team signed the game ball. I still have it."

Kevin sat back, that smile still pasted on his face. He let out a long sigh and chuckled. "That's a good one," he said.

"What about you?" I asked. He frowned, considering. "Actually, hold that thought, I have to take a leak." I stood up and started to walk toward the bathroom.

Craig walked around the corner, and we bumped into each other.

His clipboard and the papers previously attached to it went flying and Craig hit the ground hard.

Before I even had a chance to check on him or ask if he was okay, he was balled up on the ground screaming for help and begging me not to hurt him. I took a step back.

"Craig," I said, but he couldn't have heard me over his screaming. "What are you doing? I'm not going to hurt you." Maybe I shouldn't have messed with him earlier. Stephen had put everyone on edge, but Craig was the one most obviously afraid of us and it didn't take much to push him all the way over the edge. I stood there, with my hands halfway up in the air, not sure what to do. Craig kept screaming and all the patients were standing there watching him with a mix of confusion, pity, and disgust on their faces.

Charlie burst onto the ward. He wouldn't listen to me, and Craig's screams drowned out whatever I said anyway.

As he approached, I screamed, "I didn't do anything." But, it didn't matter. I left my hands hovering because any kind of movement could have been misconstrued as hostility.

He leaned down and pulled Craig's hands away from his face, which was covered in tears and snot. The look of disdain on Charlie's face would've been funny if I didn't already know I was going to spend that night locked in the Thinking Room. At least that night, but probably longer.

Charlie pulled Craig off the ground and pushed him off the ward, and then came back for me. "Charlie, I didn't do anything. We just bumped into each other. I didn't even see him."

He didn't respond, just grabbed my arm, dug his fingers into the flesh, and pulled me off the ward. I tried to convince him of what happened as he dragged me toward the Thinking Room, but he never said anything in response. After he pushed me into the room, I looked back at him. Before the closing door obscured him, I could see that he was smiling. At least I had the Percocet to keep me company.

CHAPTER 20

My frustration with the place and the knee jerk reactions to everything was driving me nuts. The most important thing was to get back into the vents to see Ava so we could start figuring out how we were going to help each other escape, but instead I was locked in the Thinking Room with nothing but a concrete floor to sit on, all because Craig was a pussy who misconstrued an inadvertent bump as an act of intentional aggression.

Someone must have told Dr. Sawyer about me being taken to the Thinking Room again, because within three or four hours, Charlie came back to get me.

The frustration I was feeling before he came back gave me an excuse to abuse the pills I had on me. Regressing back into that excuse-filled mindset fully woke up the old addict in me, and by the time Charlie came back I was high, but just as frustrated with myself as I was with them. I'd gone into the Thinking Room with nine pills, and with any indication of one's effect wearing off, I would take another, so by the time Charlie came back a few hours later, there was only one left. I was determined to hang on to it until it was time to go into the vents again.

"Come on," Charlie said. "Doc wants to see you."

"Did Craig finally calm down enough to tell you what really happened?" I asked as we walked toward Dr. Sawyer's office.

He didn't respond, just knocked on Dr. Sawyer's door and waited for a response.

"It's open," Dr. Sawyer said. Charlie opened the door and gestured for me to go in, then turned and walked away.

"Close the door," Dr. Sawyer said. I did so without responding and then sat down in the same chair I'd started my adventure at White Oaks in so many months ago.

"Has Craig recovered from his devastating injuries?" I asked.

"You think this is funny?"

"No," I said and sat forward resting my elbows on my knees. "I think this is a ridiculous joke. I accidentally bumped into him, and he freaked out."

"Well, you know Stephen…" he started, but I cut him off.

"I'm not Stephen. The only time I've ever done anything to any of your guards was in response to patient abuse. We've been over that."

"Do you want me to have Charlie take you right back to the Thinking Room?"

"For what?" I yelled, my voice shaking. "I haven't done anything wrong, and you know it. That's why you had Charlie bring me out of the Thinking Room, because you fucks had enough time to figure out that I didn't do anything."

Whether or not Ava could be trusted was still an uncertainty, but after one brief conversation, I liked her a hell of a lot more than Dr. Sawyer and had a feeling she'd earn my trust. I needed to calm down, shut up, and do everything possible to keep him from sending me back.

"If you don't calm down right now, you're definitely going back, and I might just leave you in there. You've been nothing but trouble since you got here."

"Sorry for raising my voice," I said and had to swallow my pride to do so. "I'm just frustrated."

"So, what were you doing prior to assaulting Craig?" he asked with a small grin.

The smile was not returned. "I didn't assault Craig."

He held up his hands. "I was only joking."

"Hilarious."

"So?" he asked.

"So what?"

"So what were you doing before running into Craig?"

"Talking to Kevin."

"What were you talking about?"

I hesitated. "Baseball."

"Was there a game on?"

"No, we were just talking about childhood memories."

"You and Kevin are becoming close."

"I guess. He asked me to tell him a fond memory, the first one that came to mind. I told him about the time I pitched a two-hitter against our in-town rival. It was my last game on the team before moving to Colorado."

He nodded and scratched his beard. "Was there something painful tied to that memory? Is that why you left and ran into Craig?"

"I just had to take a leak and we didn't see each other coming."

"You didn't answer my question."

I wanted to deny him the satisfaction of being right about that memory, but what was there was fresh and on the surface and it must have been obvious.

"There is something else attached to that memory. Something painful," he said. "I can tell."

"It's nothing really. My dad left for Colorado early to get us situated. Base housing at Fort Irwin was short and there was a new family coming in so we volunteered to leave base housing a week early so they could move in. There was a little nothing-town right outside the base. We stayed in a motel for a few days before leaving."

"Mhm," he said and crossed his legs. He may have been trying to mimic my sitting position to disarm me in some way, or maybe it was coincidental. Either way, I didn't like it and adjusted.

"There was a swimming pool in the middle of the parking lot in front of the motel with a cinderblock wall built around it. I spent my last week in California, mostly alone at the motel, pitching and catching a baseball off that cinderblock wall, hour after hour."

"Why were you alone?"

"My mom was still working."

"And?"

"And nothing. I told you it wasn't much. It was just a lonely time right after a triumphant moment. All my teammates were getting ready for their first ever Little League World Series tournament and I was pitching against a wall waiting to leave town forever."

"Just in case you thought you were getting away with something," Dr. Sawyer said. "I know Craig gave you a bunch of Percocet."

"I didn't think it was a secret he'd be keeping."

"Well, don't expect to get more." His face was slowly turning red. He shuffled some papers on his desk and tossed them into an inbox. "Charlie," he shouted, and Charlie opened the door a few seconds later. "Mr. Miller is ready to go back to the ward."

I stood up without saying another word and left his office. Charlie unlocked the ward door and watched me walk in but didn't follow. He shut the door and locked it behind me.

On the opposite side of the ward, leaning against the wall not far from my bed, James was standing there like he was waiting for me to get back. He had the bottom of one foot resting against the wall and when we made eye contact, he pushed away from it and started walking toward me. I didn't know what he had on his mind or what he might want from me, but I had no interest in reigniting the feud with him the second he was back. His left arm was in a cast going halfway up his forearm. It was grimy and the fabric parts were frayed unevenly at the edges.

Before he had the chance to start our interaction off wrong by opening his mouth, I said, in a soft faux concern voice, "Hey, James. How are you doing?"

He raised his one good hand in the air, gave me a thumbs up and stopped in front of me.

"I'm sorry about Randall and Lee," I said. "They never said exactly what happened to them, but it must've been bad if they were both put on a medical leave of absence. I'm glad you weren't hurt as bad."

"Are you?"

"We may have had our differences," I said and crossed my arms. "But that doesn't mean I wish harm on you or anyone else."

"No one?"

"No one," I said, then reconsidered, shrugged my shoulders, and said nothing else about it.

He smiled and picked at his teeth.

"Anyway, welcome back," I said. "Craig could certainly use the help."

"So I heard," he said and laughed.

Needless to say, I still found no humor in it. I shook my head and walked around him

"I'll see you later," he said as I continued walking away.

I got to my bed, lay down, and let out a long sigh. I needed to rest a bit. My back had improved considerably, but it still felt like something was going all kinds of wrong inside me. I had stopped taking the meds Dr. Sawyer had me on, and hoped that whatever was going wrong in my body wasn't permanent. I dug my tongue into the hole where my tooth used to be and then fell asleep. It was almost impossible for me to ever nap during the day, but I was exhausted and had enough drugs in my system that it was more like passing out than falling asleep.

***

A few hours later I woke up with a start and sat up in bed. My vision was blurry, and I was disoriented and unsure of where I was. The dream, whatever it was, left little tendrils of fear whipping around inside my mind, and I tried to pull away from them. I shook my head, looked around the room, and rubbed my eyes. I let out a groan and buried my head under the pillow.

When evening medication was given out, I was able to slide the pill up into the back of my mouth, between my cheek and teeth. A couple minutes later, I went into the bathroom, spit out the pill, and flushed it down the toilet. After dinner, I crawled back into bed to get as much rest as possible before my evening trek. After pulling the sheets over my head, I heard footsteps. They stopped right next to me.

"Jason? Are you all right?" Michael asked.

"I'm fine," I said, a little muffled under the covers. "Just trying to rest my back."

"Okay," he said and gently touched the curve of my shoulder covered by sheets and then shuffled away. I never got back to sleep the rest of the night. My mind floated in between the world of the conscious and subconscious as I lay there ignoring the ward and whatever might have been going on in order to focus on the task at hand. I was glad there was time to rest, but had gone without any kind of medication the whole day after overdoing it with Percocet. The one pill I had left sat heavy in my pocket all day, and the hours passed slowly as I waited for the right time to take it and go find Ava again.

The ward had been dark for a couple of hours, and all the typical sounds of the day had faded into shadows. I was so anxious, both to get off the ward and to take the medicine, that I was sweating and tensing up all over. I caught myself flexing like I was practicing for a bodybuilding competition and had to force myself to relax. Every time my shoulders snuck up toward my ears, my neck got tighter, and the need to take the meds and get out of there drowned out everything else.

I pulled the pill from my pocket and stuffed it into my mouth.

Before it was all the way down my dry throat, keys rattled somewhere outside the ward. It sounded like someone going into the pharmacy, or maybe Dr. Sawyer had forgotten something in his office. There was muffled laughter, a door opened, and then the lights in the pharmacy came on. After that, the pharmacy door leading into the ward opened and a faint light spilled into the room.

Charlie and James came in hanging onto each other and trying to silence each other's laughter. I didn't move. They slowly closed the door behind them, but not all the way. I continued to lay still, my eyes half closed, trying to make out what they were doing.

At first, they just walked over to the first window on the far side of the room, each one of them leaning against the wall on opposite sides of the window. Their faces were half illuminated by the moonlight. They talked in hushed tones and gestured toward any number of different beds. They could have been talking about Michael or Leonard, maybe even Clint. Maybe me, lying still in my bed under the window on the far side of the room away from them.

Their voices rose for a moment, they must have been arguing about something, but it was still unclear what they were saying. They walked off the ward and quietly closed the pharmacy door behind them. A few minutes later, the door opened again, and they crept back in.

They walked low, like they were trying to be sneaky, but were giggling and shushing each other loudly. They were clearly drunk and whatever they were doing was eating into my time off the ward, taking away my chance to talk to someone who made sense, and reducing the possibility of getting help to escape White Oaks.

Charlie and James slowly approached Leonard's bed. James chuckled again and Charlie lunged back and smacked him hard in the chest. "Shut up," he buzzed.

"Asshole," James said. "You almost hit my arm."

Charlie said something in response, but had lowered his voice again, and I couldn't make it out. James approached Leonard, leaned over him, and seemed to be listening for something. He whispered and Charlie nodded.

A bead of sweat rolled down the side of my face to the back of my neck. It dangled there, tickling me. My hand was starting to go numb and there was a light thud behind each eye that usually meant a bad headache was coming. The longer I lay there without moving, the more uncomfortable I got. The sweat dripped from the back of my neck and the tickling started to subside, then another bead of sweat rolled slowly down to replace the first. Unable to silence the discomfort any longer, I shifted, and the bed squeaked. Charlie and James both froze. After a few seconds they each whispered something to each other. James shook his head and shrugged. I stayed still.

The moonlight made Charlie's dark hair glow. He leaned down and did something to Leonard's leg, maybe injected him with something and then stood back up. Leonard shifted a little, and let out a sigh, but didn't appear to wake up.

They started back toward the pharmacy and weren't whispering or hunched over anymore.

"How long will that take?" James asked.

Charlie laughed. "Twenty minutes." He pushed the pharmacy door open, and they both walked in. "Twenty minutes and that bitch…" he continued but shut the door so the rest of what he said was muffled.

Obviously, they were planning to come back. The pharmacy lights went out and the door shut on the other side. Maybe they were going to get another of whatever they were drinking or have a smoke while they waited twenty minutes for whatever.

After letting out a big sigh, I wiped my face, then sat up and walked toward the bathroom. I was about to push the bathroom door open, but stopped. I couldn't remember hearing them lock the pharmacy door.

My heart started to thud in my chest. If they left the pharmacy unlocked and weren't coming back for twenty minutes, I could get more meds, enough to last until I got the hell out of there. Maybe enough to last me a little longer. I promised myself, while slowly creeping toward the pharmacy door, that I wouldn't be irresponsible with the supply. I'd use it when in pain and only as long as it was needed to help me get out of there. My mouth went dry, and the sweat started to shed from my skin again.

Clouds covered the moon, and the ward went dark. I took that as my sign to go for it and bolted across the room silently. None of the other patients stirred. At the door, I put my ear against the old solid wood and listened for any sign of them, just in case. It was just as quiet on the other side of the door. I dropped down and tried to look under the door for feet, but the opening was just a hairline, and I couldn't see anything.

I stood, put my hand on the door handle and tried to slow my heart down. I controlled my breathing and the room got even quieter when my heart rate dropped to a normal level. I turned the knob. There was no resistance. The door was unlocked.

After a long exhale I pushed the door open slowly. The room was empty, except for the shelves and rows of pills. Having raided the place once before, I knew where the good stuff was and could be in and out of there well before the twenty minutes elapsed. The possibility that it was a bad idea, like the first time I'd gone into the pharmacy, evaporated the instant I had access to such a large volume of drugs. I filled a snack sized plastic baggie I found in one of the drawers and quickly left the room, closing the door firmly but quietly behind me. The clouds were still providing cover. I walked into the bathroom and to the first stall. I closed the door behind me, sat down, and caught my breath.

Since I stopped taking Dr. Sawyer's mystery medication, and had no intention of ever taking it again, it wasn't hard to convince myself there was a good reason for self-medicating. I had to be able to function through the pain if I wanted to make it in and out of the vents, but also to focus. Constant pain has a way of distracting a person, but I still needed to exercise some restraint. That was always the objective with me, to exercise restraint and take my pills as they were prescribed.

In the bathroom, I rested my head in my hands and tried to clear my thoughts. Within ten minutes I'd have to decide what to do, how to do it, get back in bed, and wait for the drunken jack asses to return.

I counted out six pills from the plastic baggie. Like the last time, there was a mix, but most of them were the one thousand milligram Percocet. It was the strongest thing in stock. It was a good thing they didn't have OxyContin because coming off Oxy was its own sick version of hell, but it was also very difficult to resist. I pulled a few squares from the toilet paper roll and deposited the pills to keep on hand. I closed the plastic baggie, added that to my pocket and then left the stall.

The ward was still dark and quiet. The lights in the pharmacy were out, and there were no muffled voices behind the door. I looked around the ward to make sure no one else was up, and then walked over to the vent.

I would keep a small supply of pills on me to use during the day and just in case they tossed me into the Thinking Room. The rest would stay in the vent. That way, I wouldn't have complete control over the stash at all times, just in case that old hunger got the best of me.

I slipped the baggie of pills well inside the shaft and secured the vent. Across the room, Michael stirred in bed. I stepped down from the vent quietly. He sat up and stretched. Before he got out of bed, I moved to the couch and lay still. His bed creaked and he groaned. His footsteps shuffled across the room slowly. The bathroom door opened and closed, and I jumped up, ran over to my bed, and slipped under the covers.

My heart was thudding, but for the first time in years, I was actually proud of myself. It was a bit misplaced and felt all sideways inside my head. I could have taken a handful of pills, but didn't. I could have kept them all accessible, but didn't. It was a weird kind of pride, and the realization of it was a little more than embarrassing, but it was still there, and it resonated while I waited for James and Charlie to come back onto the ward and finish whatever it was they'd started.

CHAPTER 21

The toilet flushed and Michael's footsteps echoed in the bathroom. He came out the door and it closed slowly behind him as he shuffled back to bed, got under the sheets, and was snoring gently within seconds.

I focused my attention back on Leonard. I wondered about the trauma he had suffered in his past. I knew it was something about fire. A family business, I thought, maybe a restaurant his parents owned that burned down when he was a kid. The staff knew most of our histories and often exploited weaknesses. No one was watching after all.

What were they planning?

Right on time, keys rattled outside the door coming onto the ward. The handle turned slowly, and I lay there holding my breath, trying to stay quiet, but then the door burst open and banged off the wall. Charlie and James came rushing in, screaming.

"Fire, fire, fire!" Charlie buzz-sawed the room with the warning. I shot up but didn't get out of bed at first.

"Fire!" James yelled, but the word broke off, and he started to chuckle. Charlie swatted him.

Most of the others had risen and were standing near their beds like trapped rats unsure of what to do. The laugh James let out made it seem like a joke, but he was the only one who found it funny.

Leonard was sitting in his bed fidgeting and looking around the room in fast jerking motions. He was pouring sweat and breathing fast.

"Fire!" Charlie yelled again, and that time Leonard jumped up and started to run, but one of his legs didn't want to cooperate and he fell hard to the ground. Charlie and James had an arm around each other as Leonard fell. I was watching them, and it was almost in slow motion because it was clear in that moment what they'd done. They had big grins and their eyes were wide with anticipation.

Leonard's cheek smacked off the floor with a sickening snap and the two guards roared with laughter. The other patients stood around, at first, not sure what to do or what was going on. The orderlies continued to laugh and supported each other out of the room. The door slammed, the lock slid home, and their laughter faded into the bowels of the hospital.

Michael ran to Leonard first. He was holding his cheek and had rolled onto one side. Michael grabbed his other arm and helped him into a sitting position.

"I'm all right," Leonard said and let out a hitching breath.

"What happened?" Michael asked. Kevin and Clint were standing behind him. Leonard shook his head while rubbing his leg.

"I think I know," I said and started walking over. "I didn't see what they did, but adding what I saw before to what just happened, it's pretty clear."

"What'd you see?" Kevin asked.

"They came in," I said and rubbed absently at my shoulder. "Those two assholes were hovering around Leonard's bed and sneaking around, laughing."

"And?" Clint said.

"And they might have injected something in his leg. Maybe it was to make it numb, and then they come in here screaming fire, Leonard jumps up to flee and lands on his face. James and Charlie have a nice laugh and go back to their coffee, or whiskey, or whatever it is they do."

"What were you doing up?" Clint asked.

"Not that it's any of your business what I do or why, but I had to go to the bathroom and hadn't gotten back to sleep yet when they came on the ward."

"Why didn't you say anything?" Leonard asked.

"Like what?"

"Like anything," Michael said. I was taken aback by him coming after me, but he had a point. I could have said something, but didn't want to start yet another confrontation with them, especially when they were drunk and even more so because I was waiting to get off the ward to meet up with Ava. Leonard's humiliation was worth a potential escape for all of us, but it still made me feel shitty, like I was complicit.

"I was half-asleep and didn't even see what they did. I just put it together after. Besides if I had to say something every time we saw one of them doing something suspicious we'd just be gabbing all fucking day."

"What's eating you?" Michael asked.

"I don't know, Michael. Maybe it's that we're doing this in the middle of the night just because they wanted a laugh. I'm tired."

That was true, but in reality, I was pissed that my trip through the vents was being delayed. If the ward didn't get calmed down and with everyone back to sleep in a reasonable amount of time, I'd have to wait until the next night to see Ava again.

Leonard stood up, still holding his cheek. "I'm going to get cleaned up and go back to bed," he said. "I think we're all tired."

Michael started to walk with him, but Leonard put a hand out to stop him. He looked back at Michael and nodded his thanks. "I'm fine," he said.

One by one, everyone else got back into bed. Leonard came back, no longer holding his cheek. He got in bed without another word. Eventually the room was filled with overlapped deep breathing. There would be enough time to see Ava.

There was another bed check and while I was still doing the math in my head, trying to figure out what time it was, the door opened, and James came in alone. His flashlight was on, but he kept the beam pointed at the floor. He slowly walked around the room, never really getting close to any of the patients, and didn't flash the light in anyone's eyes or holler out a false fire alarm. He walked out the door, closed it quietly, and locked it.

None of the other patients had stirred when James came in, but I waited a few minutes just to make sure. I was so tired, and wanted to sleep, but forced myself to stay awake. I had to get out of there.

After a short debate about whether or not it was necessary, I went into the bathroom and got a handful of water to swallow another one of the pills, and then relieved myself, but didn't flush.

Inside the vent, I clicked on the pen light, which I always left in there, stuck it in my mouth, and started crawling.

I got to Dr. Sawyer's office and waited to make sure there was no activity there. The room was dark and quiet. I shined the light through the vent and around the room. It was empty. I lifted the vent cover and set it on the other side of the opening, then dropped down into his office.

I shined the light around the room. The only other place that he'd keep anything Ava might want, other than his file cabinets, was in the desk. I wanted to search the place, but it was already hours later than she'd been expecting me. I turned to leave but heard approaching footsteps and talking outside the door. It was James and Charlie.

"That was hilarious," James said. "Just don't ever do that to me."

"I won't," Charlie buzzed. "Got a couple other things in mind we should do. The night shift is boring. Have to get our entertainment from somewhere."

"Want to smoke?" James asked.

Charlie grunted in response. Their footsteps and conversation faded.

I eased away from the door and let out a breath. After a minute of waiting to make sure they didn't double back for some reason, I left Dr. Sawyer's office and then headed in Ava's direction. Since the only two on the ward I wanted to avoid were outside, I wasted no time and ran down the hall.

Ava heard me coming and stepped out into the hallway. She threw her hands up and whisper-yelled, "What are you doing?"

I gave her a thumbs up and shook my head to try and let her know it was okay without shouting it down the hall. When I got to her she pulled me into the room with her.

"You can't be doing that," she said.

"They're outside smoking."

"Who?"

"James and Charlie. They're the only other ones here, right?"

She nodded. "Yeah. How do you know they're out smoking?"

"Heard them outside Dr. Sawyer's office before I came out."

She nodded again and let out a long breath.

"They came onto the ward a couple extra times tonight."

"What do you mean?" She pulled me further into the room, then walked back over to the door and stuck her head out into the hallway before coming back.

"They came onto the ward through the pharmacy once and were just talking over by one of the windows. They started arguing a little and went back into the pharmacy, then came out with a syringe."

She threw up her hands and shook her head. "What in the world?"

"They were sneaking around and eventually stopped at Leonard's bed and injected something into his leg. Then they left."

"What happened to Leonard?"

"Nothing at first. James and Charlie came back onto the ward about twenty minutes later shouting *fire, fire, fire!* When Leonard got up to run, he collapsed. James and Charlie just laughed their asses off and left.

Leonard couldn't move or feel his leg for a few more minutes. He smacked his face really hard on the floor, but he's okay. After a while, everyone went back to sleep."

She sighed. "I'm so sorry, Jason."

"Don't need to apologize to me. You didn't do anything."

"I know," she said and shrugged. "Still."

"My point in telling you that is that they're being unpredictable with the schedule. If they're going to start coming onto the ward randomly at night to mess with us, I don't know when it'll be safe to come here."

"It's a risk we'll have to take."

"Easy for you to say."

"Not really," she said and frowned at me. "None of this is easy."

"It's easier for you than it is on us."

Her look softened. "I know."

"Are there any other employees here?"

"You already asked me that. I said no."

"Not just tonight though. Are there others at all? Maybe certain days are better to come here than others?"

She shook her head. "No, right now it's just me, Dr. Sawyer, Craig, James, and Charlie. They were talking about bringing in some other people, but I don't think they're close to a decision on that yet. The company keeps this place pretty close to the chest; it's hard to get approval to come here."

"Where do James and Charlie hang out when they're not on the ward?"

"There's a break room on the other side of the building. This side is unofficially mine. This is where I sleep and do most of my work when I'm not in the lab. Of course, I have my own break room. That's where I found you."

"I know the area you're talking about, if they stay away from your side of the building, for the most part, that should make things easier, but," I trailed off.

"But what?"

"What are we doing anyway? And if you're an employee, why can't you get out?"

In the distance, we both heard footsteps. We stood up straighter and our eyes widened in sync. She put a hand on my shoulder and pushed me around the corner. I followed her lead. She stopped at a counter. "Get behind there," she said and walked back into the area we'd just come from. I got behind the counter and sat on the floor.

The sound of the footsteps, two sets of them, came and went, but never got close, then Ava came back to me. "They're gone," she said, leaning over the counter. "Must be going to their break room."

My trust in her was building. She just had another opportunity to turn me in and chose not to. Still, she worked there and needed to answer some questions before I trusted her completely.

"You haven't answered my question yet," I said. "What are we supposed to be doing here? Why are you being kept here? Did you see something you shouldn't have? And what is this place? There are plenty of signs indicating something wrong and two patients have died that they claim are still alive, but I can't piece things together."

"Slow down," she said. "Slow down, one thing at a time." She sat down on the floor across from me. She started to say something but got flustered and stopped.

"God, where do I even begin?" She got up, went over to the door again, and scanned the area, then quietly closed the door behind her and came back to me.

"We all work for a company called Bowman Pharmaceuticals," she said, looking down at the floor and nervously tugging at her fingers before looking back up at me. "White Oaks isn't a mental hospital."

My heart sank and I realized how bad of a situation we were in before she even finished telling me.

"It's a pharmaceutical research and development lab. I swear I didn't know the truth about this place when I took the position."

I let out a long breath. "You've got to get us out of here."

She held up both hands to still me. "This is not a place you simply walk away from."

At first, I didn't know what to say.

"The company picks up people like you every once in a while," she said.

"People like me?"

"People with no one," she said and dropped her gaze to the floor.

"White Oaks has all the proper credentials and proper appearing officials. The system was ready to send you up for a psych eval when Dr. Sawyer scooped you up. No significant other. No parents or siblings. Same as all the others in there," she said, nodding in the direction of the ward.

"So, what's your part in all this? Why do you want to help me?"

"I had only been working for Bowman about a year. Dr. Sawyer was a legend in the company. I was working on a pain reliever, something to replace opioids. That got Dr. Sawyer's attention, so he pulled some strings and got me assigned here to work with him. It was like a dream, coming here." She checked her watch. "He was very supportive and encouraging, at first, and let me focus all my attention on the pain reliever. But it didn't take much time for things to start feeling a little off."

"How's that?"

She shrugged. "It was just little things at first. We couldn't use computers, cell phones, or even a landline. For the first several months, we collaborated on the pain reliever I'd dedicated my life to. I lost my dad to an overdose. He'd worked at the train yard for twenty years. One day he got caught between two cars and lost an arm. Couldn't work anymore. Got hooked on opioids and that was it."

"I'm so sorry." It was always difficult to hear people talk about loved ones they'd lost to opioids because of the ever-present realization that it could just as easily be me they were talking about. I thought this while absentmindedly playing with the pills in my pocket.

There was a loud crashing noise coming from the other side of the building where James and Charlie were. She jumped up and rushed over to the door, opened it, and went into the hallway. In the distance, they were laughing.

She came back to me, eyes wide and full of concern. "We don't have time for this right now," she said and knelt down in front of me. "We might be able to get out of here if I can get my hands on a key, but I've already tried, and I really think the only way it'll happen is by force. Either way, Bowman is too rich, too powerful. If we're really going to escape and be safe, we need to expose this place."

"How are we going to do that?" I asked.

"Dr. Sawyer has all the records in his office."

I nodded. "I've seen them. That's how I found out CJ and Stephen were dead. Dr. Sawyer told us CJ had been transferred to another facility. He had horrible side effects from his medicine. He looked awful when I first got here, and only worsened. He had a seizure, went blind and almost all his teeth fell out."

"Jesus," she said.

"I don't know if I'm taking the same kind of thing CJ was on, but I lost a tooth the other day too."

"What does he have you on?"

"A non-narcotic pain killer, I assume a version of yours that you mentioned the other day."

"Did it work? What kinds of side effects did you experience?"

"It worked really well, actually. I had several symptom free days and that's something I hadn't experienced in a long time, but I had severe hallucinations, and he switched it up on me. He changed the medication a couple times until we settled on what I've been taking. It worked really well for the pain, but then I started feeling sick and weak and lost that first tooth."

"Do everything you can to avoid taking it. My pain medication never would have involved any kinds of symptoms like that. Hearing of your relief makes a lot of this seem worth it. Still, don't take it if you can get away with doing so."

"I already stopped taking it, but sometimes they're more diligent about checking. As far as CJ, Dr. Sawyer told us he was transferred, but I saw CJ's file in his office stamped *patient deceased*. Same kind of thing with Stephen. He attacked the guards, and we were told he was being held in another area of the hospital indefinitely, but his file had that same stamp. There were files for Randall and Lee in there too, stamped for archival."

"Randall was killed," she said.

"You were there?"

"I saw the aftermath. Randall was dead; it looked like his neck was broken. Lee was blinded; he's on permanent disability as far as I know. Stephen was on the ground. His head was cracked open and there was so much blood. It looked like Dr. Sawyer and James stomped him to death."

There was another noise from down the hall, and we both lost our nerve at that point.

"Next time you come down here," she said. "Bring some of Dr. Sawyer's files. I have a copier. Once we have everything copied, everything we need to expose this place to the world, we'll have to get a key."

"How?"

"I doubt it, but maybe I'll be able to sneak one off James or Charlie. If not, well," she said and trailed off. "I guess we'll just have to take one."

I shifted my weight from one foot to the other and rubbed at the small of my back, then pulled a pill from my pocket and cracked it between my teeth. She seemed to consider saying something about the pill, but decided against it. I wasn't sure why I'd taken the pill in front of her; it was an almost automatic reaction to the presence of the drug in my system, to take more. Some of the pride I'd felt earlier when I exhibited restraint melted away.

"I'm working on a new formula right now, something to treat and hopefully cure PTSD. We can copy the files and make plans for escape while I finish that formula. It could help both you and Kevin. I've been working on it for a while. Dr. Sawyer really pushed me to get it done so he could try it out on Kevin, but it wasn't ready yet. I gave it to him and told him I wasn't comfortable with where it was at, but he insisted."

I didn't know if she was telling the truth or buttering me up because she had other plans. The doubt must have shown on my face or maybe she just sensed it.

"Jason," she said and took my shoulders. "I swear, I mean you no harm."

"I guess I don't have much of a choice. I don't know what else the doc has Kevin on, but even your incomplete PTSD drug has helped, Kevin has been doing really well."

"I'm glad," she said, but looked troubled. "Though I wouldn't expect that to last. He might get some initial relief, but the formula as it stands isn't going to do much more than help some of the symptoms. The aim was a cure. Anyway, by the time we're able to copy the records, the formula should be ready."

"Do you develop all the other stuff we take?"

She shook her head. "I'm not entirely sure what Dr. Sawyer has been doing. He's altering the formulas in some way. Up until you got here, I wasn't even allowed in the lab. Now he has me doing all his manufacturing." She checked her watch again. "Look, you've got to go. If you get caught now, we're all screwed. They're going to do their bed check any minute. We'll have more time to talk later, just don't forget to bring some of the records from his office, and be careful."

I hesitated for a second. There were so many more questions to ask, but she was right, there wasn't time, so I left and jogged down the hall, bouncing off my tiptoes while holding the pills in my pocket with one hand. I slipped into Dr. Sawyer's office, pulled myself up into the vent and closed the cover behind me. Knowing they could show up any second, I paid less attention to the noise and shimmied quickly toward the ward.

It was still dark and quiet on the ward. I got down, replaced the cover, ran over to my bed, and slid under the blankets. I pulled another pill out of my pocket, chewed it, and reveled in the bitter chalkiness of it until Charlie opened the door a few seconds later. He checked the beds and left the ward. I lay there sweating, my heart pounding and mind reeling.

CHAPTER 22

Pharmaceutical R&D is what she'd said. Not a mental hospital. It seemed as though we were all pretty much fucked, barring some miracle. Our only hope was that we could copy all the records without getting caught and then, somehow, obtain a key to the outside world. When I first heard about Ava, I didn't imagine her also being a prisoner, as powerless as any one of us. I stayed awake all night going over the different scenarios. Even if we were able to escape the facility, would we ever be able to escape the clutches of one of the richest and most powerful corporations in the world? Would exposing them change anything, or, like most other scandals, would the country's attention be easily diverted, with all of us forgotten?

Although the hallucinations had lessened when Dr. Sawyer last adjusted my medicine, and went down even further when I stopped taking it all together, the whole scenario still seemed too fantastical. I had to at least consider the possibility that either I was hallucinating, or Ava was a patient as well, and everything she'd told me was just a part of her delusion.

The worst part was that I didn't really know what the worst part was. Maybe she was real and telling the truth and we were all going to die in some secret laboratory. Or she was lying or maybe hiding something even worse. Or, she wasn't real, and I was crazy and would never leave White Oaks. Assuming she was real and did want to help us, and that's what I was trying to believe, I still wondered how she got there and what her full role was. She didn't explain enough for things to make sense. Granted, we didn't have the time, and if I'd left any later Charlie would have seen me for sure.

Even though I was having doubts about myself, what she said matched up pretty well with what had been going on since my admission to White Oaks. It seemed possible that I could have hallucinated *some* things, but it couldn't be possible that I hallucinated everything. The treatment of the patients, the ever-shifting list of medications with inexplicably terrible side effects, getting tossed in the Thinking Room over and over again, the conversation between Charlie and Dr. Sawyer, them lying about Stephen and CJ. There was a mountain of evidence to support what Ava told me, but it was so much to process at one time that my brain just froze.

What I knew with absolute certainty was that we, the patients, had no power or control. We had no say in anything that was happening. I might be able to escape on my own if I magically came across a key or was able to surprise and overpower James or Charlie and take one of theirs, but if she was telling the truth, the corporation would probably have me back there or in a shallow grave within hours, and I would still be abandoning the others. I had no idea how to get everyone out, but had to make a move in some direction and stick to it.

If there was any chance that she was real and telling the truth, I couldn't just leave the other patients behind. I had to do something. There was no real choice but to help Ava and hope for the best.

There was still medication in my pocket, and I realized that after getting out of bed when I started fondling the pills absentmindedly. After realizing what I was doing, I took my hand out of that pocket and made a pact with myself to keep my shit together in that regard, at least for the time being. If there was ever a time to figure it out, it was then. I'd take what was needed, and only what was needed, when needed, if at all. As soon as the decision was made, an unsurprisingly familiar voice of protest sprang out of my mind and tried to convince me that I needed some then, *that I really did*, but I shut it down as quickly as it popped up and continued on with my morning routine.

Another uncertainty was whether or not to tell anyone what I'd found out. Not only about what White Oaks was, or wasn't, but that CJ and Stephen were dead. Kevin was the most likely person to confide in, but his gaunt expression didn't serve as a comfort, so I turned from him, and gnawed my fingernails. I wouldn't tell anyone, at least not yet.

The day passed slower than any I'd experienced in that place previously, even in the Thinking Room. Every episode of *Law and Order* and *The Powerpuff Girls* dragged on. Every game of checkers extended into a seemingly timeless space. Every smoke break I'd down four or five in the time it took everyone else to smoke one. The sun lingered in a cloudless sky that was so bright it brought on a crushing headache, and I had to hide in the stall in the far corner of the bathroom with the lights off to escape it. I sat tightly squeezed into the corner, between the tile wall and steel toilet. The smell of bleach was so heavy that my nostrils burned. I finally caved a few hours later and swallowed a handful of pills to help the time pass. The relief was almost instantaneous, but so was the regret and shame.

When I emerged from the bathroom, night had fallen, and the guys were setting up the chairs for evening group session. I grabbed one and set it in the circle.

"Where've you been?" Michael asked.

"Bathroom."

"For five hours?"

"I guess so," I said and sat down. Michael sat next to me. He continued to watch me for a minute, then sighed, crossed his arms and directed his attention elsewhere.

Dr. Sawyer came onto the ward, sat down in his designated seat, and rifled through some papers. "Good evening," he said. No one responded, and he looked at us over his reading glasses. There was an indistinct rumble from somewhere deep inside each of us. Dr. Sawyer shook his head and checked the list to see whose turn it was to share.

"Clint," Dr. Sawyer said, looking over the top of his papers. "You ready to share tonight?"

Clint shifted in his chair and picked something off his pants. He nodded slightly and looked around at the group.

"I was thinking of that day," Clint started. "The day we had the cornbread Michael liked so much."

Michael looked at Clint and they shared a smile, a short one, but noticeable.

"What about it?" Dr. Sawyer asked.

"Him being so excited about the food, it just reminded me of when I was a kid. We were really poor, and food was a big deal, especially good food or a new food." He went quiet for a minute, and Dr. Sawyer cleared his throat softly.

"There was a time when I was about ten and we didn't have money for anything but potatoes. That's all we ate for six months. Potatoes, potatoes, and more potatoes. I hate potatoes."

A low murmuring laugh was followed by quiet stillness hovering over the ward. Clint rarely shared anything other than conspiracy theories and hostilities. For as long as we'd all been around each other, we barely knew him.

He glanced around the room and saw that he had our attention. He fidgeted for a minute, and I could see that his cuticles were bloody in places. Dried flecks of lavender spotted one fingernail.

"Every once in a while, my mom would get a cheap cut of meat and pound it out so thin that it'd look like three or four good sized hunks of steak or pork if you didn't know they were thinner than paper."

He chuckled softly and shook his head, saying something indistinct under his breath. "One winter we got so cold our mom took us down to the rail yard: me and my brother. She had us take one of the cross ties so we had something to burn. Told us to be grateful we lived in a house that had a wood burning stove," he said and settled back in his chair.

"We had a wood burning stove in my house when I was a kid too," Dr. Sawyer said. His beard barely covered the smile on his face. It seemed genuine. On occasions like that one, everything seemed normal and even welcoming, but I had to remind myself that he was performing illegal experiments on us, and that two patients, including CJ, who was a friend, had died or been murdered under his care, and he lied to us all about it. As I sat there, perplexed by his duality, he continued. "I'll bet you still can't stand the sight of potatoes, can you?"

"No, sir," Clint said. "Well, other than French fries. I love those."

"Of course."

Clint smiled and stared off into the distance, saying nothing, for a long time. The smile slowly faded, and his eyes filled with tears. In a barely audible whisper he said, "I sure miss my brother."

"Did something happen to him?" Dr. Sawyer asked, his voice calm and soothing.

"Don't know," Clint said and shrugged. "I was on the streets for a long time. He didn't really have any way to find me. I would stop by his house a couple times a year and he'd take me in, get me cleaned up and fed. He always begged me to stay, said he'd do anything to get me help, but I never did. I was in a hospital for a while and didn't tell anybody. When I got out and went to see him, he'd moved. No idea where. He could be dead for all I know." Clint wiped the tears from his face.

"Maybe you'll find him again one day," Dr. Sawyer said. "Maybe we could help you with that, when the time is right."

Clint brightened at the suggestion, and it was all I could do to not lash out at Dr. Sawyer and his lies. I saw all the way through his bullshit right then and would never be fooled by it again. His previous sincerity had baffled me a bit, and there had been a number of times during my stay at White Oaks that he caused me to question myself and my suspicions about him, but now that I knew what he was doing, it was clear how fake it all was. He would have made a great cult leader.

Dr. Sawyer started organizing his papers. "Well, gentlemen, I think we'll call it a night," he said, looking around the room. When he got to Leonard, he stopped and frowned. "Leonard, what happened to your face?"

Leonard looked around the room uncomfortably and said, in a barely audible whisper, "I just slipped."

"You slipped? When?"

Leonard squirmed in his seat. "Last night."

It was obvious from the expression on his face that Dr. Sawyer thought there was something more than just a slip to the bruise on Leonard's cheek. He told us to put away the chairs, except for his and Leonard's and when we were all out of the way, the two started talking.

"They what?" That was the only part of the conversation I could hear. Dr. Sawyer almost shouted it, and then stormed off the ward. Leonard must have told him the truth about the false fire alarm.

Clint seemed off the rest of the night. After therapy, he wandered off to the farthest corner of the ward and stayed there for hours, staring out the window.

We got our evening round of meds before bedtime, but that was our only interaction with anyone else that night who wasn't a patient. At one point I even got into the vent for another handful of pills. No one was around the TV area or within sight of it at the time, but it was still extremely risky and stupid. I hated myself for it as soon as it was done. When the idea first emerged didn't seem to be a single reason *not* to risk trying to get more pills, but as soon as I did it, I realized how stupid it was. All the same, it was done, so I downed half a dozen other pills to make the time pass a little faster.

As soon as everyone was asleep, I moved from my bed toward the vent, then lights in the pharmacy clicked on. There were some rustling noises and the loudspeaker clicked on with a squawk. Several of the patients stirred. My heart jumped in my chest, and I tried to still it with calming breaths.

Static came from the loudspeaker, then the familiar pounding riff of Rage Against the Machine's "Bullet in the Head" exploded on the ward. Everyone shot out of bed. Clint cried out covering his ears and ran to the bathroom without slowing down. He crashed through the swinging door and ran into one of the trash cans. Both he and it went down in a burst of noise and swearing.

From Dr. Sawyer's reaction to the news about James and Charlie tormenting us in the night, I thought he might have a word with them. If they were reprimanded, it apparently backfired and made them even more hostile.

Michael looked around confused and covering his ears. We made eye contact and he threw up his arms. "What the fuck?" he mouthed, but I couldn't really hear it. I shrugged and walked toward the pharmacy. Behind the one-way glass James and Charlie howled with laughter and banged in unison with the drum beat on the window.

Leonard was under his sheets squeezing his pillow against his head. Kevin sat up in bed staring with open contempt toward the pharmacy. He didn't try to cover his ears or speak to anyone.

The song ended and there was a moment of silence, then a burst of wild laughter and the song started over. This went on for hours. By the end of the night, we were all exhausted and sitting next to each other on the tile floor of the bathroom, leaned up against the wall. It was the farthest we could get from the noise. The song played on and on until daylight broke through the underside of the door. It cut out in the middle of "*they say jump, you say how high,*" playing for the hundredth time. I'd heard of that tactic being used against terrorists imprisoned at Guantanamo Bay, endless loud music for hours or days at a time. It was immediately clear why it was considered torture and why there were protests and cries for justice when it became public information. The difference between Guantanamo and White Oaks was that at Guantanamo they used it as a tool to get information, but James and Charlie just did it for kicks. Neither offending parties were right to do what was done, but the pure sadism attached to James and Charlie made it exponentially worse, as far as I was concerned.

We all stood, stretched our backs and legs, and slowly walked back out to the ward. As much as I'd wanted to see Ava again and get some questions answered, I had to stay on the ward being tormented by two men that I vowed right then and there to kill before leaving White Oaks. After the promise was made, it felt righteous and justified, but as with the substance abuse, it was followed by shame and doubt. Maybe they deserved to die, but I'd already killed enough, and wasn't sure I'd be able to go through with it without some immediate life-threatening provocation. I wondered if Ava had heard the festivities and had known not to expect me.

Along with the desire to kill and the shame that came with it, my mind reeled from what Ava had told me, what'd been happening to all of us, and the potential of what was to come. I didn't know where to focus my thoughts and the lack of sleep only made things worse.

CHAPTER 23

It was another long and slow day after our evening with Rage Against the Machine. I loved that band, and particularly that song, but I'd never be able to listen to it again and not think of White Oaks.

Charlie and James didn't bother us that night. I wanted to get back to Ava and start copying files, but was so exhausted that I was asleep almost as soon as my head hit the pillow.

When I woke up the next morning someone was struggling for breath. The haze of sleep hadn't cleared, and Tony came to mind. I stretched my body and wiped my face. The choking continued. On my right, Kevin was holding his throat. Blood leaked between the fingers. I jumped out of bed and slid across the floor to his side.

"Kevin," I yelled. Everyone else was out of bed quickly and hollering for help. Michael rushed up behind me but took a step back when he saw all the blood. Kevin had wrenched a piece of jagged metal off a spring from his mattress and stabbed it into his own throat. Between his gags there was a low whistle coming from one of the holes, and there were several. His eyes bulged and he tried to grab at the spike again, but I held his hands down.

"Help me," I yelled over my shoulder to Michael. He came back and held Kevin's feet. Leonard and Clint were banging on the door shouting for help.

My hands were covered in blood. Kevin's eyes never left mine, in them a mixture of panic and pleading. I couldn't say for sure, but the pleading was almost like he wanted me to let go so he could finish the job. My face hardened and I shook my head.

Charlie and James rushed in and told me to get out of the way. When I didn't move, James shoved me back and Michael caught me. They each grabbed a side and rushed Kevin off the ward. The door stayed open for a few minutes and a silence hung over us all. After a while Charlie walked back to the opening, his hands also soaked in blood, and slammed the door shut.

I sat on the floor, Kevin's blood cold and sticky all over me. The others watched me in stunned silence for a minute and then all followed suit, flopping on the floor and exhaling stale metallic breath.

"Did he say anything to you?" I asked Michael finally. He didn't respond.

"Michael?" He looked up at me like I hadn't been sitting there next to him the whole time.

"Did he say anything to you?" I repeated.

"No."

I looked around to Clint and Leonard. "Did he say anything to you guys? Or seem off at any time?"

They both shook their heads.

"No," Leonard said. "Nothing. He seemed normal last night."

"It must be his meds," I said. "He was doing fine until recently. The doc switched his meds, and he's been deteriorating ever since. Watching him has been like watching a live action version of the side effects list on a commercial."

No one responded, except Michael silently nodding almost imperceptibly.

"May cause fatigue, sleeplessness, loss of appetite, suicidal thoughts or actions," I said in a fake TV voice.

"What are we going to do?" Michael asked.

I shook my head. "I don't know."

What I wanted to do was blurt out the truth to everyone, but it was still too soon, and my thoughts were too scattered. Plus, if I told anyone, it might get back to Dr. Sawyer or the other staff in some way, and it wasn't a risk worth taking.

The staff abandoned the ward for several hours after that. It didn't matter how much we banged on the door or shouted.

Our cigarettes and a lighter were always left sitting on a table by the door. No one had ever dared to light a smoke inside, and I hadn't even thought of it until that moment. I walked over, grabbed the pack and the lighter and lit a smoke while walking over to the TV area where I sat down.

The others came over, one by one, and lit smokes as well. Even Michael, who had never smoked before, lit one up, and puffed on it. About halfway through he started to look a little sick, so I took the cigarette and finished it myself. He smiled with sheepish appreciation.

"Maybe they'll come back and tell us how Kevin is soon," Michael said as he went over to his bed to lie down for a while.

"Maybe," I said and lit another smoke.

No one else came over or said much of anything the rest of the day. I sat and stared at the TV. About an hour after we should have been taken to dinner, Dr. Sawyer, Charlie, and James all came onto the ward at once. The door was left open. None of them said anything at first, just started organizing the circle of chairs for the evening group session like nothing happened.

Soon after, Craig walked in with half a dozen boxes of pizza. He set them down on one of the chairs, then left the room and came back with plates, napkins, red plastic cups, and two-liter bottles of off brand root beer. He stacked those on another series of chairs. Still, no one spoke, but we had started to herd around the food and chairs.

Craig left the room again and when he returned, he brought Kevin with him. He was alert and looked fine. His throat was bandaged, and though there was a spot of blood showing through the bandage, it was a small spot and didn't seem to be spreading. His eyes were bright and glassy, like he was high on something.

Kevin raised his hand as soon as he walked in, and we all breathed a loud sigh of collective relief at the same time.

"Kevin," Michael said, and rushed over to him. The two hugged for a second, Kevin with just one arm in an awkward side hug.

Kevin held his hands out and mouthed, "I'm okay," though no sound came from him. He gently touched his throat and mouthed it again. "I'm sorry," he mouthed and twirled a finger around his ear, like he was saying sorry for going crazy. We all chorused that it was okay and not his fault and circled around him as he walked slowly to his seat.

"Can you eat?" I asked. He shook his head.

"Well, the rest of us can," Dr. Sawyer said.

Kevin nodded in agreement, and we all got plates and napkins. We each got pizza, and no one was interested in complaining about how late dinner was or why they'd left us with our worried questions the whole day.

Pizza was something from the real world, and we zeroed in on it the second it was on our plates. It was barely warm, so the pizza place they got it from was probably a ways from White Oaks. We all ate in silence and gulped down glasses of room temperature root beer.

Dr. Sawyer was wiping pizza sauce from his sweater with a napkin.

"So," I said, and he looked up at me, still wiping at the stain. "What the fuck?"

"What the fuck? That's your question?"

"Yeah, I think it's pretty clear what the issue is, Doc."

He chuckled and scratched at his bushy eyebrow.

"Don't get me wrong," I said. "I appreciate the pizza party and everything, but I'm kind of curious about what happened to Kevin and why and what you've done about it." I belched and wiped at my lip with a crumpled napkin.

I lit a smoke and exhaled in his direction. He opened his mouth to protest, but just shrugged his shoulders and asked me to toss him the pack, which I did. "And the lighter," he said. He caught the lighter, pulled a smoke out of the pack and lit it. He inhaled deeply, sat back in the chair, and exhaled to the ceiling.

"So," he said, and sat up straight in his chair. He took another drag off the cigarette and exhaled through his nose. "It's pretty simple. Kevin had a reaction to his new medication. It's rare, but it happens."

"Stabbing yourself in the throat is a possible side effect?"

"Not that specifically," Dr. Sawyer said.

"This funny to you?" James asked me.

"No, jackass, this isn't funny," I said and stared at him. "Don't pretend you give a shit about it either."

James' brow furrowed, but he didn't say anything in response and eventually broke eye contact.

"Suicidal thoughts or actions," Dr. Sawyer said. "That's the possible side effect. He's been having some other issues with the new medication, so I put him on something else. Problem solved."

"Yeah, sounds like it. Solve one problem caused by a pill with another pill. That should do it."

Dr. Sawyer said nothing in response, just stared at me with open contempt.

"What are you going to do about it anyway?" Charlie buzzed at me, finally speaking up for the first time.

"What?"

"You heard me."

Of course, he had a point, there wasn't much I could do. Dr. Sawyer hadn't said anything after Charlie spoke up, but the look he was giving Charlie was full of rage and frustration, like Charlie had spoken out of turn. Charlie caught the look and stared back defiantly.

After they left, we moved around the beds so we could all be closer to each other. We pushed all the empty beds together at the far end of the room and then pushed our beds up against the back wall under the line of windows.

When everyone was asleep, I slipped from under the covers, pulled myself into the vent, and then closed the lid behind me. I grabbed the pen light, turned it on, and started the slow crawl toward Dr. Sawyer's office.

When I got close to the opening over his desk, the duct area seemed to get brighter. I stopped moving and clicked the pen light off, but the vent stayed illuminated. Someone was in Dr. Sawyer's office. For a while I heard nothing, and lay there still, praying to any deity in earshot that no one in earshot would hear me.

The door opened and closed. A chair squealed, and Dr. Sawyer sighed as he sat down. I lay in the vent and dripped sweat from everywhere. My breath was getting hot, and the walls seemed to be closing in on me. A phone rang and he answered it immediately. I pulled myself a little closer so I could look into his office. He didn't have a landline; he was on a cell phone. It was the first time I'd seen a phone since arriving at White Oaks.

"Hello."

"That's right."

Long pause. Slow sigh.

"I know that."

"I know, damnit."

Long pause.

"All right."

"I'm on it, Bill. You know that."

"Yeah."

He hung up.

"Shit," he said and stuffed the cell phone into his pocket.

After a minute he did more paperwork, then gathered his things, put them into his briefcase, flipped off the light, and left the office.

I heard his footsteps recede and let out a long slow breath. The walls breathed with me, and my space grew back to normal size. I lifted the cover, and dropped into his office, then grabbed an armload of files and crept out into the corridor.

Ava was waiting for me to stick my head around the corner, and as soon as I did, she waved me down. I trotted slowly toward her. She obviously knew where the others were and that it was safe for me to run down.

"Come on," she said, waving me toward her impatiently.

When inside and crouched behind the counter where I hid the last time I was there, she double checked the hallways and came back to me.

"We may have a problem," she said. "Or an opportunity. I don't know yet. These guys are hard to predict."

"What happened?"

"Charlie and Dr. Sawyer got into a huge fight. I kind of made it worse."

"Well," I said. "Don't leave me in suspense."

"I wanted to say something to Dr. Sawyer about Leonard and the false fire alarm, but I only knew that because of you."

"Why would you bother?" I asked. "If he cared about anything that happened to us, he wouldn't be here in the first place."

"He is a greedy, arrogant, inhumane piece of shit and you're right, he doesn't care about you, but he does care about his work and reputation. It wasn't until you got here that I knew the full truth about this place. I asked him why they would go to the trouble of running a fake mental hospital. If they were willing to illegally experiment on people, why not just go all in and not waste the time and effort with the charades." She stopped and frowned.

"What is it?"

"We're idiots," she said, staring at the file folders clutched to my chest.

"Right," I said and handed them over. She put the contents of the first folder in the copier and started the machine. The copier was inside a small supply closet that had a door. The copier was already quiet, but when she closed the door, we could barely hear it, which was a good thing since we needed to make sure we could hear anyone coming.

When she came back, after checking the hallways again, I gestured for her to continue.

"So, he told me he'd done that before. Experimented on people who were being held against their will and knew it. He said the people were so stressed and terrified that it tainted the results of the experiments. He also said it was too stressful for him, to constantly be listening to the people beg to be let out and cry and carry on."

"Yeah, it must have been so hard on him. Poor guy."

She laughed, but it was without humor and touched with a desperate sorrowful hopelessness that was completely relatable.

"So, anyway," she continued. "The morning after they were blasting that metal music all night. Speaking of which, what the hell was that about?"

"I know, totally out of left field. They seem to be getting a taste for stuff like that."

She nodded solemnly. "I heard them arguing and got closer so I could hear, this was on the other side of the building where their break room is." She stood up and tilted her head like she was listening for something. After telling me to hold on, she went into the copy room, started the next folder, and then came back over.

"Dr. Sawyer was pissed that they'd done the false fire alarm that hurt Leonard, not because Leonard got hurt, but because they weren't keeping up appearances," she said with little air quotes around the last part. "He was afraid that doing things like that would put the patients on the offensive and not be the docile willing participants he wanted to work with. Of course, he didn't even know that the previous evening you'd all been tortured with metal music blaring all night, so I just waltzed in there and told him."

"What'd he say?"

"He was furious. He didn't even bother asking me how I knew, and I think if he was younger, I think he would have taken Charlie down right then and there. Charlie was even angrier. He told me to get back to my corner where I belonged, and to watch my back."

"Great. So, yeah, we might have a problem if he's hellbent on coming after you."

"Well, if Charlie listens to Dr. Sawyer, he might stay back for a little while."

"Meaning what?"

"Dr. Sawyer said he was under a lot of pressure to finalize his results. I guess corporate is getting pretty nervous about a project so risky. He told Charlie that they needed me to help with manufacturing if things were going to get done in a reasonable amount of time, and that he'd get his chance with me. That's all I heard because they told me to get back to work."

I told her what happened to Kevin, and she was horrified. "He had been doing really well for a while," I said. "He looked wonderful. Healthy. He was growing hair in places that'd been bald for years." She frowned at that. "He didn't seem depressed anymore, he talked more and didn't exhibit the same signs of PTSD he had before. He was exercising and just overall was doing well and seemed healthy. Then Dr. Sawyer changed his meds and he just tanked. He's been on a downward spiral for days. He looks like shit, feels like shit. Now this."

"I told you I wasn't expecting his relief to last, since the formula wasn't complete. But his hair is growing back?"

I nodded. "Yeah. A lot. Or at least it was."

"That's weird. I didn't know he was working on a hair growth drug; he must really be messing with formulas."

"If Kevin is any indication, the drug could be very successful. Imagine all the ridiculous Donald Trump comb overs we'll never have to see again."

She laughed quietly. "Hell, maybe the place is somewhat justified if the cure for balding came out of it."

I couldn't tell if she was joking or not. "I don't know about that," I said.

"Yeah," she replied. "I was only kidding anyway."

I went back over the timeline of when Kevin started feeling better, how his behavior changed and how long it lasted compared to when he started getting worse.

"Even though my formula isn't complete, he was at least getting some relief from symptoms. I've always thought Dr. Sawyer was messing with my formulas, but adding this information to what you told me about the side effects from your pain killer makes it pretty obvious. Whatever he did to it made Kevin start to decline. If things are as bad as you say, we might need to do something about it, otherwise he might be dead before we're ready to make our escape."

"What do you have in mind?"

"Since you're able to get into the pharmacy, I could manufacture a batch of the unaltered medicine for Kevin, and you can swap it out with the junk Dr. Sawyer manufactured."

"Obviously, that's another layer of risk, but if it'll help Kevin, I'm in. Not sure how I'm going to be able to tell which medication is his. I don't know if they have it labeled by name, or lot number or what."

She started the last batch of copies, checked her watch and our surroundings, and came back over to where I was hunkered down.

"I could do pain meds for you as well as the PTSD medication for Kevin. If we're going to take the extra time to do that, might as well do both of you."

"Maybe. For now, let's focus on Kevin. I'll just keep pretending to take mine. I have other pain meds I took from the pharmacy anyway. Kevin has no alternative. We can get his clean meds into the system while you work on finishing the formula, and finish making the copies. After that, I guess we'll just have to play it by ear. I wonder why the doc never put me on that PTSD medication of yours."

"We just do one at a time, don't want anything else interfering with the experiment. Some of the medications can alter reactions, or even counter some of the active ingredients in one another."

The copier finished with the last batch. She gathered her copies, hid them in a box she kept supplies in under her workstation, and gave me back the folders.

The immediate plan was to go put the records back in Dr. Sawyer's office, and while there, find Kevin's file and figure out what his medication was. Since I wasn't sure if the patient bottles were labeled by name or some kind of batch or lot number, I was going to verify what he was taking first before going back into the pharmacy to locate his meds. After that, I was going to go into the pharmacy to find it, so the next time I went in there to swap out his poisoned meds for Ava's good batch, I wouldn't have to waste any time or effort searching.

We still had a lot of time on top of that, so I stayed for a while, and she told me everything about her time at White Oaks that we previously hadn't had time to discuss. I wanted to be angry with her for her involvement in things, but she'd been put in some really difficult positions where every possible outcome was a losing one, so I wasn't – couldn't be – angry.

She might have made some mistakes or been naïve about some things, but the same could be said about anyone in human history. She seemed to be a genuinely good person who hurt for us and our troubles more than for herself, and she was certainly in a situation just as dangerous as the one all the patients were in. During the course of that conversation, she earned my trust and sympathy.

I decided to do whatever it took to protect her.

CHAPTER 24

The next morning, James rolled out the medication cart. He noticed that we'd shifted beds around and seemed irritated at first, but walked over without commenting on it. Since learning about a lot of the patients' symptoms seemed to help Ava figure out what might be going on and how she could potentially fix it, I considered writing down a list of all the patients' various symptoms and side effects – especially because my memory was shit and I'd never be able to remember them all. Like a sign from above, the first thing I noticed sitting on the cart was a pencil. I looked up and caught Leonard watching me. I glanced at the pencil again, then back to him. He seemed to get the idea and nodded.

James picked up the first cups of pills and water and handed them to Clint. He swallowed without argument and gave the empty cups back to James. He crumpled them and dropped them on the cart, then picked up Leonard's pills.

"I don't want to take that," Leonard said when James held them out.

"What do you mean, you don't want to take it?"

"That's not what I usually take."

"Yes, it is," James said. He double checked the chart anyway just to make sure and then turned back to Leonard. When he did, I grabbed the pencil off the cart and stuck it in my pocket. James looked back at me.

"Back off, Jason, it's not your turn yet."

I turned and walked back to my bed without protest. After getting my pill, which I held in my cheek, I went to the bathroom. At the last stall I spit out the pill and flushed the toilet, then took out a brown paper towel and slowly documented everyone's side effects, any changes in mood or behavior and any changes in medication that I was aware of. I folded the paper towel and stuffed it into my sock. The pencil went back into my pocket and was eventually stored under my mattress.

Leonard came into the bathroom when I was on my way out.

"Thanks," I said and walked around him.

"Wait," he said. "What was that about? What are you going to do?"

"Nothing," I said and patted him on the shoulder. "Just wanted to write a few things down before I forgot. Appreciate the distraction."

He nodded, but if I trusted the look in his eyes to be telling me he didn't really believe what I told him. He didn't push the matter though, just said okay.

"Thanks." I patted his shoulder again and went back to the ward to get in line for breakfast. A vision of the pills sitting in the vent came to mind, but they passed from my thoughts as soon as the line started moving and the smell of bacon frying filled the air.

***

With the extra time to talk the previous evening, Ava gave me a full breakdown of how she ended up at White Oaks in the first place, and how she'd become a prisoner instead of an employee.

Bowman Pharmaceuticals was one of the richest and most powerful companies in the world, but they had plenty of competition, and some of those competitors were besting Bowman. They wanted to be number one in all aspects of the pharmaceutical industry, but weren't. One area they lacked in was opioids because their two primary competitors held the patents on the majority of them, the most profitable, of course, being OxyContin.

When they hired Ava and first gave her the opportunity to develop her non-narcotic pain killer, it wasn't out of concern for the public and the opioid epidemic, it was a way for them to corner the market and put their competitors in a downward spiral. Plus, they could publicly claim that the drug was developed in response to the opioid epidemic; it would be tremendous PR, which would also boost their business in that market, and other markets as well.

Opioids brought their competitors over $20 billion per year in revenue that Bowman wanted. If they could develop something to replace their competitors' opioids on the market, they would no longer just be *one* of the richest companies in the world, they had a chance at the top spot, and the men at the head of the company couldn't resist the opportunity to make such a claim.

There had been small things Ava noticed at White Oaks that made her uncomfortable, but what convinced her things weren't right with Dr. Sawyer was when he left a file behind in her work area one day.

She said the file contained a lot of troubling information about the experiments Dr. Sawyer was running that she didn't even know about, but the most troubling was a reference to a positive cell gene mutation test.

What she told me was that gene mutation can cause cancer. She said that most gene mutations happen slowly over time, eventually leading to cancer later in life. If she read the results of the test and his other notes in the file correctly, it seemed like he was trying to induce cell mutation to happen more quickly. She didn't know to what end, but when she confronted him about it, he said that's why their trials were ending.

He had asked her to stick it out with him. That if she was loyal and helped him finish the last few weeks of work, that he'd write her a glowing letter of recommendation for any position she wanted, in or out of Bowman. He promised her that they weren't bringing in any more test subjects and that she'd be free to move on in just a few weeks. So, she stayed, but within days, I was sitting in Dr. Sawyer's office, and she saw me. She finally saw Dr. Sawyer for what he was, and when she threatened to leave and expose what he was doing, she was imprisoned. Soon after, a company man came to White Oaks to help get her cooperating again. That's what I needed to discuss with Kevin.

***

After getting food, I sat down next to Kevin. "How are you doing?"

He shrugged and looked at me. "I'm okay," he said in a whisper that was an obvious struggle to get out. "Considering," he added.

I nodded. "Sorry, I shouldn't have tried to get you talking."

He let out a harsh laugh, just a short burst, and then he sighed, slow and long. The pain was clear in his eyes.

"You're going to be a hundred percent soon, and then we're getting out of here," I said and looked around the room.

He gave me a questioning look.

"Later," I said. "Just trust me."

He watched me a moment longer and then finally nodded his agreement. We finished eating without another word.

Back on the ward I set up the chess board and asked if Michael wanted to play.

"Let's go out for a smoke first," he said. "James is about to take me out."

"We're smoking outside again?"

He shrugged. "I guess. They just didn't want another thing to fight about, but he said they weren't going to just let us smoke in here whenever we wanted."

"All right," I said, and we walked over to the door to wait for James.

I was about to start talking to Michael and wanted to let out what I knew so badly, but James hollered, "Last call for smoke break." When no one spoke up, he walked around the corner. "Guess it's just us," he said and pushed past us through the door.

When we got to the smoking area, James stopped and lit up, but Michael and I kept walking until we were out of ear shot.

"That's far enough," James said and let out a plume of smoke. We stopped walking, waved our acknowledgement, and lit smokes of our own.

"You decide to start up?" I asked.

Michael shrugged. "Don't know. Haven't really thought about it." He let out a long breath followed by a series of sharp coughs. "Maybe not," he said, smiled thinly, and held the cigarette out to me. I took it from him.

"What's going on with you?" he asked.

"What do you mean?" I didn't look at him, just watched the trees.

"I don't know," he said. "Just seems like you have something on your mind lately."

"A lot going on," I said.

He nodded. "I know." After a long pause he added, "Still."

I finally looked at him. He met my gaze and didn't waver from it. James wasn't paying any attention to us, and it was a perfect opportunity to fill him in on what was going on and what to expect, but I didn't know where to start and thought it might be a better idea to talk to Kevin first. They'd known each other longer than I did, and Kevin might be able to help me figure out how and when to discuss this with all the other patients.

"You're right. Something is going on, but it's too early to say anything," I said and left it at that. He pressed for a little, but he wasn't a pushy person and knew when it was time to quit. Despite his other issues, he could read people and knew when to push and when to back off.

***

Dr. Sawyer, on the other hand, was a heavy-handed jackass who only knew how to run his mouth. He was often calculated in his dealings with us because he had to be, but he had no respect for us, and probably thought he'd never get caught, which is why it was easy to see through at times. Those in power often think they're above reproach, above the law. That night, he tried to force me to share something he swore existed but that I'd never even hinted at, and he didn't appreciate my lack of cooperation.

"It's your turn to share tonight," Dr. Sawyer said to start off our evening group session.

"I don't really have anything to share," I said.

"Nothing."

"Not a single thing," I responded. "I think we've delved into the worst of things and came out squeaky clean on the other side, so I'm good. Thanks though."

He sighed loudly, didn't even attempt to cover it up. "It's your turn to share tonight," he repeated.

I leaned forward and repeated what I'd said, only slower.

"You're holding something back, and I know it," he said.

"How exactly do you know that?"

"I've been doing this a long time, and it's not difficult to get background information on patients."

"What the fuck is that supposed to mean?"

He didn't respond, just glared at me. The light tubes overhead blinked and hummed. A plump fly lazily buzzed around the room. Leonard waved it away from his face, and the fly disappeared somewhere on the ward. Maybe it'd escape through a hole far too small for any of us. Maybe I'd find it dead on a windowsill tomorrow morning. It felt like we had a shared fate in that moment.

"There is something," Dr. Sawyer started. One finger was outstretched and pointing at me. His voice shook and rose as he continued speaking. "There is something. In your past. And you are refusing to discuss it. You're refusing to discuss it, and that refusal is hindering your progress."

"*That's* what's hindering my progress?" I almost screamed.

His eyes narrowed and he clenched his jaw. I didn't care how he looked at me. I didn't care what he thought he knew about me. I'd never tell him, or anyone else, about my dad ever. I'd told them more than anyone else by filling them in on Tony. What my dad had done to me was mine. That pain belonged to me and only me. I couldn't share it, especially not with someone like him. I'd spend the next ten years in the Thinking Room before telling him that story.

"I can just dump you in the Thinking Room for a few days."

"Then do it," I said and stood up. The way he dealt with us was so bizarre and contradictory. One day he was chastising Charlie for not keeping up appearances, and the next he was failing to do the same thing himself. Before he had a chance to respond, the other patients joined in. They all started screaming overlapping insults at him.

"You leave him alone," Leonard shouted, his face red, an accusatory finger stabbing the air.

Kevin didn't speak, but he was looking at Dr. Sawyer angrily and stomping one foot on the ground over and over.

"He said he doesn't have anything to share, Dr. Sawyer," Michael said. "You leave him alone. He hasn't done anything."

Dr. Sawyer was looking around the room like a trapped animal. He wiped sweat from his brow, stood up, and started to shuffle the papers on his clipboard. "Now you listen to me," he said, but our voices rose and drowned him out. He smacked his clipboard, but we continued to shout him down. Finally, he dropped his hands and started to leave the ward. When he got to the door, James and Charlie rushed in, but he stopped them and the three of them left the ward, Dr. Sawyer going last. He slammed the door behind him, and the echo of the lock banging home mixed with our voices and vanished into memory.

We stopped talking and stood there trying to catch our breath. I had been clenching my fists so hard there were little fingernail indentation marks on each palm. "Thanks guys," I said and looked around the room, nodding to each of them individually. Each one of them returned the nod.

With the staff off the ward and another confrontation with them behind us, it was time to talk to Kevin and see, not only if he would participate in the escape plan, but if he could help Ava. I didn't know how much of his Army training remained in him.

"Come here, man." I walked over to the couch and sat down. Kevin followed and sat next to me.

"Before I tell you anything, I need you to answer a question for me."

"Okay," he said in a harsh whisper. "Anything."

"This is life and death, no bullshit. I consider you a friend, but we still haven't known each other long. Can I trust you? I mean with my life, because that's what I'm risking by telling you this."

He slapped the dog tag tattoo on his forearm. "We're brothers, Jason. Always. You can trust me."

I nodded. "Good enough for me," I said, then looked around the ward and lowered my voice. "I found a way off the ward."

Kevin's eyes widened, but he didn't speak.

"I met a woman," I said.

His expression changed.

"Not like that. I mean I got out of the ward. I don't know what my plan was at first. I didn't really have a plan, just wanted to see if there was a way out, I guess."

I paused there for him to rebuke me in some way, but he said nothing, and his expression remained neutral.

"The night I was brought here Dr. Sawyer argued with a woman, but when I asked him about it, he tried to make me think I'd imagined the whole thing and said there have never been any women at White Oaks, patients or staff. Not long after that, Dr. Sawyer and Charlie were talking about her like she was a prisoner or something."

Kevin frowned hard and scratched at the bandages on his neck. He looked over my shoulder at something behind me and held up a finger while shaking his head. I looked back, and it was Michael. He'd turned around and started walking the other way.

"She used to be here voluntarily as one of the staff. She's a pharmaceutical researcher, or whatever those people are called, but she found out what Dr. Sawyer was doing. She's been held against her will since then and is forced to manufacture the drugs we're taking." I paused and took a deep breath, then looked around the ward to make sure no one else was around. "Kevin, they're experimenting on us."

The color drained from his face. At first, he looked scared, but then he looked around the room at the small group of men he'd come to know and love and that fearful expression transformed into one of anger.

"There's more," I said, and he looked back at me. He'd never looked so focused. "Stephen and CJ are dead. I saw their files in Dr. Sawyer's office. They're dead, Kevin. We will be too if we don't do something."

"What do I need to do?" Kevin asked.

"For now, nothing. We need to keep everything on the down low. We need to make sure Dr. Sawyer and the others don't think anything is up. The company that runs this place, they're very powerful and if we're ever going to be truly free of White Oaks, we need to expose them. Right now, this woman – Ava is her name – we're copying all the records in Dr. Sawyer's office. Once we have everything we need to expose this shit hole, we're going to have to break out. Honestly, unless she's able to obtain a key, we're just going to have to take it by force. If we team up together, that shouldn't be a problem. We're just going to have to be patient."

He nodded and seemed to relax a little.

"She developed the PTSD medication you were on, but she said Dr. Sawyer rushed her formula before it was ready. What you were originally taking is what she developed."

"When I felt like me again?"

"Yeah, then Dr. Sawyer changed it, and you got worse than ever. She's fine tuning that formula now, and I'm going to switch out your meds so you're healthy enough to help me kick some ass by the time we're ready to get out of here."

He gestured to the pharmacy. "You can get in there too?" He struggled to get the words out, but at least they were coming.

I nodded. "Yeah, I can get in there too. I've been taking the ventilation shaft. It leads into the pharmacy, and next door to Dr. Sawyer's office, but then the vents branch off and get too small to climb through, so I can get outside the ward door into the main corridor, but there's no way out of the facility without a key. For now, we're just going to get your meds fixed. That's what I'm going to see her for tonight. Can you look out for me?"

Kevin let out a long breath and wiped a hand down his face. He fiddled with the bandage on his neck and looked around the ward at the others. He looked back to me, then down at the ground and continued to silently contemplate the situation laid out before him. I didn't bother with telling him it wasn't a legit mental hospital. Just the fact that they were experimenting on us should have been motivation enough to at least try escaping.

"Yeah," he croaked. "Of course I'll watch your back."

"There's one more thing," I said.

"Dude," he said. "You're killing me here. I'm going to need blood pressure medicine after this conversation."

He was serious, but also not. He smiled a little, and I matched it. Sometimes humor was the only way to get through situations like that.

It reminded me of the Army, where you could laugh everything off and pretend you weren't scared, or worry yourself to death constantly thinking about that next patrol, or about that next friend to die.

"She's cooperating with them right now because she has no choice. She tried to leave before and threatened to expose White Oaks for what it is. She's been their prisoner since the day I arrived. In order to keep her working, they strapped a bomb to her leg. How much of your EOD training from the Army do you remember?"

The little smile touching the corner of his mouth disappeared immediately and he began fidgeting. Tears filled his eyes, he slowly shook his head and said, "I don't know, Jason. I don't know if I can do that."

"It's okay," I said and started rubbing his shoulder reassuringly. "It's okay, Kevin. We'll figure it out together."

He nodded, but said nothing else and lay down on the couch. I left him and went to see how Leonard was doing. He was lying in bed, legs curled up to his chest, holding his sheet up like a little kid holding a treasured blanket.

"Mind if I sit down?"

"Go ahead."

"Thanks." I sat down on the edge of his bed. He was looking off to the side out one of the windows. I followed his glance, but couldn't see anything special from where I sat.

"I appreciate you guys standing up for me," I said.

He nodded. "I'm not stupid."

"I know, Leonard. Why would you say that? I don't think you're stupid."

"I know something is going on."

I sighed, but didn't respond.

"That's what I thought. What is it?"

"I can't say right now. I don't even know for sure myself yet. We just need to stick together for now. I've got your back no matter what. When I know more, we'll talk."

He didn't say anything for a long time. Finally, he looked at me. "Hey," he said, and I met his gaze. "Okay. I've got your back, but if you know something is wrong, you need to tell me. You owe me that much."

I nodded. "Okay." I could have elaborated and should have based on what I'd just agreed to, but it was too soon to get everyone involved.

I walked over to Clint and thanked him, but didn't say anything else, and then went over to Michael.

"Listen," I said. "I just want you to know that no matter what might happen with them, or anyone. I've got your back."

He nodded and held out his hand. "Same." We shook and I walked back over to the TV area to sit with Kevin for as long as he stayed there.

The rest of the day blurred like any other. We got our regularly scheduled meals and smoke breaks. In the evening, Dr. Sawyer cancelled the group session and none of us protested. There was a movie marathon for the weekend on one of the channels, so we all gathered in the TV area. There weren't enough chairs or couch space for all of us, so I sat on the ground leaning up against the arm by where Michael was sitting. We watched *Die Hard* and then *Pulp Fiction*. When that was over, I went into the main area and grabbed one of the folding chairs. When I walked back around the corner and started to set it up, Clint spoke up. "You can have my spot for a while," he said. "I'll take that."

"You sure?"

He nodded and got up.

"Thanks, man."

He grunted a response and sat down.

"Appreciate it," I said and sat down. He waved me off.

After that was *Twelve Monkeys*, and what a fitting movie to watch in a place like White Oaks. Most of us squirmed during the scenes at the mental hospital.

We got dinner and another smoke break, and then meds for the night. Before Charlie left the ward and shut off the lights, I stopped him.

"What is it?" he buzzed.

"There's a movie marathon going on that we've been watching most of the day. We'd like to stay up a little later tonight and keep watching."

He sighed and crossed his arms.

"Come on, Charlie. I'm not asking much. There's been a lot going on lately, and we just need a little break from the routine."

He thought about it for a long time, then looked around me and saw the other patients watching us with anticipation. He uncrossed his arms. "Fine, just this once," he said, retrieved the remote control, and handed it to me. "Don't make me regret it."

"Thanks, Charlie."

He left the ward and locked the door behind him. I turned around slowly, smiling and waving the remote control at them. They were all beaming. It was a small moment of triumph and one we all desperately needed. I'd been there for months, and all the others had been there longer, and none of us had ever been given control of the remote, or permission to stay up late.

The next movie playing was *The Fifth Element*, and then *Armageddon*. It must have been Bruce Willis' birthday or something, not that I was complaining. We stayed up and watched movies. We talked a little, but mostly we sat there and enjoyed each other's company while distracting ourselves with one story after another. After *The Sixth Sense*, I went to sleep. I don't know how much later the others stayed up, but when it was still dark Kevin shook me awake.

I sat up and rubbed my eyes. "What time is it?" I whispered. He shrugged his shoulders and then looked around the room and back at me. He made a gesture of sleep, his hands folded together pressed under his chin, his eyes closed. He opened his eyes, pointed to me, and then to the vent cover.

I nodded and got out of bed. He stood up, tapped me on the shoulder, then walked over to his own bed and got under the covers. I went to the vent cover, lifted the lid and looked toward him. A thumbs up rose from the shadows and I pulled myself up.

After replacing the cover, I turned on the penlight and shined it on the baggie full of Percocet. I stared at the baggie for a long time, but then turned away from it and started down the shaft toward Dr. Sawyer's office.

I forgot to stop at the pharmacy first to get Kevin's pills and had to double back. I dropped them off with Ava, who rushed me out of there thinking James was going to be coming around soon, and I went back to the pharmacy to replace it with pills Ava had prescribed. Even though that was the only thing to be accomplished, it was important. We needed Kevin better so he could help us when the time came. He was a big dude, and if we had to take over the hospital by force in order to get out, his help would be necessary, especially since my back had the habit of going out at the worst times.

On the way back to the ward, I passed by the baggie of pills without a second glance, then replaced the vent cover, and saw that everyone, including Kevin, was asleep. I stood by my bed staring out the window.

Everything in the building was old and poorly sealed and the window above my bed was no exception. The smells from outside came pouring in over me every day. It kept me alive half the time, kept me human, feeling something like that from outside the walls. I stood there and smelled the fresh air while looking out over the moonlit field of unkempt grass and scattered trees on the rolling hills. On the other side of the building was the staff parking lot. That was the area that led to a freedom I longed for and missed dearly. I'd go back to Afghanistan and never come home if it got me out of White Oaks. That's how badly I wanted to leave.

There was a small flock of birds flying in a fractured formation, and

I envied them. I'd have given anything to be a bird. Free to go anywhere, anytime. When the thought crossed my mind, I didn't know if I should have felt sad for envying an animal. The more I thought about it, the more sense it made. Being a bird would solve everything. I laughed at myself, took one last look at the moon and slipped under the sheets.

CHAPTER 25

A couple days after swapping out his meds, Kevin was back to normal. He looked healthy, maintained eye contact, and exercised rigorously. His voice still had a touch of husk to it, but we all marveled at how quickly his appearance and demeanor turned around. It was a welcomed surprise. Ava and I were able to get some of the records copied, but it was moving slower than I'd have liked, and I planned to speed up the process that night.

Dr. Sawyer was equally surprised by the change in Kevin's health. Surprised and irritated. He tried to hide his irritation, but it was impossible to miss. That terrible bedside manner finding its way out again. Of course, no doctor in the world, no well-intentioned one anyway, would ever wish anything but good for their patients. Dr. Sawyer was almost mad that Kevin had improved. Not only mad that he was better but mad that he couldn't figure out why or how. He was actually flustered by it. I wasn't sure if I should be amused or terrified by this, but I felt both of those things while staring at the man with disbelief.

In addition to threatening me with more time in the Thinking Room at group therapy, and his reaction to Kevin's well-being, Dr. Sawyer, like James and Charlie, seemed to be struggling to keep up appearances. The whole system was coming apart at the seams and it made me even more eager to finish copying the records so we could figure out how we were going to get out of there. It seemed inevitable that we'd have to take the facility by force, and having Kevin healthy for that inevitability gave me some comfort, but we still had to finish getting all the documentation we could, otherwise our escape wouldn't mean much more than all of us out looking over our shoulders the rest of our lives.

After the Doc stormed off the ward, Charlie came in and offered a smoke break. I volunteered to go, and so did Michael and Clint.

Despite our vast individual differences, not only between patients, but between patients and staff as well, the one thing we could all agree on was that we were excited for the next football season to start because for the first time in any of our lifetimes the Cleveland Browns weren't the laughingstock of the sport.

All of us had been lifelong fans and were justifiably bitter and despondent about the future of the Browns, but for the first time since any of us could remember, we were all cautiously optimistic.

We finished our smokes and started to walk back in. It'd been nice to talk about something trivial and get my mind off things, if only for a few minutes, but as we walked back toward the building, I wondered if any of us would be alive to watch any of the season take place, or if we'd still be trapped at White Oaks and drooling in a corner.

Michael started to ask me something, but his words were muddled, and as I turned around his eyes went blank, and the lids descended slowly as if he were falling asleep while walking into the building. His knees buckled and he fell to the ground. It happened so fast I couldn't catch him, but fortunately he fell to the side and landed in the grass instead of crashing onto the concrete walkway.

"Charlie," I called and knelt down next to Michael. Charlie turned and then groaned when he saw Michael. We checked his pulse and breathing, and it appeared that he was just asleep.

"Grab his feet," Charlie told me. I bent down to do so, but he stopped me. "Actually, never mind, let Clint do it. I don't want you fucking up your back again."

"How sweet," I said, and he glared at me.

Clint came over, grabbed Michael's feet and the two of them carried him inside and back on the ward.

"Shouldn't we take him to the infirmary?" I asked.

Charlie didn't respond, just shook his head. They continued toward Michael's bed and set him down gently on it.

"I'll see what the doc wants to do," Charlie said and left the ward. He never came back with any advice or instructions from the good doctor. I sat on the edge of Michael's bed until he woke up.

"What happened?" he asked.

I shrugged. "Don't know. We were walking in, and you just collapsed. How do you feel now?"

"Okay I guess."

"It's almost time for group," I said and stood up. He nodded and sat up slowly. Dr. Sawyer and James came onto the ward, and we started putting out the chairs.

"All that talk about the Browns, I thought you might just be trying to con them into giving you a football helmet to walk around in. You know, protect your noggin whenever you fall asleep at random. You got lucky this time. Falling in the grass, I mean."

"Har har," Michael said with little humor, but I didn't miss the smirk. He started to help with the chairs.

"So," Dr. Sawyer said, brushing something from his lab coat. He looked at the clipboard, squinted, and realized he didn't have his glasses on. He pulled those out of one of his many pockets and put them on. "Michael's turn to go tonight."

Michael cleared his throat. "Well," he said. "I'd like to know how I suddenly developed narcolepsy."

"What are you talking about?" Dr. Sawyer asked.

"No one told you?"

"No one said anything about you today." He took the glasses off and looked at James. "What happened today?"

"I don't know anything about it," James said.

Dr. Sawyer's jaw clenched, and he glared at James, and then turned his attention back to Michael. "What happened, exactly? And when?"

"It was outside earlier today. Charlie took us out for a smoke. I just passed out as we walked back inside. I started to feel really sleepy and the next thing I knew I woke up and Jason was sitting on my bedside. That was just a few minutes ago."

"Charlie didn't mention this to you?" Dr. Sawyer asked James.

"Already said I didn't know anything about it."

The two stared at each other for a long moment. James crossed his arms and leaned back in his chair.

"Charlie was supposed to go get you and let you know what happened," I added. "Obviously, he didn't give a shit and just left Michael hanging. We're all so shocked."

"I will talk to Charlie then, and Michael, we can talk about this more, later."

"Great," Michael said under his breath. "Kind of wish we hadn't said anything."

"Moving on," Dr. Sawyer said. "What'd you like to share tonight?"

"I know what I'd like him to share tonight," James said. Everyone looked at him. "Nothing. I'd like him to share nothing." His voice was rising with every word. "I'm sick of all of you and all your woe-is-me stories. I'm sick of this fucking place."

"Welcome to the club, jackass," I said.

James stood and pointed at me. "Keep talking to me like that and we're going to step outside."

I stood up. "Any time, you piece of shit."

"No one cares about you," he screamed. "None of you. Not one person on this earth gives a shit about any of you."

"That's enough," Dr. Sawyer roared, but James paid no attention.

"And you," he said, pointing at Kevin. "What you did to your own family. You deserve to be here."

Kevin said nothing, but the look in his eyes changed, and his face started to turn red as he clenched his jaw over and over. James turned to say something to Dr. Sawyer, but before he got a word out Kevin was out of his seat.

"No," Dr. Sawyer shouted, and James turned back toward Kevin. His reaction was too slow. Kevin's right arm swung in almost slow motion as the rest of us watched with eager anticipation. He connected with James' nose. There was a sickening crunch, and blood speckled his face instantly, and then he fell back on his ass. James looked up at Kevin with an unfiltered hatred I'd never seen burn so brightly in another person's eyes.

Dr. Sawyer shouted for help, and Charlie came rushing onto the ward. He assessed the room, first looking at James sitting on the floor holding his nose. "Damn fool, you're worthless," he said, but James didn't respond. He saw Kevin, who was still clenching his fists and looking down at the broken-nosed country bumpkin, and then started toward him, but Dr. Sawyer stopped Charlie's progress, told him to help James up and the three of them left the ward. The door slammed loudly behind them, and they started arguing outside the door.

"What the hell was that about?" James asked.

"How'd you end up sitting on your ass holding a broken nose? You aren't even supposed to be talking during group."

"I'd fire you right now if I could," Dr. Sawyer shouted. "You keep your damn mouth shut during sessions. I don't care if you're sick of it or not. It's not like any of us enjoy this."

"We need more staff," James whined.

"And we'll get some as soon as we can, but right now it's all on us."

"What about Craig?"

There was a long pause. I moved closer to the door in order to hear them more clearly.

Finally, Dr. Sawyer spoke up. "Craig tried to leave and was…" He stopped and stammered, then paused, and let out a long breath. "Well, he won't be back."

Neither James nor Charlie responded to that. I turned around and looked at the other patients, who were standing there in silence, shocked to learn that yet another member of the staff wouldn't be returning. What did Dr. Sawyer mean by he tried to leave? Maybe he tried to rebel against the doc and Bowman, just like Ava, and was silenced because, unlike Ava, he had no real value to the mission.

After that I pulled Kevin aside and we agreed that we needed to let Michael in on what was going on.

We didn't want to attract anyone else's attention so I told Kevin to go get Michael and bring him to the bathroom so we'd have a little more privacy.

At first, Michael panicked and started raving about the men in suits coming after him again. Eventually, we talked him down, and either no one heard his ranting, or didn't care enough to come see what the commotion was. I reminded Michael that on my first day at White Oaks he'd warned me about the dangers there, that he'd always known something was wrong at White Oaks, and that he'd probably just been convinced by Dr. Sawyer and the other staff that it was all just a part of his delusional disorder. I didn't tell him everything, and didn't mention Ava at all, we just filled him in about CJ and Stephen and the realization that they were experimenting on us. Kevin and I agreed to hold back some of the details until later.

When Michael had fully calmed and agreed to do anything he could to help us, we started to leave the bathroom and Michael collapsed again. That time I was quick enough to catch him and was grateful to have Kevin around to help me. We put him in bed and started to count down the minutes until I could slip back into the vent to go see Ava.

CHAPTER 26

When I got to Ava's work area, she asked about Kevin and breathed a huge sigh of relief when she learned how much he'd improved.

"We told Michael what's going on," I said. "We need all the help we can get."

"Do you trust him?"

"With my life."

She nodded. "Okay. That may be what it comes down to."

I gave her the next batch of files for copying, then remembered the list of side effects that was stuffed in my sock and gave her that as well. "I don't know if this will do you any good, but I wanted you to be aware of what the patients are experiencing."

"It's helpful, but I don't think we'll have time to do much else."

"It is getting pretty spooky around here," I said. "Now that some of the other patients know, it feels like things will come to a head really soon. Also, James lashed out during a group session. The staff is about as ready to explode as we are."

"How are you feeling?" she asked while looking at the list of side effects. "You didn't write down anything about your own symptoms."

"I've been okay since I stopped taking it. I have a stash of meds, mostly Percocet, in case my back flares up."

"Do you think that's a good idea?"

"I don't have much choice. I can either take Dr. Sawyer's

Frankenstein medicine that makes me feel like a cancer patient and lose teeth, or I can risk keeping myself supplied with something that isn't quite so intentionally poisonous."

Ava looked at the clock then walked over to the door to check the area. We had to make sure, more than anything, that none of them found me with Ava. That'd end badly for both of us, which would screw everyone else.

The copier finished running, and she gathered the files that needed to be returned to Dr. Sawyer's office. "You should head back."

I hesitated, staring at her for a long time, and she finally asked what was on my mind.

"You've had many chances to turn me in, and you haven't. Because of that, you've earned my trust, but I don't think you're being entirely forthcoming with me."

"What do you mean?" she asked and started to fidget a little with the buttons on her shirt.

"You know what I mean. I have the right to know who I'm working with on this."

Her gaze drifted over my shoulder and tears filled her brown eyes. She looked down at the floor, wiped her face, and then looked back at me.

"I didn't know what this place was when I came here," she said. "You have to believe that. I thought we were doing approved clinical trials. The work was so exciting at first. We were on the cutting edge of medicine. I was so focused on coming up with an effective alternative to opioids that I probably missed some signs I shouldn't have."

The wind picked up outside and caused the old building to creak and groan in response. There was a noise down the hall, near the break room James and Charlie sometimes used, and we moved our conversation somewhere out of sight in case one of them came by unexpectedly.

"When I realized what Dr. Sawyer was doing here, I was scared. I didn't know what to do." She intertwined her fingers and twisted them back and forth nervously. "I confronted him about it, but he could be so convincing. I'm not proud of it, but I continued the work voluntarily a while longer. I thought, maybe it was worth it. If we could make the kinds of advancements Dr. Sawyer convinced me we were working toward, I don't know." She trailed off.

"You thought the ends would justify the means?" I asked.

"I guess. It was scary. I was a part of the illegal testing going on here. It didn't matter that I wasn't fully aware of it. I could have lost everything I worked so hard for, so I stayed and tried to do my best to minimize things. To keep the experimentation as humane as possible. Then they brought you in, and I knew he'd never stop."

"You could have stopped things sooner. It sounds like you had a lot of chances before they started keeping you here against your will."

"Look," she said, her tone suddenly defensive and defiant. "I'm not proud of it, but I'm doing what I can to make things right. This is just as dangerous for me as it is for you. I can't take away the past, but I'm doing everything possible to stop this from ever happening again."

That hit home and my judgmental feelings about her involvement in things at White Oaks dissipated. I had a difficult and hard-to-face past, just like she did. We were in this together.

She started to say something else, but stopped. We both heard it at the same time; approaching footsteps. She pushed me into the back room, and I waited, heart thudding in my ears.

Ava ran over to one of her workstations and started to busy herself. James walked in and I pushed myself as far into the shadows as possible.

"Hey there, Ava," James drawled. "You all right, girly? You look a little spooked."

"I'm very busy right now, James. Do you need something?"

"Aw, don't be like that. Might as well make something of our time here."

I peeked around the corner and James was too close to Ava, who looked uncomfortable, but also unsure of what to do. It wasn't until then that I saw Ava the same way I saw myself and the other patients at White Oaks. There was a sudden surge of brotherly protectiveness. It took every ounce of self-control to stop myself from coming out of the shadows and finding something sharp to stick in his troublesome mouth.

As it turned out, she didn't need me to stand up for her. Ava pushed James back with her elbow in one rough motion. James fell back, surprised by her strength, and the look on his face made me forget myself for a moment, and I almost laughed out loud.

"Out," she said and seemed to grow as she approached him, or maybe it was just that James seemed to shrink in the face of unanticipated resistance. "Get out of here right now. I have work to do."

"All right," James said. "I see how it is." He turned and walked out. I breathed a sigh of relief. She came back to where she had me stowed.

"You better go now."

"What time is it?"

She looked at the clock. "Four."

"We still have a little time. I could go get some more files."

She shifted her weight from one foot to the other and considered. "I don't know. What if he goes back to the ward?"

I shrugged. "He shouldn't. If they were going to do anything they probably would've done it by now. It'll be lights on in just a couple hours. I could get more files."

It was obvious she was uneasy, and she wasn't alone. "We're running out of time, Ava. We have to…"

She nodded. "I know. Just one more batch though, and then you have to get back."

"Have you tried getting a key?"

"I haven't had any opportunities, and I'm not sure there ever will be. When the time comes, we're just going to have to team up on them somehow."

I nodded and left without another word. Not knowing for certain where James or Charlie were was nerve wracking, and it was a slow walk back toward Dr. Sawyer's office. At one point Charlie laughed, but it was somewhere far off, and underneath the laugh was James' voice.

After retrieving another stack of files, a small one, out of Dr. Sawyer's office, I brought it back to Ava. Once she got the copier going and checked the halls for any other surprise visitors, she came over to where I was waiting.

When she didn't say anything for a while, I broke the silence. "Are you all right?"

"What do you mean?"

"Just James, I guess."

She scoffed. "I can handle that punk."

That brought out a smile on my face, and I thought she was smiling too, though I couldn't see her face from where I was sitting. As we waited for the copier to finish, I told her about Kevin's reaction to the possibility of disarming the bomb strapped to her leg. She was clearly disappointed, but understood. She said that, if we ended up having to take over the hospital by force to get out of there, she could stay behind and watch over the staff while she waited for the police to come. The police usually had a bomb squad, so if Kevin couldn't bring himself to disarm it, maybe they'd be able to, assuming the local cops hadn't been bought off by Bowman.

She handed me the files to return. "I'll see you tomorrow," she said.

I nodded. "See you tomorrow."

CHAPTER 27

Not long after the evening group therapy session, a new patient was brought onto the ward. Maybe things weren't as close to collapsing as it seemed, or maybe Dr. Sawyer was just getting desperate and trying to keep things going.

The man looked to be in his mid to late sixties and had wiry curls of white scattered throughout his beard. The jeans he was wearing were so filthy it was hard to distinguish what color they were supposed to be. His jacket wasn't quite as dirty, and I recognized the Vietnam field artillery badge right away. My Uncle Alex – or Captain Jupiter as his troops called him – had the same patch, among others, framed and mounted on his wall. Of course, Uncle Alex was dead, and I wondered what his daughter did with that shadow box he used to have hanging in his living room.

The man looked like he was just roused from a bad nightmare and wasn't quite sure if what he was experiencing was real or not.

Charlie and James pushed him onto the ward and into the bathroom without saying a word to us. When they emerged, the man was clean and wearing White Oaks issue pajamas.

"Better not lose that jacket," the man said to them as they left the ward. They didn't acknowledge that he'd even spoken and slammed the door behind them.

The man looked around at us nervously. Michael was the first to approach him.

"I'm Michael," he said and held out a hand. After a moment's hesitation, the man took Michael's hand in his own, and offered a barely perceptible smile.

"Duke."

"Good to meet you, Duke," Michael said. He looked back at the rest of us with a *what are you waiting for* kind of expression, and we slowly approached the new face and introduced ourselves.

"What is this place?" Duke asked.

"It's called White Oaks," Kevin said.

"Mental hospital," Clint said. Kevin, Michael, and I shared a glance.

"A mental hospital?" Duke said and looked around. "I'm a drunk, not a crazy person."

None of us knew what to say to that. He walked around the ward, inspecting the place. He spent a few minutes staring out the windows, and eventually we all started to drift around the ward doing our own thing.

"Where are we?" he asked, drawing his attention back to us. "I don't recognize anything."

"We already told you, bro. White Oaks." That was Clint's helpful contribution.

"I heard you," Duke said. "I mean where *exactly*?"

I assumed it was Ohio somewhere, but where exactly, I had no clue. Neither did anyone else, and it was this realization that probably frightened Duke more than anything. There was enough going on between detoxing, dealing with various personal traumas from my past, being beaten and left in solitary confinement for days, and learning that we were all being experimented on in an illegal pharmaceutical facility, that I hadn't really paid much attention to our surroundings, geographically speaking. It looked like Ohio, but the facility must have been pretty secluded. I couldn't remember ever hearing anything, traffic, airplanes, anything at all other than nature. Some of the rolling hills I'd seen around the hospital made it seem more like southern Ohio.

A while later James came back onto the ward with sheets and a blanket. He dropped them on an empty bed and told Duke to make his bed.

"How'd I get here?" Duke asked. James said nothing. "Why am I here?" James still said nothing; just left the ward and again slammed the door behind him.

Duke sat on his bed, pushing the clean sheets and blanket aside, and put his head in his hands. I went over and sat down next to him.

"Do you really not know how you got here?" I asked.

He shook his head. "Last thing I remember is going to sleep in my spot near the bridge. It's pretty secluded, and no one really bothers me there. When I woke up, I was sitting in an office, and a doctor was asking me a bunch of questions."

"Dr. Sawyer?"

He shrugged his shoulders. "Don't remember a name."

"Arrogant douchebag with a grey beard?"

Duke chuckled a little and looked up at me. "That's him."

As the evening wore on, Duke became agitated and started to pace the ward with his arms crossed, quietly muttering to himself. He was shaking and pouring sweat. Eventually, he started banging on the door begging for a drink. I'd gone through withdrawal myself, several times over the years of poor decisions and addiction and felt a wave of pity for the man. Although my detox sessions never involved alcohol, I knew all too well the pain he was in and the hell raging in his mind.

His desperate pleas for a drink went unanswered and after a while he got into the bed Michael and I had made for him and pulled the sheets over his head.

The lights in the pharmacy turned on, and we all got our meds out of the shoot again. The realization that someone was there brought Duke out from under the sheets. He rushed over to the window, knocking Leonard to one side, and again shouted pleas at whoever was behind the glass to please, for the love of god, give him a drink. I was standing behind him at the time and could almost feel the fever burning off him. He was sweating from everywhere and couldn't stand still. I put a hand on his shoulder. He reeled and shoved me back away from him, but Kevin was able to catch me.

"Shit," Duke said, turning back. "I'm sorry, man."

"Don't worry about it," I said and held my hands up so he knew I wasn't going to retaliate. "But you're wasting your breath. They're not going to help you."

He scratched at his neck and looked ready to rip his own hair out.

"You're just going to have to ride it out," I said.

"Easy for you to say." The lights went out, and he looked around the room with a frightened expression. The lights in the pharmacy went out as well, and that made him scream for a drink again. I couldn't say for sure, but it sounded like James was laughing on the other side of the door.

When he quieted down, I said, "I know it's not easy, Duke. I've been there."

He went over to his bed, dropped onto the mattress, and curled into the fetal position. It was a long night for Duke and for the rest of us because he kept us from sleeping. As the night wore on his moaning, sniffling, and coughing turned to disorientation, and maybe even hallucination. He muttered about something that seemed related to war or combat, though it was hard to make out what he was saying.

At one point, Clint lost his temper and yelled at Duke to shut up. Leonard joined in, and I jumped out of bed.

"What's going to happen to him if they come in here and take him to the Thinking Room? At least in here he has something comfortable to lie on, and us." I looked around the moonlit ward, ready for an argument, but no one said anything else. I went over to Duke's bed and sat on the floor next to him. I held my hand out and he didn't hesitate to grab hold. His hand was slippery with sweat and radiating a sickening heat. I could feel his thudding heartbeat, it was rapid and erratic.

"Where am I?" Duke asked. His eyes darted around the room and his breathing picked up.

"You're at White Oaks, remember?"

He furrowed his brow and shook his head. He opened his mouth to say something else, but instead started to weep.

"It's all right, man. I've got you."

Eventually, he fell asleep, but it wasn't long before the lights came back on. I dozed in and out while still holding his hand and leaning against the small corner of the mattress he wasn't occupying. My ass was numb and both feet had long since fallen asleep, but I didn't leave his side. I was worried what Ava might think when I didn't show up, but there was nothing I could do about it.

By the time the lights blinked on, his fever had broken, and his breathing was calmer – almost normal. He was still gripping my hand tightly, but I slipped out of his grasp. I stood up slowly, stretched, and walked in place until my feet stopped tingling, and then went to the bathroom. When I came out, Clint was waiting for me.

"What's up?" I asked.

He hesitated at first, and then sighed. "I still don't believe your stories about the war, but you're doing right by him," he said and nodded toward Duke. "I'll give you credit for that." He didn't wait for a response, just turned and walked away.

"Thanks, Clint," I said, and he threw a hand up in response. Progress, even with Clint. I could handle that.

I went back to Duke's side and waited for him to wake up. I sat on the bed next to him so it wasn't so uncomfortable. A few hours later, he finally woke up, just in time for a smoke break. I helped him out of bed and waited next to James while Duke went to the bathroom. He still looked like shit, but his appearance had improved some.

The two of us walked out with James. I lit his smoke and then my own and looked over at the line of white oak trees broken up by the black walnut ones that I often admired. He followed my gaze.

"What are you looking at?" he asked.

"Just the trees."

"Listen," he said and cleared his throat. "Thanks for sticking by me last night."

"You're welcome. Thanks for not throwing up on me."

That brought out a smile and he scratched at his wiry beard. "I hope that was the worst of it."

"Probably was," I said. "But I doubt you're completely out of the woods. The next couple days will probably be pretty rough."

"You said you've been through that before?"

"Not with alcohol. Pills. Painkillers."

He nodded.

"Coming off Oxy was the worst by far. That shit is poison. I was sick like you were last night for several days. Had diarrhea for a couple months after I stopped taking them too. I never want to take that stuff again."

He nodded again.

"Y'all ready?" James asked.

We both said yes, took the last drags from our cigarettes and put them in the ashtray.

"You play chess?" I asked.

Duke shrugged. "It's been a while, but yeah."

"Want to play a game when we get back inside?"

"Sure."

I set up the board and positioned all the pieces while he sat there hugging himself, rocking back and forth, and gnawing on his fingernails. Today would probably be a little easier on Duke, but it would still be long and difficult. I could only hope that he slept so I could go see Ava. We had copying to finish, and I was sure she was worried I didn't show up the previous night.

"You can start," I told him.

He nodded, chewed his fingernails a little while longer while staring at the board. Finally, he moved a pawn. Our first few moves were made in silence.

"Your parents big John Wayne fans?"

The question puzzled him at first. He looked at me, his head tilted. Then he got the reference and laughed.

"No," he said, and chuckled again. "Jazz. They named me after Duke Ellington."

"That was my next guess," I said.

"Folks were New Yorkers. Used to see Duke Ellington at the Cotton Club in Harlem."

"That's awesome." I took one of his knights with my bishop. He grimaced at the loss.

"You like jazz?" he asked.

"I do, but it's not something I listen to on purpose."

He frowned and studied me.

"I mean I'll listen to it on the radio and I've been to a handful of jazz clubs. Nothing like the Cotton Club though. I just don't have any in my personal collection."

"What kind of music do you listen to? On purpose I mean." He offered me a smile, and I returned it.

"Rock mostly. Some folk and indie stuff too."

A few more moves were made in silence. There was an easy way to end the game quickly, but I was enjoying the bits of conversation and his company, so I decided to drag it out a while longer.

"How'd you end up in Ohio?" I asked. "If you grew up in New York."

"I didn't grow up there. They moved here when I was little. Been here most my life." He took my bishop in a move I hadn't seen coming.

"Were you in the Army?" he asked.

"Yeah," I said. "How'd you know that?"

"Didn't," he said. "Just saw it in how you carry yourself."

"Thanks?"

He stopped studying the board and looked up at me. We both laughed.

"I'd ask you the same," I said. "But I saw the Vietnam field artillery patch on your jacket." He nodded, but didn't respond, so I continued. "My uncle was artillery in 'Nam as well."

"No shit?"

"No shit."

"When did he serve?"

I moved one of my last remaining pawns. "Toward the end. First tour was in '72, again in '74, I think."

"You know where?"

"Not sure. He didn't really talk about it much."

Michael came over and pulled a chair up beside the game table. He looked tired, but so did everyone else.

"Hi," Michael said. It was directed at Duke.

"Howdy partner," Duke said in a terrible John Wayne impression. The two of us laughed, but Michael just looked confused. He looked at me for an explanation, but I just shook my head.

"Inside joke," I said. Michael nodded.

In his normal voice, Duke said, "Michael, right?" Michael nodded. "Sorry for keeping you up last night."

"Don't worry about it," Michael said. "You better watch out for this one." He pointed at me. "He's a hell of a chess player."

"Yeah, I'm holding my own so far."

"I'll let you guys get back to your game," Michael said and started to leave.

"You're not bothering anyone," Duke said. "Feel free to stay if you want."

Michael settled back into his chair. "Glad to."

Clint was sitting on the floor in the corner. He was muttering something to himself. Duke turned around to look at him and turned back with a troubled expression. There was a gust of wind outside. The windows rattled. The sky darkened and it started to rain, the drops tinkling off the windows.

"Who'd you say was artillery again?"

"My uncle."

"What's his name?"

"Alex Miller. He was a Captain."

Duke sat up straight looking at me with bulging eyes.

"What?" I asked.

"Captain Jupiter?"

I couldn't see it, but could feel the color draining out of my face.

"Oh my God," Duke said. "It is, isn't it? Captain Jupiter is your uncle?"

I nodded. "You've got to be fucking kidding me."

"Spooky," Michael said, looking genuinely troubled.

"Yeah, Captain Jupiter is my uncle," I said. "Or was anyway. He passed a couple years ago."

The news seemed to really sting. "Damn, I'm sorry to hear that," he said. "I really am. He was a hell of a guy."

"Thanks," I said. We stared at each other for a long moment, neither one of us able to really believe in such a coincidence.

We finished our game, though I couldn't tell you who won. It didn't matter. I could not wrap my head around the fact that someone who'd served with my uncle Alex was sitting across from me talking about him. Michael drifted away at one point, and I think he said something to me, but I wasn't really listening. All I knew was that this man served with, and apparently had a great deal of respect for, my uncle, and I was going to do everything to protect him from White Oaks, from Dr. Sawyer, from anything I could.

When the game was over Duke started to get up, but I stopped him. He settled back into his chair, and I leaned forward.

"Listen to me, Duke."

He frowned, but leaned forward as well.

"This is not a good place, and I'm going to get you out of here."

"What are you talking about?"

I sighed, considered what I was doing, and looked around the room to make sure no one was listening.

"Did you trust my uncle?"

"With my life," he said, nodding emphatically.

"I want you to at least try to trust me. Can you do that?"

He shrugged. "You've done nothing but good by me so far."

"I can't go into the details right now," I said. "Just trust me. Things are not what they seem at White Oaks. Just keep your head down and do what they ask for now." I looked around the room again to make sure no one was listening. "Except with medicine. If they try to give you any medicine, don't take it if you can get away with it."

"How am I supposed to do that?"

"If they give you pills, try to hold them in your cheek or under your tongue. Sometimes they check, sometimes they don't. If they check, just swallow it and as soon as you can go stick your fingers down your throat."

"You're serious?" He started fidgeting and biting his fingernails again.

"Serious. I'll watch your back, and we'll all get out of here together."

He was obviously troubled, but eventually nodded and agreed. Later that night we had a group session. I was second guessing my decision to tell Duke anything because it just made him nervous and when the jitters hit him again and he started needing a drink, he lost his cool and threatened Dr. Sawyer openly. Charlie and James didn't hesitate to subdue him.

Duke's second night at White Oaks was spent in the Thinking Room. The only good in that was everyone went to sleep early, slept heavy, giving me plenty of time to see Ava.

In the vent, when I was on my way to see her, I heard Dr. Sawyer on another tense phone call. Though I couldn't hear the person on the other end, it was clear that they were giving him one more month before they liquidated the place. Liquidated was the word the good doctor used, and it sounded bad, for obvious reasons. We were on a clock.

I waited for him to vacate his office, then crawled down to get a small stack of files. Then I went back into the vent and inched along to Ava's spaces.

Ava hadn't been worried about me not showing up the previous evening because she knew another patient had been brought to White Oaks and thought that might force me to skip visiting that night.

I told her about Dr. Sawyer's phone call and the new timeline we had. It didn't faze her. She said, at most, she'd only need two weeks to finish improving her formula for PTSD treatment. During that time, and after if we did need the full month, she'd be manufacturing enough medication for the two of us – me and Kevin – in particular. She wanted to make sure I had enough of the non-narcotic pain killers and PTSD medication to last me a while after leaving White Oaks.

We finished the last of the copying of all records from Dr. Sawyer's office. She had also set aside a couple boxes of her research to take along with us, when, and if, it was time to stage a coup and get the hell away from White Oaks forever.

CHAPTER 28

A week passed and despite having to spend his second night at White Oaks in the Thinking Room, Duke was doing much better. He'd fully detoxed, and though he still had almost constant cravings, he wasn't sick anymore.

Dr. Sawyer had put him on medication, who knows what for; Duke had no mental or physical illness other than his alcoholism. Fortunately, because of Uncle Alex, Duke trusted me right away and wasn't taking any of the medication being pushed to him. As the days dragged on and Duke's appearance and health continuously improved, Dr. Sawyer's behavior became more erratic. He was practically hysterical because Duke was doing so well. It would have been funny if it wasn't so horrifying, and it wasn't just Duke that frustrated Dr. Sawyer. Everyone was doing better. We'd talked as a group and even Clint was on board and stopped taking his medication. Unfortunately, our secret rebellion didn't go unnoticed for long.

I planned to check up on Ava one night, but Charlie caught me throwing up in the afternoon after the medication cart came around and it was too coincidental with the timing for Charlie to accept that I was sick. He was immediately suspicious of me. Dr. Sawyer ran a test and when none of the medications showed up in my system, he was furious and I was sent to the Thinking Room where they forced me to take the medication Dr. Sawyer had me on every day, three times a day.

Almost immediately, I started feeling worse. At the end of my second day back in the Thinking Room, the hallucinations started up again.

They left me in almost complete isolation. I got a bottle of water every day, though it was never enough to satisfy my thirst. There were no meals, just forced medication and a multivitamin. Having an endlessly empty stomach, the combination of medication and the vitamins just made me feel nauseous all the time.

On the second night, while I sat up against the wall trying to adjust to the complete darkness, I saw two glowing eyes floating in front of me. At first, I could only hear raspy breathing, then indistinguishable whispers. The whispers got louder and turned to words I could understand.

"You did this," the voice said. Every time they repeated that, the voice got louder. "You did this," the voice screeched. At first, I didn't recognize who was talking but when I remembered what my dad said to me at my mom's funeral, I knew it was him. He'd come to remind me that he and my mother were only dead because of me. For the longest time, he wouldn't shut up. The accusations stung, but I'd heard enough of his bullshit to last multiple lifetimes and was done being blamed for their choices.

"No," I yelled back at him, and he finally stopped yapping. "You and Mom made your own choices and mistakes. I didn't force Mom to start using again. I didn't even know she had a past because you guys hid everything from me."

Again, he started to whisper, "You did this." I cut him off.

"No, Dad. You did it! You killed yourself because you didn't want to live anymore. If you think it's my fault that you're sitting here, you're wrong. You could have helped me. You could have done anything other than trick me into finding your body, leaving a note that blamed me for everything. You made your own choices."

"You did this," he growled.

"Fuck you," I screamed and lunged toward the glowing eyes. Midair the eyes vanished, and I crashed into the wall so hard it knocked me out.

Later that night I thought Ava was screaming, but I couldn't trust myself anymore. It could have just been another figment appearing to torment me. The medicine Dr. Sawyer was giving me was far more poisonous than OxyContin. Ava's maybe-not-real screaming picked up again, then it turned to shouting and I pressed my hands against my ears. Eventually, I fell asleep and when I woke up there was something or someone in the room with me.

"What did they tell you about me?" The voice was unrecognizable at first.

"Who's there?"

"What did they tell you about me?"

"Stephen?"

He giggled and asked if I'd started painting the walls with my own shit like he had.

"Not yet," I said. "At least I can say that much."

"So, what did they tell you about me?"

"Who?"

"Did they tell you about the heads?"

"Stephen, I have no idea what you're talking about."

He laughed again but it was a raspy struggling noise, like there was something alive in his throat trying to get out.

"They told you about the Thompson baby. I know that much."

"There was nothing else," I said.

"I used to collect heads. At first they were just mannequin heads. I liked to brush the hair."

"That's great, Stephen. Listen, I'm a little busy right now."

I couldn't see any part of him, it was so dark. Unlike my father, he didn't even have glowing eyes to focus on and the location of his voice seemed to change.

"But mannequin hair isn't the real thing." He had ignored my comment about being too busy to listen to him.

"So, I started collecting real heads. Mostly girls with thick long hair I could comb for hours on end. My refrigerator was so full I couldn't even keep food in it anymore."

There was a wet sliding noise and then I could smell his rotting corpse sitting next to me and could feel his oddly cold breath brushing the side of my face. I skittered over to another side of the room, bumping into the wall, and pressed my hands against my ears so I couldn't hear him anymore.

While still covering my ears, the lights came on. I looked around the room, and it was just me and the walls again. There was a noise outside the door, keys entering the lock, and then Dr. Sawyer stepped inside. Charlie and James were both behind him, but they didn't come into the room.

"How are you feeling?" Dr. Sawyer asked.

"Fuck you."

A humorless smile touched the corners of his mouth. "Any new symptoms to report?"

I didn't respond.

"Still having those pesky hallucinations?"

I didn't respond.

"I thought you were talking to someone in here. We've been outside the door for a little while."

"Fuck you."

"So I guess that means you want to stay in here." It was more of a statement than a question. He pulled out his handkerchief and blew his nose. "All right then. We'll see you again when it's time for your next dose."

Without another word, they turned to leave, and all I saw was the look of disgust mixed with pleasure and almost joy in James' eyes when he looked at me.

They left the lights on, and I spent the next several hours counting bricks and cracks and measuring the length of grout in the entire room in index finger segments. I guessed that my index finger was about three inches long. By the time I got to two hundred and fifty feet, or one thousand index fingers, I quit, dropped to the floor, and eventually fell asleep.

When I woke up my head pounded. I could feel every heartbeat like it was a needle being driven farther into my eye. The back of my neck was hot on the inside and there were little numb spots all over my face. It tingled a bit on the inside, but when I touched the skin, I couldn't feel anything other than pressure.

I didn't know what day it was, or how long, exactly, I'd been sitting in that cold miserable little room. I stood and stretched for several minutes, then paced the room. I had to keep moving, it was something to do. I measured out the perimeter of the room. It was a twelve-by-twelve box. One lap around was approximately forty-eight feet. I did some math in my head. It'd take one hundred and ten laps around the room to reach a mile. I walked four miles before Charlie and James came into the room to force me to take my next dose.

After that, they turned out the lights again and I sat on the floor up against the wall. The time passed slowly. My body was a vessel only for pain, disorientation and regret. Something inside me was changing, darkening. It was as if the medicine Dr. Sawyer had given me was altering my entire being on a cellular level. Nothing made sense, and it didn't help that I had to try and make sense of everything in total darkness.

Unlike previous stays at the lovely Thinking Room hotel, I couldn't track time by the activity on the ward. If they were still being taken for meals, I couldn't hear the line of footsteps leading to the cafeteria. Maybe that was just because there were so few of us left. A hospital with only six patients, excluding me, and three staff members, excluding Ava, was a quiet place.

Something happened on the ward one of the days or nights I was in the Thinking Room, but I didn't know what that something was or when it took place. I just heard mostly shouting voices, but the words were indistinguishable. They could have been watching an action movie with the volume too high, or maybe the staff just beat all the patients to death with baseball bats and would be coming for me next. Neither scenario would've surprised me. By then, I would've welcomed the latter.

They came and went; James, Charlie, or Dr. Sawyer, sometimes two of them, sometimes all three, to feed me the medication that was poisoning me. I was delirious with hunger and a thirst that couldn't be satisfied by the one bottle of water I got every day.

"The others are okay," a voice in the darkness whispered.

"Who's there?"

There was a slight brush of moving air and then he was sitting next to me. I had asked the question – who's there? – but knew the answer. It was just that, in all the times I'd seen him, he'd never spoken out loud until now.

"Tony?"

"I'd ask how you're doing, but," he said and patted my leg with a cold hand. "I know you're hurting."

Hearing his voice for the first time in so many years unraveled me. I broke down in tears and filled the room with the sound of deep wracking sobs. Despite the coldness in his touch and the smell of decay, I welcomed his embrace. Eventually, I stopped crying and sat up wiping my face and nose with a dirty pajama sleeve.

"I need you to do something for me," Tony said.

"Anything," I said, without hesitation.

"The next time they come in here, swallow your pride and kiss a little ass. Do anything you need to do to get back on the ward. The others need you."

"What's the point?"

"You want to die in here?" His tone was harsh. "You want the others to die in here?"

"Of course not."

"Then wake the fuck up and get yourself out of here."

At first, I said nothing

"You know I don't blame you for what happened, right?" he asked.

The words hurt everywhere a person could hurt, but they also freed me in some way. As much as I wanted to believe he'd feel that way, he was just a projection of my own mind – *wasn't he?* It was also hard to believe because I could hear bugs skittering around inside his clothes and skull. A million tiny feet crawling around the decay.

"We were brothers then," Tony said. "We're still brothers."

A hot ache in my throat strangled any ability to respond. I leaned my head on his shoulder, and though it brought the insect sounds even closer, it was also a comfort so complete that no words could ever describe it.

"It's obvious Dr. Sawyer is up to no good, but I don't think his objective is to cause you – or any future patients – to deteriorate the way you are. Cooperate and tell him about side-effects. Maybe he'll be able to alter your medicine enough that it at least slows things down."

If the advice had come from anyone else, I probably wouldn't have listened. What Tony said did make sense. It was obvious that Dr. Sawyer was trying to make us all sicker with his medications. Maybe he was trying to develop a way to give people cancer more rapidly, as Ava had suspected. Cancer was a booming business. Almost as big as opioids. But, the way the medicine was working now, what he was trying to accomplish was happening too fast and too aggressively.

Tony stayed with me for the next three days. Having his company made the Thinking Room tolerable. We talked about the war, but only the good parts. When we talked about the dead, it was in happy remembrance, not in mourning. There was plenty left out of the conversation, like the scores of dead civilians and the young girls burned with acid, raped, or murdered for simply wanting an education. We didn't talk of all the lost ground and wasted efforts or of the regret over sacrificing so much for a cause we never understood.

Dr. Sawyer was pleasantly surprised by my sudden cooperation, and, to Tony's credit, the good doctor was able to alter my medication enough to slow down whatever poison was growing inside me. After that, Tony and I said our goodbyes and Dr. Sawyer took me back to the ward. Despite the improvements, I planned to throw up or pocket every single pill they gave me. I just couldn't get caught doing it again.

CHAPTER 29

As soon as I walked through the ward door, and it was closed and locked behind me, the other patients circled around, all of them talking at once.

In my absence everything on the ward had changed. It could have been that Charlie's and James' behavior had done too much damage to the image they were trying to maintain or because of the new clock Dr. Sawyer and the entire facility were on, but they dropped the veil and stopped pretending White Oaks was a mental hospital.

There was no explanation given to the other patients, they just stopped doing therapy, taking people out for smoke breaks, or even taking them to the cafeteria for meals. Everyone was still fed, but the meals were brought to the ward. The only other time any of the staff came on the ward was to force them all to take their medicine. So much for my plan to avoid that again. It looked like we'd all be short of choices until Ava and I could get everyone out.

Duke was clearly the most frightened, because he'd only been there a week or so and didn't even have a chance to realize on his own that things might be off at White Oaks. When the group finally stopped talking over each other, Duke went to his bed, sat down, and put his head in his hands.

Leonard looked like he lost twenty pounds since I'd left. Even though they were still being fed, it was only small portions. When I pointed out his weight loss, he called attention to mine.

"You look awful," Kevin said, and Michael nodded in agreement, though it was clear my harshness of Kevin's assessment hurt his feelings.

They told me James and Charlie had kept them up all night the first night I was gone, again with loud music, but with the Barney the Friendly Dinosaur theme song instead of Rage Against the Machine.

On another night, the two of them came onto the ward, clearly drunk, and forced the patients to entertain them with a White Oaks version of Fight Club. I hadn't noticed it initially, maybe I was just overwhelmed, malnourished, and exhausted, but they all had injuries of some kind. Duke's nose was twice its normal size. Leonard and Clint both had double black eyes. Michael had a split lip and Kevin looked fine except for his knuckles.

"What do you mean they forced you to fight each other?" I asked looking around the room at each of them. "You could've refused."

"They had cattle prods," Michael said.

"What?"

Kevin nodded. "We all refused at first, but they kept hitting us with the cattle prod. I'd like to see you withstand a few of those and still keep refusing."

I opened my mouth to respond, but he was right. They'd been forced into a corner where the only way out was through each other.

"It's not like we hit each other that hard," Kevin said.

Leonard chimed in. "But we had to do a good enough job to get them to stop with the cattle prods. They just wouldn't stop until we satisfied their sick little minds."

By that point, Clint had wandered away and was sitting on the floor in the corner farthest from us. Soon after, Leonard joined him. They each put an arm around the other. Clint rested his head on Leonard's shoulder.

"What are we going to do?" Michael asked.

"Get out of here," I said, and Kevin nodded his agreement.

"How?"

I told him everything about Ava previously left out. He was thrilled to have someone on the inside helping us, though he wasn't sure how much help she'd be if she couldn't even free herself, but we outnumbered the staff and would be able to take them down. It was the first time I was truly thankful for Stephen, because if Randall and Lee were still working at White Oaks, we probably wouldn't have been able to take over.

Michael wasn't mad at me for withholding some of the details before, just relieved that we might actually be able to get away from White Oaks in one piece. He asked why we hadn't already taken out the guards if that was our plan in the end, and I explained that in order to permanently escape the clutches of White Oaks and the company that ran it, we needed to expose the facility to the world and that we'd been working on that for weeks by making copies of all the records.

"If we're going to take over the facility anyway," Kevin said. "Why bother copying all the records, we can just take the originals, right?"

"Assuming we're successful, we're going to be calling the cops to come here and they'd be taking the originals as evidence, and we want to make sure they have that in order to build a case. But, if they're going to get out to everyone, we need copies. Our plan is to make copies of our set of records and send them to news organizations and maybe even some politicians, all over the world. This is one of the most powerful companies in existence we're talking about. You know how easy it would be for them to squash this if all they have to deal with is some county Sheriff? No, we need to get this information out fast so they're being attacked from too many directions to put up an effective defense."

"Okay," he said. "Seems like you have it pretty well figured out."

"I hope so." After that, I went to talk to Duke.

"How are you doing, Duke?" He looked up at me with unmasked fear.

"I can't die like this," he said. "Not after surviving 'Nam and decades on the streets."

"You're not going to die here. We have a plan."

I filled him in on the details, then went over to Clint and Leonard and did the same. We were all working as one. We'd talked before, enough to agree on not taking the medication, but I hadn't told them all about Ava until then.

Later that night I slipped through the vents one last time to see Ava. It was a slow crawl, but after getting my first meal in over a week I had enough strength to make it happen. Dr. Sawyer's office was empty, as were the halls, and I ran down to Ava's work area.

Seeing me walk through the door just about unraveled her. She thought for sure I was dead and that the others were never going to get out. We hugged hard and frantic, like siblings separated for decades and finally reuniting.

"They caught me throwing up medication," I said, and that was the only explanation she needed.

She wiped tears from her face and her expression hardened. "We're going to get these bastards."

"Things have changed on the ward."

"How?"

"They're not even pretending it's a mental hospital anymore. All the patients are being force fed their medication. No one is allowed off the ward for any reason, not even to eat, they're just bringing meals onto the ward now. No therapy, nothing."

"Then we don't have any more time to work with." An odd silence came over her and she dropped her eyes to the floor.

"Did something happen to you?" There was a vague memory of hearing her scream while I was in the Thinking Room, but at the time I dismissed it as one of many mental concoctions.

"Things have changed for me too," she said. I waited for her to elaborate. Seeing her pained expression carved a pit in my stomach and I feared the worst.

"What happened?"

"James and Charlie came in here a few nights ago." She paused for a long time, and I didn't try to force it.

"Technically, they didn't do anything, but they tried."

"Ava, please tell me what happened."

"They were drunk. I tried to fight them off, but Charlie held me down. James tried to rape me, but he…" She paused. "You know, he couldn't make it happen." I clenched my fist so hard that it almost broke the skin on my palm.

"Charlie thought it was hilarious. James got angry and told Charlie if he was such a big man to do it himself, but Charlie declined because he said he wasn't into black girls."

She had deep bruises on both wrists. "I'm so sorry, Ava."

Her face contorted and we hugged again for a long time. She wept and I wept along with her. The tears weren't just for Ava. They were for all of us and were hot and bitter and determined.

When we separated, I said, "Pretty weird for a black man to not be into black women."

She shrugged.

"Not that I'm complaining," I said.

She nodded and wiped her face.

"I'm going to kill those motherfuckers," I said. "All of them."

She shook her head. "Killing isn't the answer. It'll just make you like them."

"Some people don't deserve to live."

"I don't think it's up to us to determine who is and isn't worthy."

"I've killed before."

"War is different, Jason. You know that. If it's self-defense, that's one thing. Murder is another. You're nothing like them. Don't change that now."

There was no point in arguing about it. I didn't agree with her at the time, but also didn't dismiss the possibility that she might be right.

"How close are you to being ready?" I asked.

"Close. We have all the records. I have a large supply of meds manufactured and ready to go with us. Give me one more night to get my affairs in order."

"You have access to tools?" I asked.

"No, but there's a supply closet with tools. Why?"

"Kevin is going to need some if he's going to disarm that thing and get it off you. I don't want to leave you behind."

"Do you think he's going to be willing, or more importantly, do you think he'll be able?" she asked.

"Honestly, I don't know."

"I could just stay behind and wait for you guys to get clear. You could call the cops and I'd be here watching over Dr. Sawyer, Charlie and James, until the cops came."

"Maybe that would be best. I don't know though, if you come with us, you're definitely going to be safer. If we have to leave you alone with them, who knows what could happen in the time it takes for us to get away, call the cops, and for them to get here. And that's all assuming the local cops aren't paid off."

"Let's just focus on one thing at a time," she said.

"I guess we don't have a choice."

"You'd better go back," she said. "Now that things have changed, you never know when they're going to show up on the ward."

"You good?" I asked. "I can stay a while if you like."

She smiled. "I'm good. Thanks. Now go."

James, Charlie, and Dr. Sawyer had all earned death, as far as I was concerned, but a small part of me recognized the truth in what Ava said.

If I killed them in cold blood, it might change me in a way that could never be undone. Self-defense was another matter.

I ran down the halls until reaching Dr. Sawyer's office. As soon as I locked the door behind me, there were footsteps out in the corridor. They approached the door, and I could see the beam of a flashlight in the crack under the door.

Slowly, I backed away toward his desk. There was a gentle knock on the door, and I held my breath, pushed Dr. Sawyer's chair back, got under his desk and pulled the chair up against me.

A key slid into the lock. The door slowly creaked open and the beam of a flashlight illuminated the room. My heart was thudding so hard I could hear it and was afraid that whoever was in the room with me would too. I held my breath to slow it down.

The beam of the flashlight went from one corner of the room to the other. Sweat poured off me and my back started to itch. If they looked up at the ceiling and noticed the missing vent cover it'd all be over. The flashlight swept the room again, and then whoever was holding it clicked it off and shut the door. They locked the door from the outside, and I continued to hold my breath until their footsteps receded.

In the morning, as soon as the medication was forced upon us, I pulled Kevin off to the side and gave him more details about the bomb strapped on Ava's leg to see if he might feel more comfortable with the idea of using his Army training one last time. He seemed to know what to do, none of the details threw him off, but he was still clearly uncertain about his ability. Maybe when he met Ava face to face, he'd feel more comfortable and be willing to try. As she suggested, we could always leave her behind to wait for the cops, but that option made me extremely uneasy, as it probably did her too.

"It might be a couple more nights, depending on how things go around here. At least one night anyway. She's manufacturing enough of her unaltered medications, the stuff for PTSD and the pain medication

I've been taking, so we'll have some kind of foundation once we're out of here."

"Tell her not to bother making anything for me."

"Why?"

He didn't answer at first.

"Come on, Kevin. Talk to me."

"I don't have anything to go back to," he said.

"None of us have anything to go back to, but starting over is better than dying in here."

He stared at me. His look hardened. "I deserve this place."

"No you don't."

"You don't know what you're talking about," he said, fists clenching and opening.

"Then enlighten me. We've all done things. Believe me, I have a lot of baggage and regret. Tony isn't the worst of it."

"Come on," he said. "Let's sit down." I nodded and he guided me over to the couch in the TV area.

"Remember me telling you that my wife and two daughters were dead?"

"Of course."

"After I came home from my last deployment, I was all messed up. I couldn't function in any way and my volcanic mood swings were doing irreparable damage to my marriage and the relationship with my girls."

I nodded but said nothing.

"One night, this was really late, maybe three in the morning, I woke up in a panic and wasn't thinking clearly." He stopped talking and dropped his head and sucked in a hitching breath. "I don't know why, but I started choking my wife. Almost killed her, but I finally snapped out of it and released her. She was justifiably upset. Said she couldn't take it anymore and was going to go stay with her folks for a while and take the girls with her."

He looked back up at me and the pain in his eyes was almost too much to bear. I let out a long breath and nodded, encouraging him to continue.

"They all left the house that morning because of me. When they were just a couple blocks from her parent's house, they were hit head on by a drunk driver. All three of them died on the scene."

I opened my mouth to say something, but he interrupted me.

"Don't you dare tell me it wasn't my fault, Jason. If you say that I'm going to beat your ass."

"I am so sorry, Kevin."

"It sounds like that bomb has a proximity sensor, like if she managed to escape and got far enough away from the building, it'd detonate. Maybe I will take it off her, and when you're all gone and safe, I'll take a little walk with it."

"I've done a lot of messed up stuff too, man. We deserve, we all deserve, a chance to start over. Maybe one day you could meet someone else and start a new family."

Before I even knew anything was coming, he punched me in the face. The light in the room brightened and there were a million black spots floating around me. I sat there for a couple hours, rubbing my cheek, contemplating what he'd told me and what I'd never told anyone. The weight of it all was suddenly unbearable and I didn't know if I wanted to leave or stay behind and take that final stroll away from White Oaks at Kevin's side. Eventually, he came back over and apologized.

I suddenly knew what had to be done.

"It's okay, man. Can you sit down?"

He did so without responding.

"Kevin, do you remember when Dr. Sawyer was prodding me at group therapy, saying he thought I was holding something back from my past?"

"Vaguely," he said.

"I didn't realize it until just now, but I don't know if I'll ever be able to move on with my life if I don't tell someone about this. Maybe it'll help you find some peace with your past as well."

"What is it?"

After pausing for a long time, I nodded, wiped a hand down my face and started talking. I told him about my mom and how she'd relapsed and overdosed after my own struggles with substance abuse surfaced. Then I told him about my father and the suicide note.

I'd sworn to take the secret to my grave, but as soon as it left my mouth it felt like the hope I'd been holding on to for so long was real and that recovery was possible. My friend shared the burden of the pain with me, taking little pieces away so I could start to heal. He assured me it wasn't my fault and that it was horrible of my father, of all people, to put such a burden on me. Then he thanked me for trusting him with that information, stood up, and started to walk away, but then he stopped. He let out a long breath, and then turned back to me.

"Okay, Jason. Maybe I will go with you."

CHAPTER 30

Hours after lights out, I was still awake. Ava had asked for one more night to get everything ready to go, so there was no plan that night to go anywhere. As I lay there, staring up at the ceiling, my thoughts were shaken into consciousness by a noise.

From the other side of the security door a key slid into the lock and turned. The door opened with only the slightest sound. Charlie and James sneaked in, and it was obvious just by their gait, that they were drunk.

"Wake up!" Charlie hollered.

At first none of the other patients woke up, despite the tremendous, silence-shattering, noise of his buzz saw voice. Michael and Leonard slowly twisted and groaned under their sheets. One by one everyone woke up as the beam of James's flashlight slapped light across every face in the room.

He pointed the light at me. I covered my eyes with an extended middle finger. When he moved the beam to the next groggy face, I sat up.

"Everybody up," Charlie buzzed. "That means you too, Michael," he yelled. Michael rose and rubbed his eyes.

"Charlie and me came up with a new game y'all might like," James drawled and then let out a little giggle like he was a kid with a great new toy to play with.

"What time is it?" Michael asked.

Charlie walked over to Michael's bed and leaned down so close they almost touched noses. "It's time for you to get out of bed, like I told you." Charlie stood up straight, towering over Michael, and dared him with vacant bloodshot eyes to argue. Michael looked at the floor and got out of bed without another word.

"What are they going to do?" Michael asked me in a barely audible whisper.

"I don't know. Don't worry, man. I'll watch your back."

Despite the assumption that whatever was coming wasn't good, Michael managed to smile when I promised protection. His good-natured, open smile was one of the few things that got me through my time at White Oaks. I nudged him with an elbow and smiled back.

"This isn't right," Duke said. His voice quavered, but he looked more angry than afraid. They ignored him.

"Here you go, Jason." Charlie underhand tossed the ball he was holding. The weight of it smacked into my palm, heavy and destined to break teeth. The ball, best I could tell, was a baseball wrapped in a couple inches of duct tape. "Dodgeball, gentlemen." He beamed with sinister pride.

"Damn, Charlie," I said. "You could kill someone with this."

"Nah, it's not that hard. Besides, killing wouldn't be anything new for you, would it?"

"Killing in a war is a little different than this. Less sadistic and assholey," I said. He lit a cigarette, took a deep drag, and blew the smoke in my direction, squinting at me with conspicuous contempt. He took the cattle prod off his belt and hit the trigger a couple times, making it clear that refusal would end up for me the same way it did for everyone else when I was locked in the Thinking Room and they staged their own Fight Club on the ward.

"I'm not throwing this at anyone; I don't care what you do. You guys are sick."

Charlie stepped toward me. "Maybe I won't do anything to you," he said. "Maybe I'll just toss your buddy Mikey in the Thinking Room."

"You leave him alone," I said and took a step closer to him.

"Does that mean you're going to play?"

The ball sat heavy in my hand. A bead of sweat dislodged itself from the thick mat of hair on Charlie's head. It zigzagged down the side of his face and, in slow motion, dripped off his chin and onto the floor.

"Let's go!" he yelled, but I didn't move.

In the distant echoes of a life long forgotten I heard the crunch of dirt beneath boots and could almost smell the old outpost in the mountains of Afghanistan.

"You want me to use this?" Charlie buzzed, holding out the cattle prod.

The drop of Charlie's sweat on the floor turned red. The surrounding air changed into brown dust I could barely see through or breathe. My teeth buzzed and ears rang and I stared at the spot of blood on the floor; it was all I could see clearly.

Charlie brought me back to reality when he jammed the cattle prod into the base of my rib cage. The drop of blood turned back to sweat, and the air cleared of everything but the endless dust particles that danced in the harsh beam of his flashlight. James turned the overhead lights on, and everyone blinked to adjust to the room full of light

"You back with us, Jason?" he asked with a touch of concern that was as fake as their entire operation.

I blinked, focused on his eyes, and nodded.

"Good, then throw. Every man for himself. Last man standing is the winner," he said and stepped out of the way.

I backed away from everyone and looked at each face. I wasn't sure who to throw it at. For a long moment I considered throwing it at Charlie and taking my chances in a fight, but wanted to at least try giving Ava the time she asked for. Besides, everyone was still half asleep, and it was hard to know how they'd respond to it.

Apparently, I was taking too long because Charlie stepped up and got me with the cattle prod again, that time in my lower back. I dropped to one knee, but stood back up immediately and glared at him.

Clint was the only one I could bring myself to throw the ball at. He was the one I had the least attachment to, and his insistence that I was lying about my military service to cover up my cowardice on the alien mothership had rubbed me the wrong way since my arrival at White Oaks. Still, I didn't want to hurt him, or anyone else.

I tried to throw it hard enough to be convincing, but not so hard that it'd do any real damage, but the ball slipped out of my hand and went off target, hitting Clint right in the mouth. The room went silent, and Clint clapped his hands over his split open lips, his eyes wide and surprised. Blood started to pour through his fingers, his knees buckled, and he hit the floor with a dull thud.

"Ah shit," I said and was about to go over to check on him when there was movement on my side and a rush of air as Duke ran over to where Clint fell, picked up the ball and shimmied back to where he was.

He threw the ball at Leonard. It hit him right in the stomach with a sickening thud. Leonard bent over and vomited on the floor.

"You're cleaning that up, you son of a bitch," Charlie screeched.

Duke stood there with his hands on his head, clearly disturbed by what was going on, but his expression changed quickly. His eyes bulged and he rushed toward the ball, which had rolled to one corner. He had no intention of getting hurt like he had when they were forced to fight each other.

Michael, Kevin, and I all spread out, ready to dodge his throw. Duke faked it toward me and threw it at Kevin. He was almost able to move out of the way, but the ball clipped his foot and he crashed to the ground. At first, he didn't move and it looked like he was hurt for real, but then he groaned, rolled over, and pushed himself up. He went back to his bed and sat down.

The ball rolled toward Michael, and he picked it up. First, he turned toward me with an apologetic look on his face. I stood up straight and nodded to him. “It’s okay,” I said.

He dropped the hand holding the ball and welled up. Tears started to pour down his cheeks and it was all I could do to stop myself from walking over and hugging him.

Charlie had no patience for this and jammed the cattle prod into Michael’s back. He screamed, reared back, and threw the ball at me. I wasn’t looking when he threw it. I was busy glaring at Charlie and James, who were both roaring with laughter.

The ball hit me square in the nose. The bones crunched and there was an explosion of pain throughout my face and head as blood poured down my chin and onto my shirt.

I stumbled backward and fell onto one of the cheap coffee tables by the television, breaking it into about as many pieces as my nose was in. There was a loud gasp from the others when I went down, but then Duke went for the ball again. It was just him and Michael.

Charlie looked at me for a long minute after I crashed to the ground though it felt more like he was looking through me. I wasn’t real enough or worth enough to be seen by him or anyone else. He winked at me before returning his attention to the two left in the game.

They each made throws that went wild. Michael had the ball back and was ready to finish the game, but something in Duke’s expression made Michael pause. He straightened and looked uncertainly at Charlie.

Suddenly, Duke charged and tackled Michael. As he fell, in what seemed like slow motion, Michael’s head clipped the fire engine red knob on the metal radiator, and then he crashed into the ground and went limp. Duke jumped off Michael and screamed in triumph, then picked up the ball lying on the floor and dropped it onto Michael's chest to solidify his victory.

Charlie and James laughed and cheered and clapped Duke on the back. I sat there in a pile of coffee table limbs watching the blood pour out of Michael's head and pool on the floor while they celebrated.

The others were huddled in the corner staring at Michael. Even the sane, the normal ones outside those walls, wouldn't know how to react to that, so everyone stood in silence gaping at the gore. I shouldn't have waited to go after Charlie and James. I shouldn't have hesitated.

Though Michael's brain was a tragic wasteland of misfires and bad connections, he was the sweetest, most genuine human being I'd ever met. I had seen too much death in my lifetime to not know it as soon as I saw it. Michael, who'd never hurt anyone, just a victim of circumstance, was dead, and those motherfuckers in front of me were responsible. Not Duke. He was a victim the same way Michael was.

They hadn't noticed that their game had done more than bruise each of us on the outside and scar what was left of the inside. They didn't notice me stand up with a coffee table leg in one hand. They continued to recount the game with Duke until I hit Charlie in the back of the head with the table leg.

James was too busy being pleased with himself to realize anything had happened until I stepped in front of him and swung the table leg at his face. It connected with his still smiling mouth, sending teeth in every direction. The sight of a toothless James reminded me of CJ which made me want to laugh and cry at the same time. James was screaming as blood poured from his mouth.

The only thing I wanted was to permanently silence him. I wanted to hit him over and over again until his skull cracked open and exposed the spongy innards. But then I thought of Ava and realized she was right. I couldn't kill them and still be me. There was a lot in my life I wasn't proud of and carried so much baggage I often didn't know what to do with it or myself, but murdering them would make me something else. Something I couldn't come back from. For so many years I'd held out hope that some kind of life was out there waiting for me to discover. That I could recover from the war, from Tony, my parents, and all the drug abuse. Killing them, I realized, would destroy that hope forever.

James stopped staggering around screaming and lunged at me. I faked a high swing and he flinched back, then I lowered it and hit his knee. There was a loud crack and he collapsed, holding his knee and screeching.

"Make sure they don't move," I said to the others.

I took Charlie's keys and ID badge off his belt. There was a supply closet by the bathroom, and I used Charlie's keys to open it. There was a toolbox in the closet. I pulled it from the shelf and set it on the floor, then pulled out a roll of duct tape, and sealed James' big mouth with it.

Kevin came over to help me lift the squirming hillbilly into a chair, and we secured him to it with the duct tape.

Charlie lay motionless on the floor, but I kicked him in the side a few times to make sure he wasn't feigning unconscious. Some ribs cracked, but he didn't move or make a sound. We lifted him into a chair as well and taped him to it.

I looked at Michael lying on the floor. Kevin walked over slowly and dropped to his knees beside him. He checked for a pulse, looked back at me with an expression of total defeat that was just about as terrible as anything I'd ever seen.

Clint started to move on the ground. Leonard went over to help him up.

Duke stood off to one side with his hands on his head. He was weeping openly. I wasn't sure at that moment if it was something he'd ever recover from. Having accidentally killed my best friend Tony, I knew how Duke felt. We barely knew the man, but the time I'd spent with him convinced me that he had a good heart. Seeing the expression of grief and shock and bewilderment on his face made me hurt in a way I never thought I'd have to experience again.

Forcing one foot to go in front of the other, I walked over to Duke and grabbed his face with both hands. "It's not your fault," I said, though I could barely get the words out.

He tried to respond, but couldn't. The panicked desperate noises coming from him would follow me for the rest of whatever life I had left. I hugged him for a long time, telling him over and over again that it wasn't his fault. Eventually his cries ceased, I let him go and he slumped down onto the nearest bed.

CHAPTER 31

If Dr. Sawyer kept to his usual schedule, we had a couple hours before he came to White Oaks. We'd moved Michael's body out of the pool of blood and onto one of the empty beds. Everyone was sitting around him, holding a makeshift wake.

I told the others I'd go inform Ava that it was time to go. I ran down the halls to her workstation but didn't really know what to say.

"Oh my god, Jason, what happened?"

I couldn't say anything and my hands were shaking. She rushed over and hugged me, caressing the back of my head, not asking any more questions until the sorrow had run its course and I could speak again.

"Please," she said. "Please talk to me. Tell me what happened."

I nodded and wiped my face, grimacing after inadvertently bumping my destroyed nose. "James and Charlie came onto the ward tonight. They had cattle prods and forced us to play a game of dodgeball. That's what happened to my nose."

"What kind of dodgeball were you using?"

"I think it was a baseball or maybe a big rock wrapped in duct tape."

"Where are those bastards now?"

"They're still on the ward. Both of them are taped to chairs. Charlie's unconscious, but James is still awake." I paused and the next words caught somewhere in my throat. I took a deep breath and let it out.

"Michael is dead."

"Oh no," she said and covered her mouth.

"It was an accident. The new patient, Duke, knocked Michael down and he hit his head on the radiator. Cracked his head open." I let out a choked sob. "I had been hit in the face with the ball and fell into a coffee table. After Michael went down, James and Charlie were laughing and celebrating Duke's victory. I grabbed one of the legs of the coffee table and took them by surprise."

She didn't respond, just continued to look at me with competing expressions of shock and exhaustion.

"It's time to go, but we need to wait for Dr. Sawyer."

"You can't kill him, Jason. You're not a murderer."

"I know. I could have easily killed those two, but didn't. We can't let him get away with this though."

She nodded in agreement.

"I want them to pay for what they've done to all of us, but I'm not going to give him an opportunity to run for it either. We need to get all the records together, and whatever meds you have. After Dr. Sawyer shows up, we'll leave."

"Then let's get you cleaned up," she said. "We have time."

She walked me over to the sink. I wasn't entirely sure whose blood was on my hands, probably a mixture. I washed them and she slowly cleaned my face.

"I can set your nose, if you want me to."

"Do it," I said and clenched my teeth in anticipation.

She snapped it back into place and wiped the thin line of blood that ran out of it afterward.

We gathered the boxes of records we'd copied from Dr. Sawyer's office and her research files and walked down to the ward. No one paid any attention to us when we came into the room and stacked the boxes inside the door. James was still making an awful racket. We went back to her office and got the box of medication, which had at least a couple dozen bottles with handwritten labels.

Ava looked around the room she'd spent the better part of the last several months in. A single tear rolled down her cheek and she brushed it away angrily.

"That everything?"

She nodded, turned out the lights and we walked back to the ward.

I introduced her to the others and said she was helping us all get out of White Oaks and that we'd be leaving for good tonight.

Leonard, Duke, Clint, and I each grabbed a box and went out to the employee parking lot. James' and Charlie's vehicles were the only two out there and we'd be using one of them for our escape. I opened the back of the larger of the two vehicles, a minivan, and we loaded the boxes. Kevin stayed on the ward with Ava to watch over our prisoners and to get a closer look at the bomb secured to her leg.

I had taken one of the two-way radios with me, and left it with Leonard, Duke and Clint, who didn't want to go back on the ward.

I handed the radio to Leonard. "That's fine if you guys want to stay out here, just stay in the car and stay down. The other radio is in the ward. Let me know when you see Dr. Sawyer coming in, okay?"

"Sounds good," Leonard said. He was shaking. Clint looked rattled, but alert. Duke was staring off into the distance.

"Get in the car and stay down," I repeated.

"Okay," Leonard said and then turned to Duke. "Come on, Duke, let's get you in the car. This will all be over soon."

When I got back to the ward, Ava was comforting Kevin.

"What's going on?" I asked.

"I don't know if I can do it, Jason." Kevin said. "My hands won't stop shaking. I don't know if I can disarm it."

"It's okay," Ava said and shushed him. "When you guys are gone, just call the cops and tell them to send a bomb squad. No biggie. It'll be fine."

I knelt down in front of Kevin and told him it was all right and to not worry. "She'll be fine, Kev."

The radio came to life on the other side of the room. "Jason," Leonard said on the other end. "He's here."

I stood up, walked across the room, retrieved the radio, and pushed the button on the side. "Okay, thanks. I'll let you know when we're on our way down."

"Please hurry, Jason. We really want to get out of here."

It was probably a good thing I didn't leave the car keys with them.

"Hang in there, fellas. We won't be long." I handed Ava the radio.

"Come on, Kevin, I might need your help."

He nodded and stood up. We left the ward, closed the door behind us and waited in the corridor for Dr. Sawyer to come in.

When he walked around the corner toward his office, he didn't see me standing there. He was deep in thought and fumbling in his pockets.

"Morning, Doc," I said cheerfully.

He looked up at me with bulging eyes. "What are…"

That's all he got out before Kevin came up from behind and put him in a choke hold.

Dr. Sawyer clawed at Kevin's hands until I punched him in the stomach. There was a loud barking escape of air and his hands dropped. The doc went limp. We moved him onto the ward and secured him to a chair.

After radioing to the guys in the van that everything was all right and we'd be out soon, Ava tossed a cup of water in Dr. Sawyer's face to wake him up. He reacted to it, but didn't open his eyes until she slapped him hard across the face. He cried out and looked around the room frantically. He settled on Ava and his expression hardened. I pulled the tape off his mouth.

He took a few gasping breaths. "What's going on? Where are James and Charlie?" He struggled against the tape and stopped when he heard his two guards' muffled voices behind him. "Answer me, damn you. What happened?"

"Your henchmen came onto the ward in the middle of the night, drunk and armed with cattle prods."

"What?" Dr. Sawyer roared.

"They forced us to play a game of dodgeball with this," I said and tossed the ball into his lap. I was hoping for a shot to the balls, but it hit his leg and dropped to the floor. He still flinched with pain and looked up at me with a defeated expression.

"Michael was killed." I looked over at the bed he was laying on; a sheet had been used to cover his body.

"What do you want?"

"Well, to be honest, Doc, I want to kill you and your minions." I paused for a long time and stared at him. He was starting to sweat. "Fortunately for you, Ava has convinced me not to."

"Then what do you want?" he asked again.

"I want to hear you say it. What this place is and who runs it."

Dr. Sawyer glared at Ava. "You are one dead bitch," he said. In response, Ava slapped him across the face again and then rubbed her hand.

"Curious thing to say to the person who convinced us to let you live," Kevin said.

"Now," I said. "Answer my question. What is this place?"

"You already know the answer to that, clearly."

What he said was more true than he realized, he didn't really have any idea what I knew. What *he* didn't know was that when Ava was still free to come and go as she pleased, but had begun to suspect things weren't on the level at White Oaks, she'd bought a micro stick voice recorder online. You can get anything on the internet. A micro stick was some James Bond shit; an easily concealed, easily hidden recording device that did not look anything like a recording device. She'd hidden it in her work area weeks before I arrived and before she was taken prisoner. If the records we'd copied weren't enough, the recorded admission he was about to give would certainly help.

"Still. I'd like to hear you say it. And I might not kill you, but that doesn't mean I won't beat you within an inch of your life if you don't cooperate."

"Tough guy picking on someone taped to a chair," he said in a mocking childlike voice.

"Says the person who's been tormenting and torturing everyone in his care."

He scoffed at that but provided no further response. I pulled up a chair and sat myself in front of him. "Well?" He didn't respond immediately, so I punched him in the nose. That felt good.

When he finished yelping, he started talking. "It's pharmaceutical research and development," he said.

"Why the fake mental hospital? What was the point of all this?"

"Why a mental hospital? Because I didn't feel like running a prison. Making things appear somewhat normal got you people to cooperate. Besides, I enjoyed the therapy sessions. You all had such interesting stories. Better than any book I've ever read. You know what they say, truth is stranger than fiction." He smiled at me defiantly, so I punched him in the nose again. His face was a shattered bloody mess and he was taking great big gulps of air through his mouth.

"I've worked in prison-like laboratories before, and it's never worth the trouble," he said and then spat blood on the floor. "They were always begging and crying, and, *oh my god why are you doing this to me*, and that's just exhausting. It hinders the research."

"What were you trying to accomplish with this place? What were you doing to the medicine?" He hesitated, and I made it look like he was about to get punched again.

"Okay, okay. *Shit.*" He sighed and let out a series of hacking coughs.

"I was trying to induce cell mutation." I looked up at Ava and she was staring at him intently.

"Meaning?"

"Cell mutation causes cancer, or can cause cancer. My primary objective was to find a way to induce cell mutation. I tried to find something we could add to any and all medicines we manufacture to induce that mutation. CJ was our first big success, but it happened too quickly. Too aggressively. And the FDA is a joke. They only have a fraction of the resources they need to monitor the industry, and we have plenty of political friends that make things even easier on us."

"Why would you want to induce cancer in unsuspecting patients?"

"Do you have any idea how much money is in cancer?"

I punched him again, and for a long time he wailed and cried and made empty threats.

"What happened to Stephen and CJ?" I asked.

"They're buried on the hospital grounds."

I got out of my chair and punched him in the stomach as hard as I could. He vomited all over himself and struggled to catch his breath.

"That's not what I asked you. I asked you what happened to them."

For a minute, he just cried, and I almost felt sorry for him. James and Charlie were squirming and drowning out any useful dialogue. Kevin picked up the cattle prod and quieted them both immediately.

"CJ just died. You saw how sick he was."

"I saw how sick you made him."

"Yes," he shrieked. "Yes, I made him sick."

"And Stephen?"

"He had just killed Randall. Lee was out of commission after Stephen gouged his eyes out. James and I killed Stephen."

"How?"

James started grunting distorted syllables at us from behind the duct tape around his mouth, and Kevin hit him with the cattle prod again.

"We stomped him to death."

"What company do you work for?" I asked.

"*Fuck you.*"

I punched him again, that time in the jaw, and it knocked him out. While he was out, we dragged Charlie and James up in line with Dr. Sawyer so we could bind them all together. All three of them were very well secured individually, but just to be safe we taped all three of them and their chairs together. I found some rope in the supply closet and we tied them all up in an intricate layer of varying types and sizes of knots. They'd never be able to free themselves.

The radio let out a burst of static that scared the shit out of me. It was Leonard.

"Is everything okay in there?"

"Yeah, we're good, Leonard. We'll be down shortly."

"Thank god," he said. "We really want to get out of here."

Dr. Sawyer woke up and looked around at us, dazed.

"You ready to tell me what company you work for?"

When he didn't answer right away, I punched Charlie and James in quick succession and then made it look like he was next.

He let out a long sigh. "What difference does it make now?" he muttered to himself. "Bowman Pharmaceutical."

"See, that wasn't so hard. Do they know what you're doing here?"

He hesitated and I punched him again. He was barely recognizable. There were lumps and cuts all over his face, which was drenched in blood. His grey beard had stripes and splatters of red all over it.

"Of course they know. Bowman has the largest chunk of the cancer industry. If I can double revenue within five years, I'll get a one-billion-dollar bonus. Even that amount of money is nothing to them. Do you really have any idea who you're fucking with?"

"Do you?" I asked, and he laughed.

"We've been buying funeral homes too, you know why?" he asked.

"I can take a guess, but go ahead, enlighten me."

"So when the people die from the cancer we give them, we get to squeeze their bank account one last time."

Behind me, where Ava was standing, something beeped. I turned around and looked at her. She was looking down at her leg. The beep sounded again, and she looked up at me.

"Oh shit," Dr. Sawyer said. "Get her away from me."

Beep.

"What is that?" I shouted.

Beep.

Dr. Sawyer was doing everything in his limited power to move away, but secured as he was, and with Charlie and James tied to him, there was nowhere he could go.

Beep.

"What is that?" I asked again and grabbed him by the shirt.

"The bomb is on a timer," he said. "If I don't check in every twenty-four hours, it gets activated."

"Jason," Ava said, but I ignored her.

Beep.

"If you check in now, will it be deactivated?"

"It's too late. You have ninety seconds. Get her away from me."

It was almost comical seeing him panic that way. A man who desperately wanted to give the whole world cancer just so he could profit from it, but couldn't face his own demise with an ounce of courage or humanity.

Beep.

"Jason," Ava said again, only much louder. I released the doc and turned around to face her.

"Just go."

"No."

"You have everything you need to make this right, and now you have this too." She held out her James Bond recording device. I took it and put it in my pocket.

"*Go!*"

Kevin ran over to the toolbox sitting outside the supply closet door, the one I got the duct tape from. He grabbed it and another chair, and then set the chair next to Ava. "Sit," he said.

Beep.

"Please," Ava said. "You guys need to get out of here."

"Sit," Kevin shouted, and she did.

Kevin carefully rolled her pant leg up so it was out of the way. He wiped his hands on his shirt, and then shook them out as if to rid himself of the nerves.

Beep.

He pulled out some tools and got to work.

James, Charlie, and Dr. Sawyer weren't making the situation any calmer, as they shouted and grunted and cried and tried to squirm away, like the snakes they were.

Beep.

"Jason, tell him to stop, please. I want you to stop. I want you to go. *Please.*"

"He's got this, Ava. He can do it."

Beep.

I had no idea if my pseudo-confidence in Kevin had any credibility whatsoever, but I hoped my saying it reassured Ava – at least a little bit.

Beep.

That sound was getting really annoying really fast. I liked the way I felt the last time I said it, so I said it again, "He can do it."

Kevin was in some other zone.

Beep.

"Shit." I lost my own reassuring tone.

"Go!" Ava said, suddenly aware of my confidence being a pretense.

Beep.

Is it getting faster?" I asked. I could have sworn it was getting faster.

Kevin glanced up at me with a look of what I could only describe as "shut the fuck up, you pitiful amateur." He smiled – or smirked – in the professional zone he was in, it was tough to tell, but it was in his whole face…he slowly turned back to his task, and I saw his head nod.

Then I heard him whisper, not to me, but to someone unseen, "Too easy, Staff Sergeant, too easy."

Beep.

Ava gasped.

He clipped a wire and paused.

The beeping stopped and we all breathed a sigh of relief. Dr. Sawyer was crying, and James had wet himself. It dripped from the chair he was secured to and puddled on the floor.

Ava grabbed Kevin's face and kissed him long and hard. Kevin blushed and said he just needed to detach the bomb from her leg. It didn't take long.

"Got it," Kevin said and pulled the device off her.

He stood and looked at me with a big grin on his face. "Thanks for believing in me, Jason," he said and then the device beeped. The smile slowly faded.

Beep.

The color drained from his face. "*Shit.*"

Beep, beep, beep.

Kevin hugged the device to his chest and ran for the bathroom door. Ava jumped up and tried to go after him, but I knocked her to the ground, and covered her body with mine. The bomb went off while the bathroom door was still swinging shut.

My ears were ringing, and I could barely see through the thick fog of dust and smoke. The smell of smoldering flesh was something I hoped to never experience again, but there it was. James had blood coming from his ears, and Charlie looked like he got hit in the back by shrapnel. The wounds weren't bad, but they were plentiful.

Doctor Sawyer had caught the worst of the blast. If the mangled, blood-covered piece of metal sitting a few feet away from me was what went through him, then it had been a piece of the door Kevin ran behind that Frisbeed through Dr. Sawyer's throat. His head was tilted all the way back with his mouth gaping open and his eyes glazed over in an unnatural final stare, not at the ceiling, but at me. His severed neck was barely attached to his body and thick blood was oozing out, dripping down to the floor.

Ava was crying and screaming something, but I couldn't hear her over the ringing in my ears.

Eventually the ringing started to subside, and Ava was checking me over for injuries. I could hear Leonard shouting over the radio, trying to find out what happened. I picked up the radio and, in a shaky, breathless voice I didn't recognize, I told him we'd be right down.

***

"What now?" I asked Ava after we pulled out of the White Oaks parking lot. Duke was silent. Leonard and Clint were both crying over the news of Kevin's death. I was still too stunned by the sudden act of selflessness to mourn him properly.

"We're going to need money," I stated.

"I have some," she said. "We're going to my house. I have a place near Columbus and have money there, about ten thousand dollars."

I whistled. "That should help."

"We can go to my place and get the money. Then we'll go somewhere we can scan all these records and copy them onto thumb drives. We could send them out to thirty or forty newspapers and law enforcement agencies. Maybe even a few members of the Senate and Congress."

We only stayed at Ava's house, which was cold and dusty, long enough to get the cash. A company as big and powerful as Bowman surely knew her address, and though no one knew that we'd fled and left the employees bound and secured, we weren't going to take any risks.

I called the Columbus Dispatch, then the police, and twice told our story about the facility and the staff members we left behind, as well as the details of what happened to Michael and Kevin, and that there were other former patients buried in unmarked graves somewhere on the grounds.

A few hours later on the news, we saw film footage of ambulances leaving the scene. The reporters said there were four bodies confirmed dead and one in intensive care. I wondered which one had survived long enough to realize that I didn't really care.

The policemen were seen in the background taking out boxes. All the original records that we left at the hospital had been seized and the story started to develop quickly through the news cycle.

After that, we sent the thumb drives everywhere. Fifteen went to the largest newspaper companies in the world. We sent some to local papers as well. Not just the records of the misdeeds at White Oaks, but all of Ava's research. She had no interest in patents and wanted everyone to have free access to her work. Maybe in time, the world would be free of opioids, and millions of people struggling with PTSD would be cured while the entire pharmaceutical industry would be significantly overhauled.

Thumb drives also went to universities, the Veterans Administration, and mental health organizations. Every place we could think of got a thumb drive and a letter in the mail, including several members of the Senate and Congress. It took two very long days of work at a random hotel in the heart of Columbus, but we did it. The backlash was going to be so beautiful.

When we were finished and it was time to go our separate ways, there wasn't a dry eye among us. We'd all gotten a couple changes of clothes and other miscellaneous supplies. Leonard, Clint, and Duke all said they had distant relatives they hadn't seen in decades or old friends that they could stay with.

"What are you going to do?" Ava asked.

"I have an old friend down in Florida who should be able to help me secure a new identity. We used to forge documents in high school, and he's still at it, last I heard. After that, I honestly don't know."

Ava handed me a grocery bag with a large supply of medicine and a roll of cash. She offered me the keys to her rental car, but I told her I'd just take the bus or a cab to the airport and get a flight to Florida. After that, I'd get a car in my own name, my new name.

I hugged her. "Thank you."

"Thank you," she said. "Are you going to be all right?"

"Yeah. For the first time in a long time, I really think I am going to be okay. How about you?"

"I think so," she said.

"Good luck with this circus. I assume you'll be reaching out to some authorities?"

"Yeah, should be fun."

***

The next time I saw her was on television. Well, I knew it was her, though no one else could tell. Her face was darkened out in a silhouette and her voice was technologically altered to sound like she had a throat full of lawn mowers telling the story. She and Bowman were the top news story all over the world. The records had been received, Senate hearings were being arranged, arrests were made and some of the wealthiest people in the world were caught trying to flee the country.

Before the news broke, I'd connected with my old friend in Florida, and he set me up with a new name, birth certificate, social security card, and driver's license. From a little outdoor bar along Florida's Emerald Coast, I had a beer and watched one of the press conferences with a little smile on my face.

As the day wore away, I walked down to the beach and sat in the sand. I watched the sun go down and listened to the waves. Rows of pink and orange light shot out of the western horizon and mixed with the darkening blue sky that revealed distant stars. Tight formations of birds flew overhead. The waves crashed on an endless loop. The milky foam slipped to my feet buried in the sand, and then retreated to start all over again. I could have listened to those waves forever.

Down the beach a ways, Tony walked off into the distance. His pants were rolled up to the knee and the waves splashed his legs. He turned back and looked at me. He didn't wave, and it was dark enough that I couldn't see his expression, but I thought he was smiling. It was then that I decided to head west, and on my way to wherever I was going I'd stop in the small town of Alpine, Texas where Tony was buried and say one final goodbye to my old friend…and to my old life.

Jordan earned an MFA in Creative Writing from Miami of Ohio. His non-fiction essay *Lost Time: A Road Trip Journal* was published in Adelaide Literary Magazine, February 2019. *White Oaks* was a finalist in the Ohio Writer's Associations' Great Novel Contest of 2019, and is Jordan's debut novel. He lives in Central Ohio with his wife and son.

Learn more at www.runningwildpress.com